She knows how to unravel secrets, but getting to the bottom of this one might just kill her.

Magic is for fools, television news reporter Caitlyn believes. And she's no fool. She's determined to prove master illusionist Shay a fake. Somehow though, with Shay the lines between magic and reality blur. Perhaps it's his charisma, or being in Ireland with him, but now she's dreaming of a magical place. One that seems oddly familiar...

Shay hides a terrible secret. He's to blame for Caitlyn's separation from her family and the world she doesn't remember. She must go home to the Sidhe, and to recover his honor, he must be the one to bring her. He'll willingly lose everything he is to help her break the curse binding her. But time is of the essence--the old evil has surfaced. He must make Caitlyn believe in magic, and his love, before she becomes its prey.

Books by Judith Leger

Enchanted

Published by Kensington Publishing Corporation

Enchanted

Judith Leger

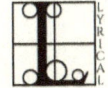

LYRICAL PRESS
Kensington Publishing Corp.
www.kensingtonbooks.com

Lyrical Press books are published by
Kensington Publishing Corp. 119 West 40th Street New York, NY 10018

First Electronic Edition: September 2012
eISBN-13: 978-1-61650-401-4
eISBN-10: 1-61650-401-3

First Print Edition: September 2012
ISBN-13: 978-1-61650-882-1
ISBN-10: 1-61650-882-5

Printed in the United States of America

To Terri with love

Chapter 1

Caitlyn. Two weeks until her birthday. Two weeks until her death.

The words seeped through Shay's mind, filling every fissure to overflowing. He had to save her. Time ran too fast, and even magic couldn't slow the days ahead.

Hoping for distraction, he glanced out the tinted window as the limousine glided along the curb in front of a sleek, mirror-glassed building where his agent, Lance Parker, leased office space. There, an array of reporters, with their corresponding photographers, milled about on the sidewalk.

Shay likened them to wolves, seeking to devour him whole. He hated the rangy beasts, having been attacked and severely wounded many years before. Now these human canines waited, some in dull wrinkled clothes, others in expensive suits or dresses. Yesterday, his requested press release had informed them of his arrival in Los Angeles for tonight's performance. Today, they lay in wait for him at all the places listed on the press release where he might show up during his stay. He doubted Lance had missed a single tabloid with the announcement.

The limo pulled to a stop at the corner. The dark tint on the windows dulled the camera flashes as the photographers rushed forward. His heartbeat accelerated with excitement when he noticed his dark-haired agent elbowing his way past the crowd.

A bodyguard's suited arm appeared and pulled the door open. Crisp, cold air mixed with exhaust fumes poured through the opening, ruffling Shay's hair. Heels clacked on the concrete, and shouted questions spewed from the crowd as they shoved and pushed to take advantage of the chink in his protective barrier.

Shay shot a glance at the golden-haired man sprawled on the leather seat next to him. Rhys, casually attired in dark slacks and navy sweater, lifted a brow in return. Sudden panic came over Shay, bringing a contrary need to laugh. Uncontrollably. His freedom would soon end. Rhys would see to it. His long-time friend's faith had ended years ago, and it was his fault.

With his power, Shay had been lucky he still lived. If only he'd not listened to one woman, none of this would have happened. With the news he hoped to get, for the first time in twenty-five years, hope for Caitlyn bloomed, but also for a possible healing of his friendship with Rhys.

Until he met Rhys's eyes.

Was that hatred he saw darkening the blue? Shay swiped sweaty palms over the leather pants encasing his thighs, but his hands stuck for a second. No doubt, it'd take much more than saving Caitlyn for Rhys to forgive him.

When he faced the door's opening, Lance dove through the crowd, stopped for a second to speak to the guard, then ducked into the limo. The door swung shut, muting the clicks from the cameras and the onslaught of questions. Shay studied his agent as Lance settled against the seat backing the driver. His skin prickled in anticipation for whatever news Lance brought him about Caitlyn.

Lance extended a plastic case containing a DVD. "I knew I could count on you to be on time. This just arrived by special courier. Reiley's last newscast. All the arrangements have been made." Breathless from his dash to the vehicle, he spoke faster than normal. His gaze shifted to Shay's left and snagged on the other occupant of the limo. "So. Who's your friend?"

Glad for the distraction, Shay held back a smile and took the case. He stared at the silver disk through the milky cover. "He's an old friend of mine. Rhys. Lance Parker, my agent. Rhys is in town on business."

"What do you do? Acting, music? Illusions like Shay's?" Lance reached out with a neatly manicured hand and shook Rhys'. He shifted back and tugged his suit sleeves. Charm oozed from the practiced smile plastered across his face. When Rhys didn't reply right away, Lance surveyed the slender blond man and continued, "If you need an agent, let me know. With your looks and body, you can go a long way."

Unable to think of a better profession for Rhys, Shay commented. "He's a gardener."

His long-time friend deserved a reduction in status for arriving in Los Angeles without warning. Shay angled a remote at the divider next to his agent. A built-in, flat-screen DVD player rose from the seat and the drawer slid open. Handling the DVD with care, he placed it in the tray and closed the drawer.

Lance frowned. "Gardener?"

Shay glanced at Rhys and resisted the urge to grin. Rhys wouldn't like the idea of everyone believing he worked for Shay. The slender man sat relaxed, his long legs propped up on the opposite seat. His finely etched features complemented the white-blond hair tied back with a black leather strip. He radiated quiet confidence and superiority, belying the tension seething beneath his calm facade. Muscles taut, Shay waited for the first words from Rhys. The older man had to follow his lead or all his well-laid plans would fall apart.

Rhys's keen gaze turned toward him for a moment before moving onto Lance. "Yes, a gardener. I supervised the landscaping for Shay's home."

The low, accented voice flowed over Shay. He loved sounds. Loud, quiet, tinkling, clunks, all sounds. Even silence pleased him. Some, like heavy machinery, distracted him. Listening to Rhys's lyrical Welsh tones soothed him. He needed soothing. Time was disappearing too fast.

"*You* did that?" Lance stared open-mouthed.

Ignoring the two men, Shay focused on the voice coming over the speaker. His heart pounded once before speeding up. He tried to slip from the leather seat, but the leather on his pants caught and halted his forward motion. As he teetered on the edge, an urge to fall to his knees in respect came over him. Instead, he leaned closer to the screen and stared at the dark-haired reporter, his breath suspended at the back of his throat. Excitement over finally finding and seeing her filled him, and he had to struggle to keep his expression noncommittal.

Caitlyn Reiley.

Her name meant pure beauty. Shay searched for the evidence on her face, but from what he could tell, her years in the human world had concealed her true beauty. Plain, perhaps dull, better described her.

Her slender figure was adorned in a simple navy suit. She appeared fragile. The genuine texture of her skin lay hidden behind a coating of makeup. The light coloring seemed wrong on her, and even caused her features to appear vague and unattractive. Dark-rimmed glasses obscured the beauty of her green eyes. Those eyes lacked the magical vitality that existed in every daughter of the Sidhe. Yet, she was the one he had been searching for the past four years. He sensed a different aura about her than what he noticed in normal humans. Almost as if her powers leaked through the cracks in the spell placed on her.

Lance frowned as he turned to the screen. "Why her? You could have anyone--Barbara, Joan, Maria--but you chose this."

Rhys coughed, and Shay sensed his friend's increasing hostility at the unintentional insult to the woman. Lance didn't need to realize how important Caitlyn was to him, so Shay murmured, "I want to keep the viewers focused on me, not the reporter."

With his gaze centered on the young woman reporting in clear and precise phrases, he waited to see if he had succeeded. He held his breath, not sure of what to expect with Lance's response.

His agent stayed silent for a few seconds. Shay's eye twitched as a bark of laughter erupted from him. "I should have known. You don't want to share the limelight with a famous reporter."

Excellent. He exhaled a slow breath, releasing the tight knot which had formed at the back of his throat from holding in the air. His agent had responded just the way he wanted. Greed and egotism were two human aspects Lance Parker understood. He would never comprehend any other motive behind Shay's choice.

"This is great." Lance grinned and tapped on the window behind him. "I'm out of here. I told your bodyguard to drop me off. Have a lunch appointment. Do me a favor?"

"Hmm?" Shay didn't look away from the screen. Caitlyn was talking to another woman. In a span of one moment, she smiled. His heart skipped a beat, and an answering smile budded on his lips, but he stopped. His body swayed closer to the screen. In that brief second, he witnessed a fragment of her beauty. He remembered her smile.

"Keep your secrets. Remember, the more mysterious you are, the better your fans love you," Lance remarked, slapping him on his shoulder before the limousine stopped. The door opened and with a backward wave, the agent was gone.

Shay eased back into the seat.

Rhys lowered his feet and sat forward, gaze trained on the screen. "Is it her?"

"It's her. I can feel her. She and I--we don't have much time."

"No, she does not." When Rhys spoke, his voice trembled.

Hearing the words from him served to emphasize Shay's need to help her. Rhys took a deep shuddering breath and turned a cold gaze on him. "For you, though, eternity is before you. In hell, I hope. Remember--bring her home no later than two weeks from today. You should, at this time, have had some luck in releasing her from the curse. Otherwise, she will be lost." He waved his hand in a helpless gesture.

Shay didn't respond. He had to find a way to help Caitlyn. She was doomed if he failed. He stared at the screen, concentrating. He knew where she was and now he could focus on capturing her attention.

The low hum from the limo's engine helped alleviate some of his tension. Pressing the Pause button on the remote, he narrowed his eyes and stared past the dark frames into Caitlyn's. He wished he could freeze her life as easily. Pity for her ignorance concerning her fate engulfed him. He switched off the player, faced the window next to him and tried not to think about the future.

Chapter 2

"Hey, Reiley. Kramer wants to see ya." The male voice came from the opening to Caitlyn Reiley's cubicle, reaching her over the cacophony of others speaking, phones ringing and keyboards clicking in Channel 52's newsroom. She groaned and pivoted toward the opening. By the time she turned to question the unseen messenger, he had disappeared.

She exhaled slowly, faced her desk and set her purse down. Sharp pains radiated from her tired, cramped feet and sped to her brow. She rubbed her fingertips against her throbbing temples. With a glance at her wristwatch, she frowned. She had just stepped into the newsroom from reporting on a tiny-tots pageant seminar for most of the day. The seminar had taken longer than she'd originally planned. Now, when she should have been able to sit and go over her report for the seminar coverage, she was told to see Kramer.

The station's business manager, Mike Kramer, didn't like to wait. First, though, the makeup had to go. She reached inside her purse for her compact. Ever since she was old enough to wear cosmetics, she'd tried but failed to grow accustomed to the pasty feel of it on her face. Added to the fact her biological mother wore heavy cosmetics, Caitlyn refused to associate anything in her life now to her turbulent childhood. An image of her mother's face loaded with thick foundation and sky blue eye-shadow appeared in Caitlyn's mind. She shoved the picture aside, cringing at the remembered texture of the cracked lipstick and flaking mascara.

The dull ring of the telephone set off tingling explosions in every nerve ending connected to her skin. Frowning at the compact, she shoved her purse out of the way and jerked up the receiver. With a deep breath, she answered, trying to keep her voice calm and even. "Caitlyn Reiley. May I help you?"

"Catey? What's up, girl?" Marcy's chirpy greeting caused Caitlyn to sag.

"Oh, not much. Just about to face Kramer in his office," she said with a sigh.

"Huh?"

"My boss wants to see me. We're not a major TV station locally, and the management's making cutbacks. I think I might be one of them." Caitlyn sat down at her desk and twisted and untwisted the telephone cord.

"Is it that bad over there?"

"Yes. When they opened this station six months ago, they hired too many people. The administration let four people go last month. They weren't reporters, but that doesn't mean management isn't going to start cutting us next. Why today? This rates as one of the worst days of the year for me."

Marcy released a short laugh. "Come on, it can't be that bad."

"Wanna bet? I just finished filming a piece on tiny-tots pageantry. I didn't know there were so many little Miss America wannabes in this area. When I arrived back here, someone told me Kramer wanted to see me. He never sends for me."

Dropping the cord, she pressed the compact latch and it opened with a snap. She glanced at her image in the small mirror and wrinkled her nose. Still the same. Nothing spectacular there. Dark hair held tight in a bun at the base of her neck, black-rimmed glasses framing dull green eyes, rouge-covered cheeks and matte lipstick. With her glasses, she didn't need the added cover of eye shadow and liner.

"Calm down. You're overreacting. They're not gonna let you go." Her friend's voice took on the familiar big-sister tone she used on Caitlyn when she wanted to get her point across. "You worry too much. Get your butt up and go see the man. You told me the other day the polls chose your segments above all the other stations. He might have an achievement award for you, not a pink slip."

"I doubt that," Caitlyn muttered. Not wanting to pass her rising depression onto her friend any longer, she tried to sound cheery. She needed the makeup off before facing Kramer. The cakey stuff made her uncomfortable and vulnerable. A minute or two wouldn't hurt. She hoped.

"So, what's up with you?"

"I just went shopping and bought the cutest shoes. They're wedges, red skinny straps, very sexy. You'll simply die to have a pair..."

Half-listening, she allowed Marcy to rattle on so she would have time to remove the makeup. She held the phone to her ear with her shoulder, tugged open a desk drawer and removed a box of damp wipes. Makeup was a necessity in front of the camera. She didn't mind making concessions like that if it meant moving forward with her career. Since she wasn't scheduled to film again today, a few swipes with the damp cloth and the face paint disappeared. Satisfied after another quick pass over her cheeks, she closed the compact and threw the cloth away.

"--Shay Evers--"

At the mention of the famous illusionist's name, Caitlyn grabbed the phone in her hand and straightened. "Wait, what did you say?"

"The performance. Tonight. Front row seats. Backstage passes. Erica bugged out, going south to meet Paco." Marcy stopped and groaned. "Let's not go there. You're second on my list of stand-ins. You simply have to go with me. So, be ready by six, okay? You're gonna love Shay. He's fabulous to look at and after tonight, I hope he'll be all mine."

Heart racing, Caitlyn struggled to control quickening breaths. This physical reaction had become normal for her during the last four years at the very mention of the illusionist's name. From the moment she had turned on her television that warm summer night four years ago and caught one of his performances, she had developed a strange dislike for the handsome Welshman.

Her heartbeat would speed up, sharp twinges would shoot through her middle and heat often soared through her veins to the degree she had to sit down and fan her face. She refused to call what she experienced an infatuation, and she didn't believe in love at first sight. She didn't believe in that overrated emotion at all. All her life, she had seen the results of that sappy feeling. Her mother and father had cared about her so much they both lost her to the system and never came back to claim her. Honestly, she didn't know what love comprised, but it certainly wasn't what she experienced when seeing the illusionist.

She was tempted to take Marcy up on her offer, but she resisted. When she answered, she kept her voice even, refusing to allow her emotions to show. "I can't believe you've fallen under that guy's spell."

"Everyone has. I thought for sure you would too, but--"

Caitlyn interrupted her. She didn't want to open a conversation concerning Shay Evers. "Thanks for the invitation, but no. If Kramer doesn't do what I know he will, I want to go home and relax in a hot bubble bath. Given a choice between Shay Evers and suds, I'll take the suds."

Without meaning to, she mentally compared her tub filled with warm water and brimming with bubbles to meeting and speaking to the superstar. An image of Evers reclining in the tub appeared in her mind, his dark hair shining in candlelight, a lean hand raised, beckoning her to join him. She straightened, fighting the sudden heat pumping through her veins. "Listen, I hate to cut you short, but Kramer doesn't like waiting."

"Oh, sure thing," her friend said. "Call me in the morning so I can fill you in."

Caitlyn agreed with a laugh and placed the receiver on its cradle. No use putting it off any longer. She needed to accept the fact that after she left Kramer's office she would probably have to start job hunting. After a deep breath she stood, locked her purse in her desk and tugged at the hem of her business suit jacket.

With her chin up, she headed for Kramer's office. The labyrinth of the newsroom outside her cubicle stretched in front of her. Desks and hinged partitions sectioned the area for the reporters and other employees. The huge room, flanked on one side with windows, smelled of burnt lint from the heating unit. The unit didn't do a great job keeping the chill out, but the sheer number of the bustling news people kept the temperature bearable. When she reached the far end and came to a short hallway, she slowed. Kramer's office was the second door to the left.

For a moment she considered how she would respond if he laid her off. Not good. She gritted her teeth as pride forced her forward. Her knock landed harder than she intended, stinging her knuckles.

She'd worked relentlessly on her college degree in mass communications just to become a reporter. She wasn't going to exit this job with meek submission. Her inner strength had sustained her through the time social workers removed her from her parents' house and placed her in several foster homes. She'd been bounced around, but she'd never allowed the fear of the unknown to show.

Even at this moment, her fear remained hidden. She wasn't about to let Kramer see any weakness in her now. She swiped her damp palms over the sides of her jacket, hoping he wanted to compliment her and not lay her off.

The low response through the door tightened her nerves. The knob twisted under her palm, and she pushed the door open. When she crossed the room, the burnt smell from the furnace heating the building sharpened in the enclosed space. Her eyes burned. Afternoon sunlight poured from the windows behind the manager's desk and filled the office. She stared for a second at the shiny spot on top of Mike Kramer's bald head, amazed at the slickness of the surface.

"Reiley. Take a seat."

Caitlyn tried not to stare but after not seeing her boss for a few days, she had forgotten his size. The middle-aged manager's abdomen ballooned from an excessive habit of fast food and more than a few beers. The buttons on his white shirt strained for freedom. With him sitting forward, his belly nearly flowed over the edge of the desk. He filled his chair like a packed sardine.

For several moments, a calculating expression covered his ruddy face. The dark moustache over his upper lip twitched as he stared at a yellow tablet centered in front of him, his right fingers sliding back and forth along the paper's edge.

She took another deep breath, mentally preparing her rebuttal should her job be threatened. With her back straight, she moved to one of the two chairs angled in front of the desk.

After she was settled on the edge of the leather chair, she glanced up and found Kramer still sat unmoving. Silence filled the room for several minutes. The faster the seconds flew by, the tighter her insides coiled. He had asked to speak to her. Now that she was here, he sat daydreaming.

She covered her mouth and forced a little cough.

Sharp gray eyes focused on her. "Oh, Caitlyn. Sorry, I still can't believe this," he muttered. "The sponsors will go nuts for a time slot."

"Believe what?" She relaxed enough to scoot back in the chair and cross her legs.

"I received a phone call."

When he didn't continue, she leaned forward and studied him. His coloring seemed paler than normal. Two months ago, shortly after the station opened, he'd suffered a series of light heart attacks.

"Kramer, are you okay? Do you want me to call someone?" She half rose to go to the phone, but he motioned her to sit.

"No, no, I'm fine. Do you know Lance Parker?"

"The big-name agent?" Settling once more, she frowned. Everyone in Hollywood knew the name. He represented the best performers in film, stage and music. He even represented Shay Evers.

"What about him? Did he die?" She didn't understand what Parker had to do with Kramer wanting to see her.

"No, he called me." His gaze dropped to the tablet in front of him. "He wants you."

Chapter 3

Caitlyn stared, her mind turning and twisting the words. Every path they traveled failed to reveal a reason why Parker would want her. When she spoke, she tried to keep her tone even and under control. "Excuse me?" The high pitch in her voice as she answered clearly told her she'd failed.

Kramer's head jerked toward her, and he frowned. "Not you, personally. Seems Shay Evers is his client. Evers saw your piece on money-saving coupons and liked it. He wants you to interview him."

A gasp escaped her Caitlyn leaned forward, mouth open, staring hard at her boss. "He saw what?"

With a shake of his head, Kramer snorted. "You know where you interviewed…"

She waved a hand back and forth to stop him, and then grimaced. When had Evers watched that segment? The piece wasn't a fine example of her work. Her racing thoughts came to a slow stop. Doubt raised its ugly head. Winning the lotto seemed more possible than what Kramer had just told her. Every top name reporter sought a coveted interview with the illusionist, yet none had succeeded.

Now Kramer expected her to believe Evers's agent had requested she do the segment? She never dreamed her boss was capable of playing such a horrible trick on her.

Her temper flared, causing heat to rise to her face. "Is this a joke?"

"No joke." Kramer pushed away from the desk and stood. He picked up the notepad, moved to her side and handed the tablet to her. She focused on the top page.

Stubby finger pointing at the writing on the page, he explained, "You were the one chosen over every reporter in the world to do the interview. Everything's set. You leave in the morning in one of his private jets to go to his home in Wales. I've decided to send Blake with you to oversee the filming. You two work well together."

"You're serious." Surprise returned, battled with her temper and won. "Dead."

"I can't believe it. Do you realize what this means to my career?" She smiled as the realization struck her, and she gazed at the words written on the paper. There, in Kramer's bold script, was the charismatic performer's name, then a double slash followed by her name. When she glanced up at Kramer, a glint from the window caught her attention. She shifted her head to the right.

Through the glass, a billboard attached to the side of a building refracted a ray of sunlight. Her mouth dropped open as she stared into the deep amethyst of Shay Evers's eyes. Blackness formed around the edge of her vision. From a distance, she heard Kramer speak.

Evers lay on his side in a field of purple pansies--his slender, leather encased legs stretched out and crossed at the ankles. The white shirt draping his lean form gaped at the neck and fell in soft folds, exposing a large portion of his chest as he rested on one elbow. Long strands of tousled black hair floated in the wind around his perfect features. The picture, arresting and arousing, and obviously targeted for women, achieved its purpose. The smiling intensity in his purple eyes struck her to the core of her mind and left her breathless.

"The station's ratings are going to go through the roof. Parker remarked about this being an hour-long documentary with you doing the report. We'll have sole rights to it. The advertising alone will be astronomical." His abrupt laugh sounded harsh and loud.

With a shake of her head, Caitlyn tore her gaze away from the billboard, yet when she blinked she still saw the image.

Kramer snapped his fingers in front of her eyes. "Are you listening, Reiley? You leave at four in the morning for Wales. Evers owns a place, and I mean a big place, there. Somewhere in the mountains. Refurbished an old castle. Heard rumors it's like a faery tale castle. Plants and whatever all over. I've called Blake. He'll go by accounting to pick up the paperwork and credit cards."

Caitlyn shut her eyes for a moment. The thought of staying at Evers's home thrilled her, but what if she did something stupid? The idea of falling under his spell did not sit well with her. She'd kept her deepest emotions concealed all her life. What if she couldn't hide her attraction to him? So many women across the world were enamored of him.

She bit her lip, a frown tugging her brows together. Could she take the chance? Insecurity flared and for a moment she didn't know what to do. She glanced at Kramer, hoping to find some guidance.

Her decision appeared, solid and firm, in the set of his jaw. She nodded and said with a forced smile, "This is great. He's a fake. There isn't any real magic, and I'll prove it."

Kramer's eyes widened. "What did you do? Read my mind? Listen, Reiley, I don't care if he's fake, but I do care about what this means to this station." He propped a generous hip on the desk before he continued. "Parker gave the station full authority with this interview. Didn't even argue when I told him what I wanted to do."

"Which is?"

"Reality or illusion? Shay Evers, the man behind the magic."

Caitlyn studied him for a moment. "That's good. This gives me leeway to find out the truth about his acts."

"Thought you might approve. Come on, you need to start packing." He stood, grasped her by the upper arms, forcing her to her feet.

"Go home. Now. Grab what you want to take. Go shopping for anything you don't have. Charge it and put it on the expense account."

He guided her to the door and opened it for her. "I'll pick up you and Blake in the morning and take you to the airport. Three o'clock sharp. Bring warm clothes. And don't forget to call me. Often. I want a daily update."

The door clicked shut behind her, and she twisted around to stare at the knob. The word interview would have satisfied her goal to further her career, but the man she was selected to interview made this her first major assignment.

She tried to recall all she knew about Evers. He had shot to the top of the entertainment world four years before, and to date, showed no signs of falling. His performances were interlaced with his own music and lyrics. This music caught on and now it rang across the world. Caitlyn couldn't think of a single place she'd gone where she hadn't heard at least one of his songs.

All the tension drained from her body as she glanced at the tablet. For a moment, she stared at the name. She straightened and gasped.

Marcy.

Caitlyn had to let her friend know she changed her mind about the invitation. Tonight she would have the chance to observe Evers without anyone noticing. First objective on her agenda: call Marcy and, right after, do a search for any information about him she might have missed during the years. At least, now she could surf the web for him without waves of guilt washing over her.

She half-jogged to her desk. Dropping into her chair, she grabbed the phone and punched in Marcy's number. "Hey, I changed my mind. It's not too late, is it?"

"You wanna go?"

"Yes."

"Sweet. Come by my place at five thirty. We'll get ready together. I'm not letting you out in public dressed in one of those stiff suits," Marcy said. "How'd your meeting go? It must have turned out okay for you to change your mind about tonight."

Caitlyn grinned. "Yes, Kramer had some good news for me. I've been assigned a major interview. Listen, I've got a lot to do before five thirty, so I'll see you then."

After placing the receiver on the hook, she faced her laptop and clicked several keys, typing out the superstar's name for an internet search. The end results, though, left her with little more information than she already knew. All the sites she glanced through showed numerous photographs, but told her nothing about his personal life except to say he was a private person. There was never any mention of a love interest, no hint of a secret scandal hovering in his closet, nothing out of the ordinary.

Caitlyn shook her head. She'd take notes on the flight so she wouldn't have to wing the most important interview of her lackluster career. This assignment could either make or destroy her, and she refused to allow the latter to happen.

She touched a small card taped on the left-hand corner of her laptop.

Trust in your own abilities--the force behind your goals. Take each day, one by one. Look for the strength in your soul and believe you will move forward, past tomorrow. Trust that all things will work out and believe you have the power to succeed.

This card with the inspiring words was her only concession to what she considered foolishness. As practical as the loafers on her feet, she stayed away from frivolous activities. Yet, this card with its sweet phrases reminded her to stay on track with her goals. Most of these she had completed, but the one large goal, to move out of the small interviews and into the larger, more serious ones, had passed her by.

Until now. She was on the right path, and she would not allow anything or anyone to stop her.

With one last glance at the notepad, she ripped out the page and pulled her purse from her desk drawer. The sheet fit perfectly over the laptop keyboard before she closed the lid. She wanted to keep the paper as a memento of her success.

She remembered what Kramer said about shopping. She'd purchase a few of the illusionist's videos. Excited about the changes this interview promised with her future career, she glanced about her cubicle one last time. Laptop in its carrying case and with her head high, she left the newsroom without a backward glance.

Chapter 4

In an attempt to attract buyers, the video store played the current movie trailers for shoppers browsing in the mall. All the monitors in their showcase displayed the same clips. Caitlyn ignored the screens. She started to enter the store, when a white flash caught her eye, and she swerved toward the window.

The screens lit up with the opening to a Shay Evers performance. On stage, he paced back and forth speaking to the audience. Caitlyn smiled and tilted her head as anticipation for the approaching interview built inside her. She savored the soft lyrical words spoken with a Welsh accent. Shay, with that gorgeous, sexy voice, asked the audience who among them believed in magic.

An unbelievable urge came over her to raise her hand. Surprised, she stopped the movement in mid-air and shot a look around, hoping no one noticed. Tearing her gaze from the screens, she marched into the store, determined to find some videos of Evers so she could study his acts. She refused to allow the thought of the man to distract her from the assignment. When the tall figure of a man appeared before her, she came to an abrupt stop. Blinking, she stared at his strong neck. Her gaze roamed over his strong jaw and ended at his laughing amethyst eyes.

Life sized, the cardboard cutout of Shay Evers stole her breath. His gentle, bewitching smile captured her senses. She leaned closer, and her gaze dropped to the sensual lines of his lips. Pulse pounding, she raised a finger and touched the curve. She pulled away with a jerk. The impression of being haunted by the illusionist crossed her mind. A strong premonition of someone watching her crawled over her neck, sending chills rippling across her shoulders.

"May I help you?"

Caitlyn jumped and turned to the sales clerk. A spiked-haired young woman stood with a customer-ready smile pasted on her ring-pierced lips.

"As a matter of fact, yes. I need some of his--" She pointed to the poster board. "Videos."

At the clerk's knowing look, heat raced up her neck and into her cheeks. When the salesgirl turned to lead the way, Caitlyn narrowed her eyes and grimaced at the poster. Frustrated but still curious, she wanted to discover what made her desire to reach out and feel the smoothness of his skin. His long silky-looking hair, his flawless skin--no, the reason behind her reaction centered on the sensuous sparkle in his gaze and the way he curved his sexy mouth into a smile. Combined, they pulled at her in an almost physical manner. She shook her head, attempting to erase the thoughts. Worry sliced through her. She had to remain in control tonight or she would ruin her chance for the interview.

Determined to ignore the tingles rushing through her, Caitlyn followed the woman to the far side of the store. The clerk pointed out the correct section and left her alone.

After a quick search of Evers's selections, Caitlyn found three current releases. She hoped they might contain some new information on the illusionist. Satisfied, she made her way around the aisles to the front of the store where a cashier waited.

While checking out, Caitlyn refused to glance at the life-size cutout. The more she tried to ignore it, the more the urge to look increased. Unable to resist, she peered over her shoulder. The grin on his features called to her. She faced the counter again.

"I have a friend who's crazy about Evers," she told the cashier with a tilt of her head toward the cardboard figure. "What are you going to do with that? Can I have it to give to my friend?"

The woman lifted her brows. Caitlyn leaned her elbow on the counter, trying her best to act professional while she waited for the girl's response. After a moment, the clerk smiled and winked. "You want it for a friend? Sure, why not?"

Caitlyn straightened, ignoring the insinuation that she was the one who really wanted the cutout. Unable to stop, she grinned, imagining the shock on Marcy's face as she carried Evers into her apartment.

The woman went to the back of the store and returned with a plastic-wrapped fold-up. Handing it to Caitlyn, she shrugged and said, "For some reason, the promotions department sent us two of these."

Caitlyn paid for the videos, trying to keep her excitement under control. On the way out the door, a surge of foolish embarrassment shot through her. She had never done anything like this in her entire life. Not even for a friend. Yet, Marcy would love the life-size picture of Evers. Happy that she'd bring Marcy some joy, she carried the cutout under her arm, holding it tight with one hand.

She couldn't wait to arrive at Marcy's apartment and give it to her. Caitlyn hurried through the mall, out into the parking lot. When she reached her car, she unlocked the passenger side door. Setting the cutout of Evers in the front seat, she removed the plastic to study his eyes and face. A gush of heat rushed through her body. He was just too handsome for his own good. The desire flaring within her at the mere sight of his face made her uneasy. She shifted the poster so it would remain sitting upright without getting damaged and pulled around the seatbelt to hold it in place. Once behind the wheel, she headed for Marcy's.

Caitlyn glanced at her watch. Four-thirty. She had time. As long as the traffic didn't pile up, she'd reach Marcy's apartment in a few minutes.

Stopped at a red light, she grinned, ignoring the apprehension flowing to her nerve endings. She'd never been nervous about an upcoming interview, but she had never interviewed someone so famous. She glanced over at the cutout. "You'd better watch out, pretty boy. I plan on uncovering all your secrets. Then I'm going to receive fantastic offers from the major networks. I'll be on my way to the top."

At the next light, she continued her one-sided conversation. "I have my life planned out perfectly. There's no room in it for extra emotions, especially not for famous illusionists, so whatever you're doing to me, stop it."

The quiet rumble of her car answered her. She nodded and faced forward, smiling. She took the next right and drove for several minutes, satisfied her little speech had worked on her imagination.

Marcy's building loomed along the left side of the street. Caitlyn sped up and pulled into the slot next to her friend's red sports car. An elderly woman, walking toward the parking lot from the apartments, glanced from her to the cardboard picture.

With a grin and a wave at the woman, Caitlyn turned toward the cutout of Evers and froze. The two dimensional lines blurred, then stretched and thickened into a living, breathing man. The air in the car filled with the scent of wildflowers.

She jerked away and pressed back against the door. Staring at the now fully-formed Shay Evers resting his head against the seat, she couldn't even scream. With relaxed ease, he rolled his head on the headrest to face her. The vein in his neck pulsed with the beat of his heart.

Breathing became impossible, and all she managed was a low croak of protest.

Lyrical words filled the air surrounding her. "Hello, Caitlyn. It's been a long time."

"Oh God, I've lost it," she muttered. "You're not real." Her right hand gripped the back of her seat while her left hand clutched the steering wheel.

"Am I not?" The alluring Welsh accent permeated her skin, soothing the distressed nerves throughout her body. Lean fingers reached out and brushed her cheek. "Open your heart to me. Let me help you find what you have lost."

His words, added to the tender, compelling light in his eyes, diminished her shock. A strong but gentle hand cupped her jaw and put just enough pressure to draw her toward him. Unable to resist the temptation, she closed her eyes and allowed the intensity of the moment to sweep her away.

Sharp tapping came from behind her. Caitlyn snapped upright, her gaze bouncing about the interior of her car. The cardboard poster sat in the seat next to her. What had just happened? Her heart pounded, and she couldn't draw in a deep breath. Glancing over her shoulder, she met the watery eyes of a silver haired woman. Caitlyn didn't recognize her. The poor woman continued to peer at her through the window, a concerned frown on her aged face.

Heart racing, Caitlyn waved to show she was fine. After the stranger walked away, Caitlyn peeked at the cutout. Still there, only cardboard.

Hands shaking, she clasped them and squeezed, trying to calm her racing pulse. The upcoming meeting with Shay Evers had caused her imagination to overreact. Oh God, if this kept up, she'd be a babbling idiot in front of the illusionist.

She sighed, grabbed her purse and stepped out of her car. Retrieving the cutout, she doubled the layer of plastic over his face, and hurried up the sidewalk leading to Marcy's apartment. She would not look at the handsome features. Once she finished this assignment, all thoughts of him would disappear. Obviously, this strange new compulsion to touch and do more with the man would vanish after she'd met him in person, and she could live a normal life. Within the next year, she would achieve her dream, and Shay Evers's shining star would fade from her memory.

* * * *

When Shay opened his eyes, a smile flitted across his lips. He pressed his head against the back of the sofa and turned to the opposite side of the hotel suite toward the terrace doors. He needed the sky to anchor to as old familiar sensations flowed through him. Using his magic to contact and project his physical form to Caitlyn had been so simple, yet the sight and sound of her surprised him. The desire within her gaze had been real. A complication he had not prepared for during his four year search.

A puff of breath escaped his lips in a quiet sigh. He stood. Pacing, he rubbed at his burning eyes. Sleep evaded him during the night, and his days were filled with constant activities, planning and practicing for his performances. Now he had found her, and she wanted him. To make matters worse, he felt the answer to her passion rise inside him.

Rhys would have his head.

Shay's half-lowered eyelids shielded his gaze from the four men sitting at a round conference table in the hotel suite's living room. He closed his mind to the human sounds in the room and concentrated on the wind rustling through the trees outside the half-open terrace doors.

Hoping to take his mind off what had happened a few moments ago in Caitlyn's car, he inhaled. He missed the smell of wild flowers, green grass and the rich earth of the Sidhe. Here, in this place, all he scented was the sterile fragrance from the air conditioning unit and the germ-killing cleanser the maids used. If only he could go home.

Fool. Going home was impossible as long as Caitlyn's life remained in danger.

He kept his back to the few men who made up his personal entourage. "Everyone, leave. I want to be alone for a while."

No hint of complaint came from any of them. They stopped their planning for tonight's show and bustled out, closing the door behind them.

The room, so cool earlier, turned hot. He needed air. His stride ate the distance between the sofa and the French doors leading to the terrace. He gripped the handles and pulled the portals wide. Cold air, filled with the pungent odors from the human world, coated his body and cleared his head. A few more steps and he grasped the brick balustrade, breathing deep. He ignored the stench of polluted oxygen and raised his face to catch the midday rays of the winter sun.

Caitlyn Reiley. Her name echoed in his mind.

His freedom would cease the moment he brought her home. He would, once more, resume his prison term. He deserved his punishment for the part he had in Caitlyn's disappearance. He would bring her back for no other reason than to assuage his guilt. Any other option was out of the question. Rhys wanted him punished for how he had assisted in her abduction.

During his search for Caitlyn, freedom had become more than a word to Shay. He valued the ability to move when and where he wished. To return to the Sidhe meant his freedom would end.

Sharp pain sliced through his gut. Imprisonment for twenty years was enough for him, but to Rhys, a thousand was a better punishment for his crime. His sentence would never justify what he had done to Rhys, a friend since childhood.

"Why hasn't he killed me?" Shay muttered. At least, then his misery would end. Yet, if he died, any hope for Caitlyn would die along with him.

She played the victim in this sordid affair. The fault for her kidnapping lay on the sorceress who'd used him to succeed in her wicked plan. Gwyneth still lived. He knew it. Here, in the human world, she'd made it difficult for anyone from the Sidhe to discover Caitlyn's location. Somehow, he'd kill the witch and repay the wrong done not only to Caitlyn, but also to Rhys.

Shay gritted his teeth. The skin covering his fingers tightened as they curled into fists. He was her solitary hope for salvation.

Unfamiliar presences brushed against his senses. The hair across the back of his head prickled, and his back tensed. With slow precision, he rotated his head to the right and stared at the potted hibiscus next to the terrace door. Dried leaves stirred in a soft gust of wind. Nestled in its pot on the opposite side of the door, the plant's twin crackled in response.

He moved closer to the doorway. A slow smile tugged at his mouth. There wasn't any threat. The dead plants were simply responding to the magic in his blood.

"Rejoice," he murmured to the dying plants. "Reveal to me your pleasure."

Seconds slid by. Green leaves sprouted on the hibiscus. Dozens of buds formed and opened in vibrant beauty. The white trumpet flowers curved toward him.

"Rejoice, precious ones, for your princess has been found. Soon she will return and reclaim her crown, and I will be no more," he whispered into the cold breeze.

The flowers turned their faces to the open balcony doors. Shay stiffened. He raised his gaze to stare into blue eyes.

Leaning against the door jam, Rhys commented, his tone calm and quiet, "You shouldn't work your magic in the open. A human might see."

Shay quirked a brow. "I'm an illusionist. Just practicing my art."

Without answering, Rhys stepped outside and moved to stand beside him. "I don't care for this cold. It's out of place here."

"Gwyneth?"

The blond met Shay's gaze. "Don't you think it's odd you discovered Caitlyn on television in San Francisco yesterday--and today, we arrive in Los Angeles to find her and there's an unusual, severe cold front to greet us?"

Shay snorted and nodded. "Gwyneth."

"Of course. She doesn't want the plants to reveal where she and Caitlyn are located. She can't control the plants, but she has the capability to destroy their abilities to inform us of the witch's whereabouts." Rhys inhaled, his chest expanding with the deep breath. "How can humans live in a world so soiled?"

With a low chuckle, Shay turned, returned to the railing and rested his elbows on the balustrade. "So you prefer the Sidhe?"

A smile fluttered at one corner of Rhys's mouth. "Don't you?"

The question sobered Shay. Of course he did, and Rhys knew it. The Sidhe had been his paradise until twenty five years ago. At that time, the place he loved became his prison. Then, four years ago, Rhys had surprised him by giving him a chance to atone for his crime. He had to find Caitlyn and bring her home. During the last four years, Shay had learned to value his freedom with each new day, but he'd also experienced a loss of not being able to travel back and forth to the Sidhe. So now Rhys's question was double-edged because of his guilt. Shay nodded.

"Are you ready for tonight?" Rhys looked over at him with one pale eyebrow raised.

Shay met his gaze for several moments. "Yes. I have only to gather my magic tighter about me for this work, but otherwise, I'm ready."

Rhys gusted out a low laugh. "Reminds you of all the times we went to battle, doesn't it?"

"I suppose. Only then, we had no fear of dying and losing our fellow fighters. There is too much at risk here. I want to make sure all is ready. She has to come willingly or she will be driven insane."

"True. I will hold you to her safekeeping."

For a moment, Shay savored those words. His joy at knowing Rhys gave him a measure of trust pleased him. Almost as fast, the past reared its ugly head, and he quirked a brow at the older man. "Trust? Is that what you're giving me?"

Several seconds ticked off while he waited for Rhys to answer. When he lifted his gaze to meet his, Shay shifted away, the tension becoming a barrier between them. "I gave you my trust for all our lives. You were like a brother to me. Yet in a brief moment, you threw our friendship away because of Gwyneth. I will hold you to your word concerning Caitlyn's safety. Just know your punishment will be greater if you fail."

Unable to form words to justify his action, Shay broke eye contact. "I will return her home."

"Good."

They stood side-by-side on the balcony. Neither spoke for several more minutes as the quiet of the afternoon surrounded them and eased some of the friction. Rhys released a deep breath and commented. "I sent word to Myrielle. She will be happy to hear her daughter has been found."

The words, spoken low, belied his own excitement, but Shay sensed it. Guilt reared inside him like one of the wild wolves from years ago that had desired to tear him apart. Without responding, he entered the hotel suite to dress for tonight's show.

Chapter 5

Arriving at the amphitheater where the show would take place, Caitlyn twitched the gauzy hem on the hip length tunic Marcy had insisted she wear. She tried to figure out what was wrong with the casual burgundy slacks and white sweater she had selected. There was a logical reason why Marcy found her attire inappropriate, but she never thought of her friend as a logical person. Instead, she had allowed Marcy to persuade her into wearing something slinkier, even sexy, for the extravagant magic show and backstage party. The more outfits Marcy had pulled from her closet of stylish clothes, the more skeptical Caitlyn had grown. Once her friend had chosen the right ensemble for her, she had agreed or she'd have hurt Marcy's feelings.

Deep midnight blue with a flowing flower print, the clingy material of the tunic and pants seemed too soft against her skin. She felt stripped, with nothing between her body and the outside world but the thin gauze. And the shoes were even worse. With each step, the sharp-toed mules with the two-inch heels made her want to hold onto the wall in case she slipped off them.

Caitlyn surveyed the open space of the amphitheater. Row after row of seats brimmed with excited people. Just ahead, Marcy sashayed down one of the side walkways, glancing at the tickets in her hand and then for the corresponding seats. Her skintight red dress accented every curve of her body and the crimson spiked heels added height to the leanness of her model's build. Thick, waist-length hair piled high on her head with straight strands falling here and there only accentuated Marcy's classic California looks. Sexy was the only word Caitlyn could think of to describe her beautiful friend.

"Here we go," Marcy said over her shoulder. "Told you these were great seats."

Front row. Caitlyn's heart raced. She'd take this opportunity to study him. Her main goal was to watch his behavior and see the flaws in his performance. Hopefully, after tonight and this interview, her curiosity about the performer would be satisfied.

Marcy eased into her seat with a graceful display of leg and arm. When the bald man next to her friend noticed her and gulped, Caitlyn swallowed the laugh which threatened.

"I'm so glad you came tonight," Marcy said, sending her a dazzling white smile. "I can't wait to meet him. Look, chill bumps. I'm so excited. Why didn't I bring a camera? I'd love to take a picture of you with *him*. Wouldn't that be grand?"

"You're rattling," Caitlyn remarked, shaking her head over her friend's enthusiasm.

"Can't help it." Marcy glanced past her to the people sitting on the other end of the row before turning her gaze back to Caitlyn, her bright eyes rounding. "Hey, you never did tell me what happened today."

"With Kramer?"

"Yeah."

Caitlyn stared at her friend for a moment, trying to decide if she should tell her. Marcy had so many friends in the entertainment world that the temptation for her to tell someone about the assignment could cause problems. The friend part of Caitlyn wanted to shout the news to everyone who would listen, but the journalist in her wanted to keep the information quiet so her report would be a success.

Marcy rested her chin on her palm and leaned closer. "Well? Who are you interviewing? Come on, Catey."

"It's confidential. The station wants to keep low key about it," she hedged, wishing the show would start.

"Wow. This person must be really big for them to do that." Marcy started to say more, but the lights dimmed and the audience quieted.

Multi-colored laser lights flew across the auditorium, circling, slicing and twirling as the orchestra played. The semi-circle stage remained dark except for the thin strips of lights racing across. Ceiling-to-floor curtains glinted as they glided open.

Caitlyn, nerves on edge, jerked when fireworks exploded in brilliant sparks along the back of the stage. The musical notes accelerated. Someone began to speak. At first, the words were low, but the sound increased in volume and lyrics became clearer with each note. Foreign words which she didn't understand. Was he singing in Welsh? She frowned. What did the words mean?

The spotlights focused all at once on a suspended platform in the middle and top section of the stage. The figure of a man stood high above the floor, silhouetted against the lighted background. He stepped down off the platform.

Caitlyn's gasp echoed the audience's cries of awe. Shay Evers. Dressed in black leather pants and a white, billowy shirt, he moved with feline grace. From her vantage point, he appeared as though he walked on air, but after a second, she noticed a thin cable stretched from the top back to the middle front of the stage. He strode on the cable as if on solid ground. Midway, he performed a perfect cartwheel on the wire.

She scanned the area above his shoulders and head, searching for other wires attached to him, but didn't see any. Intrigued, she made a mental note to research his balancing ability. She couldn't remember a mention of acrobatic training in the background information she'd found. His balance was perfect.

As the show progressed, she remained still with her hands clasped in her lap, observing every move the illusionist made as she tried to rationalize his performance. After an hour of logic-defying feats, Evers stopped in the middle of the stage. His gaze roamed over the spectators.

"A volunteer from the audience." Evers strode across the stage, stopping every few steps to study someone. He talked and joked with several front-row people along the way. When he reached the end, he doubled back and paused in front of Caitlyn and Marcy.

His amethyst eyes caught and held Caitlyn's gaze. The hair on her arms stood.

He moved down the nearby stage steps to a place not far from where she sat, took a young woman's hand and tugged her to her feet. This close, Caitlyn could see every line of his handsome face. Her breath caught in her throat as she struggled to suppress her reaction to his nearness. She blinked, and he was striding back to the stage. A large prop had been rolled onto the center of the stage. Concealed by a white sheet, the huge piece stood alone. Shay led the young woman to the object and commented about taking a leap of faith.

Shay turned to the woman and she giggled. Her bright smile and sparkling eyes were obvious signs that she'd fallen under the illusionist's spell. With a practiced flick of his wrist, the sheet billowed out and away from the prop. The deep mahogany framing a mirror glinted in the light. Carved Celtic figures roamed across the arch. Spiraling wooden pillars encased the sides, holding the glass in place.

The audience responded with appreciative sighs and murmurs.

"God, I'd love to have it in my apartment. It's gorgeous," Marcy whispered.

Caitlyn nodded, admiring the craftsmanship. "Wouldn't fit at your place. Now mine, that's a different story--it'd go perfect in my bedroom."

Marcy smothered a laugh, and Caitlyn patted her to be quiet. "Shush, I want to hear."

Taking a step toward the stage's edge, Evers glanced about the audience. "There was once a faery tale about a witch and her magical mirror. Well, she's not the only one to have a magical mirror." He moved back to the woman waiting by the mirror. "Do you want to see what my looking glass can do?"

The woman nodded, her expression one of wonder as she stared at him.

"It is the doorway into the faery world. Do you believe that?"

Her expression changed into a curious frown. She shrugged and shook her head.

"No? Perhaps you'll believe once you go there." Shay took hold of the side of the mirror and rolled it around, touching the air about the frame. "See? Nothing there. No fake doors. Floor is solid."

Shay stopped and positioned the mirror so that it was facing the woman and the audience. Rapping on the glass with his knuckles, he grinned and spoke to the audience. "See? Nothing out of the ordinary. But if I do this..."

He placed his palm flat on the glass. Ripples started on the surface below his palm. Liquid silver rolled away like in a calm lake. Caitlyn straightened, studying his every move.

"Come with me," he told the woman. He held his hand out and she placed hers in his. With his free hand, he sliced down with the side facing the glass. His hand disappeared into the glass. The woman gasped and started to giggle. His arm slipped beyond the glass all the way to the shoulder; the entire arm now inside the mirror.

Next, his body tilted toward the glass, vanished from the stage and reappear within its depths. He glanced at the woman whose hand he clasped and grinned. "Come, sweetheart, follow me to a world only dreamed about."

Caitlyn's chest tightened. Captivating, his voice pulled at her. The urge to stand, make her way to his side, caught her unawares. Nothing in her past had prepared her for the battle she fought to remain in her seat. Holding her breath, she couldn't tear her gaze from his face as he assisted the woman into the glass, guiding her inch by slow inch.

Once inside, Shay waved. As he lowered his arm, the mirror's glass blackened. No Shay, no woman, nothing.

Spotlights danced over the audience. People about her and Marcy twisted in their seat, equally looking for the illusionist and his volunteer.

Shay's laughter rang out from the rear of the theater. All eyes focused on the main aisle leading to the lobby. The curtains pulled apart. He strode through, the woman's hand still clasped in his. Behind them a unicorn, head high, coat shining a glimmering white and a horn glinting gold in the light, followed. Gasps, cheers and excited shouts rose from the audience.

Shay stopped halfway down the aisle and held up the woman's hand. Her clothes, no longer the one she'd worn on stage, sparkled with tiny shards which caught the light and flickered. The off-the-shoulder floating gown, a pale blue, hung on her body.

Caitlyn stared, unable to drag in a single breath. This performance was nothing like she'd ever seen. Something tugged at her from deep inside her chest. The sensation seemed familiar, while at the same time, foreign. She managed to pull herself together once she realized how focused she'd become with watching Shay. Still, the impression that something had awakened within and remained out of sight on the outer edges of her mind bothered her, like she needed to remember something she'd forgotten but couldn't.

The illusionist, amid the applause, escorted the woman back to the stage, the unicorn on his heels. Once on stage, Shay motioned to the mirror. The unicorn pranced to the glass. Its horn touched the glass and waves moved across the surface from the point of contact. Like Shay did before, the unicorn stepped into the mirror. Caitlyn held her breath, waiting until the animal was completely through the glass. She shook her head as the silky tail swished once before it disappeared from the stage.

Waving goodbye to the audience, Shay led the volunteer off stage with a laughing comment about changing her clothes. Handing her off, he faced the audience again. After a final bow, he strode toward the wings.

Chapter 6

Once Shay's assistants removed the mirror, the band started playing a new tune. Scantily dressed dancers performed during his absence.

Marcy leaned over and spoke close to Caitlyn's ear. Her designer perfume, floral and alluring, floated about them. "Well, didn't I tell you he was wonderful?"

Caitlyn swerved her head toward her friend and grinned. "I'm glad I changed my mind. He boggles my mind with trying to figure out how he does his acts. It's amazing."

Excitement shone in Marcy's gaze, her bright smile was as white as always.

"I know." She tapped Caitlyn's arm and laughed. "I have to admit. I was a little disappointed he didn't choose me."

Caitlyn shook her head. Leave it to her friend to think only of herself.

She opened her mouth to respond but stopped as Shay walked onto center stage dressed in a different pair of pants, still black leather but with fringe and silver disks hanging on the outer sides of his thighs. The first white shirt had been exchanged for a different one with lengths of lace flowing about his neck and wrists.

Uneasy with the rapid way her heart beat each time she saw him, Caitlyn narrowed her gaze, seeking some flaw with the entertainer. How he managed to dress in such a feminine fashion and still ooze sex appeal stunned her. The neck of the shirt gaped to mid-chest and parts of solid muscled skin peeked out with each of his movements. Tawny skin called to her, stoking a fierce desire to reach out and stroke the smoothness. She swallowed and clenched her fingers into fists.

He strolled past where she sat, and she waited for him to glance at her but he didn't. His accented voice rang out over the speaker system with a question. "Who believes in the fountain of youth?"

Shouts and clapping answered him.

From both ends of the stage came ten attendants. Each rolled a large disk which they positioned across the front of the stage. Five on the left and five on the right, lining them up in a semi-circle. On the top of each disk, a senior citizen stood, sat in wheelchairs or leaned on walkers or canes. They smiled and waved at the audience.

Shay strode behind the aged people from one end of the stage to the other. A new song started, and he sang. The lyrics spoke of timeless youth and to never give up on feeling young. His assistants covered the elderly with satiny white sheets. Once the elderly were hidden from view, his attendants rolled them about the stage on the disks to verify there were no wires or trap doors.

Midway through the song, Evers wove through the ten sheet-covered people, sprinkling glittering dust over them. Her heart pounded in anticipation. Unable to pull her gaze away, she barely breathed, watching every movement, listening to each note. Her hands ached where she clenched them in her lap. The music escalated. For each deep dip in the song, Shay ripped the sheets one at a time from the covered people.

The audience cried out in surprise. Instead of the elderly figures, children stood and sat. A small girl sat on a tricycle where before a walker had been situated in front of an elderly woman.

Caitlyn swallowed, the ever growing sense of something opening up inside her returned, like a doorway cracking open. A frisson of fear went through her. She didn't understand what had happened and no matter how she tried, what he'd done was beyond explanation. The children even resembled the older people. The old man on the end had worn glasses and freckles had covered his lined face. The boy, now in his place, wore similar glasses and his red hair matched the freckles which spread over his nose and cheeks.

Marcy's hand gripped Caitlyn's wrist. Her friend glanced wide-eyed her way for a brief second. Caitlyn forced a smile and quipped, "You're right. He's fantastic."

A frown crossed the blonde's brow. She leaned closer, not taking her gaze from where Evers played pied-piper to the children trailing behind him. "How did he do that?"

Caitlyn shook her head and shrugged. "Illusion?"

Over the last few years, the networks had aired a few of his shows. The ones she had watched consisted of one or two incredible magic feats. This was the second extraordinary act in a row for his performance tonight, and with excitement, she waited to see what others he would perform before the end.

The rest of the show careened past her as she struggled to rationalize all that had occurred onstage. An hour and a half later, she leaned against the wall in the amphitheater's ladies room and waited as Marcy applied fresh powder and lipstick. In a matter of seconds, they would go through the hallways to the special room in the building for the backstage party.

Her blood continued to rush through her veins, and the mirrors behind the sinks beckoned her to look and verify they were solid glass and not a doorway to a different world. No, she refused to believe what happened on stage earlier held even a small measure of reality. His act thrived with the spectacular illusions. Only illusions. Evers was a fake, and her determination strengthened to discover all his little tricks.

She turned and smiled, concentrating on her friend's reflection. Marcy's beauty amazed her sometimes. Flawless tanned skin enhanced the striking blond streaks in her hair. Bright blue eyes rose and met hers in the mirror.

"Excited?" Marcy compressed her lips to smooth the fresh coat of frosted pink lipstick.

"Maybe--a little. I haven't had time to think about it." Caitlyn stepped away from the wall. "Hurry up. I want to get this over with."

"Oooh, she's anxious. Why?" Marcy wagged a finger at her. "I know you, Caitlyn. Don't give me that strong I'm-not-nervous attitude. You're shaking inside. I can see the vein pulsing in your neck. Don't be nervous, he's a man, just like all the rest. Of course, he is famous, rich, has gorgeous looks and his body--I can't wait to get my hands on him."

Caitlyn rolled her eyes. She seriously considered the same thing, but she would never say the words out loud. They sounded vulgar and full of raw emotions, two things she excluded from her life. "Did it ever occur to you that maybe he won't even notice you?"

Marcy laughed, a nice throaty sound, and stepped closer, slipping her arm through Caitlyn's. "Does it matter? How many women do you know can say they had the chance to proposition Shay Evers? To me, that's more important than actually getting him in the sack."

"It's good to know you're not as bad as you appear." She patted Marcy's hand as they walked, arms entwined, from the ladies room. Caitlyn blinked several times to adjust her sight to the dim light in the corridor. Decorative lights hanging fifty feet above did little to dispel the shadows along the edges of the hall. Darkness lined the way. The eerie atmosphere gave her a chill.

Several teenage girls dressed in sparkling shirts and tattered jeans brushed passed them. Their overpowering perfume and excited giggles grated on Caitlyn's frazzled nerves.

Marcy swung her head toward her and winked. "Did I tell you how fabulous you look? From now on, you'll wear your hair down. Even without any makeup, this outfit and your hair make a big difference. Of course you still have a long way to go before you'll match me in looks. Who knows? Evers might notice you and ignore me. Wouldn't it be wild?" Her eyes lit up with her laugh, and she hugged Caitlyn's arm tighter against her side. "Just imagine the headlines. Illusionist falls head-over-heels for aspiring news reporter. You'd be set for life."

Blood rushed to Caitlyn's cheeks. Marcy managed to dig her point deep into Caitlyn's flesh with her words. No matter what she did, she'd never match Marcy in the looks department. Angry, Caitlyn's answer came out stronger than she'd meant. "I have no intention of ever getting married or falling love. You know how I feel about the subject."

Marcy rolled her eyes. "Oh calm down, I was just teasing. You'll change your mind one day. Who knows? Today might be the day and Shay Evers the man."

She shook her head, denying Marcy's words, but her friend had planted the seed. Deep within her heart, she wanted a relationship with Shay, but in reality, something so fabulous would never happen. She maneuvered Marcy to the right, avoiding a group of giggling fans. The crowds thinned, but a large number of young girls still roamed the halls.

Marcy pointed to a hallway branching off ahead of them. "Take a right up here. The elevator is there. Second floor and it's our turn to perform."

Caitlyn's stomach rolled. What was wrong with her? She shouldn't feel so anxious. Evers was, like Marcy said, just a man. A sharp pang sliced through her. The rational side of her accepted her friend intended to tease her, but now the idea whirled in her head. The schoolgirl jitters inside her refused to go away.

Lost in her thoughts, she let Marcy monopolize the conversation. The elevator doors opened to a huge social area, and she forced her attention to her surroundings.

People pooled here and there. Smiles were pasted on everyone's faces, white teeth flashing and battling for brilliance with all the diamonds and jewels in the room. A few groups wandered from one side of the room to the other. She stepped from the elevator and cool air smacked her in the face, relieving her internal rise in temperature from her thoughts of Evers. Marcy guided her toward the tables set up on the far side of the room.

"Omigod there he is." Her friend's excited murmur reached her above the quiet conversations around them. "Come on, hurry. I've seen turtles move faster than you. I don't want to miss him. These parties don't usually last long. If you don't speak to the star at the start, he'll disappear and you'll miss your chance."

Caitlyn frowned. How had Marcy spotted Evers in the crowd? They shifted right to avoid a group of people, and when she glanced toward the tables, she saw him. With his rear resting against the edge of the last table, he smiled and nodded at the small crowd of people huddled in a semi-circle in front of him.

Once she noticed him, the room's perimeter darkened while the light surrounding him took on a luminous glow. A clear glass, half-filled with brown liquid hung loose from his fingertips. Long dark eyelashes hid his eyes for a second, and then gleaming amethyst met and held her gaze.

The air in her lungs ceased expelling. She failed to force it out. Caught within his brilliant stare, she battled against a wave of dizziness. The slow lowering of his right eyelid released her.

He'd winked.

She froze. Did he wink at her? Yes, he had.

He looked away.

Freed from the hypnotic spell he cast on her, she exhaled.

Narrowing her gaze, she studied him. What kind of game was he playing? Her mind screamed to turn, run away. She'd find the quiet spot, phone Kramer and tell him she couldn't go through with this interview.

And he'd blow up and fire her. She shut her eyes for a second, trying to find a place of calmness inside her.

When she opened them, Evers nodded in response to something someone said. Even though Caitlyn believed he'd stared into her eyes, there wasn't any proof he focused on her. More than fifty people roamed about the room. Her imagination was playing with her, and if she wanted to succeed with her career she would have to learn to handle her reactions to his every move.

Satisfied with her analysis of the situation, she focused on the illusionist once more. Someone stepped away from him, allowing her a few moments to study his every move.

One long leg, covered in black leather, stretched away from the table while the other bent back under the wooden edge. Thick dark hair framed his features and hung over and behind his shoulders. Inhaling, she glanced at his face. The real man was far sexier than the cutout had been and, unlike the cardboard picture, he moved. The left side of his mouth twitched. He glanced in her direction again.

Marcy freed Caitlyn's arm and glided to Evers's side, squeezing past the people in front of him. The sexy blonde stopped less than six inches from him and leaned close. The side of her friend's breast brushed against his arm, and Caitlyn clenched her jaw, determined to rise above the sudden surge of jealousy bubbling within her.

Rolling her eyes, she refused to watch his reaction to her friend's overtures. She hoped no one had seen her enter the room with Marcy. The woman was a great friend, but her wild streak bothered Caitlyn.

She moved toward a buffet table not far from them. She kept her gaze on the cheese tray in front of her. Without having to look, she imagined how well Marcy was coming on to the man. Her friend had no shame when it came to men.

"What is it about him that attracts beautiful women?" A man's said from behind her in a deep, accented voice.

Curious to see the man asking the question, Caitlyn swiveled toward the speaker. Tall and slender, pale blond hair tied at the back of his neck, the middle-aged stranger stood less than a foot away from her. He stood like a monolith, his arms crossed over his chest. A frown marred his handsome face. He reminded her of a Greek statue, his features perfect and cool.

The man tilted his head and raised an eyebrow at her.

She shrugged and bit off a piece of cheese she took from the platter. "I have no idea. I'm not sure I want to know, either." She smiled and accepted a glass of wine from a passing waiter. Rich burgundy aroma rose from the fluted glass.

"It's as if he has a scent about him which attracts women," the man continued.

An image appeared in Caitlyn's mind of a stag in rut. Yes, perfect comparison for the illusionist. She raised the glass to her lips and wine shifted toward her lips. She took a small sip, the rich aroma streaming up her nose.

The blond man snapped his fingers and smiled at her. "I know. A stag in rut."

Caitlyn choked.

Chapter 7

Heat seared her throat, and she tried to draw in a tiny bit of air to cough.

"Oh my. Here, take another drink." The stranger took her hand and brought the glass to her lips. Her breath rasped as she tried to shake her head.

Strong hands came from behind, caught her under her arms and lifted them above her head, glass and all. The gentle touch slid down to grasp her ribs below her breasts. "Keep your hands up and try to cough. A good deep breath and you'll be fine."

Through the burning pain, realization hit her. That voice. Evers. He was helping her. Oh God, she liked his touch. So nice--no, more than nice. She coughed. The next second, she stiffened, the burning in her windpipe forgotten. Warmth coated her body from behind. From the top of her head, down her back, blanketing her legs, her entire backside rested against him.

His body against her should have bothered her, but the feel of his strong hands under her breasts, cupping them up, his thumbs at each side, distracted her as sharp pangs traveled to the tips of her breasts. Her nipples hardened, and she forgot to cough. With a choked groan, she turned her face toward him. Oh, why did concern shine in his amethyst gaze?

"Would you please remove your hands from my breasts?" Throat raw, her words came out husky and low.

His eyes widened, and he jerked his hands away with a grin, shifting away from her. "Sorry. I didn't realize."

"It's okay," she muttered as heated blood rushed to her face.

His eyes narrowed. "I know you. You're the news reporter, Caitlyn Reiley."

Caitlyn tried to smile, but felt cornered. She looked past his handsome face and saw Marcy. Her friend stood a couple of feet behind him, her face expressionless.

Marcy's gaze met hers and a chill raced up Caitlyn's spine. Gleaming with a strange internal fire, Marcy's eyes glowed bright. Malice aimed at her through the look sent an unexpected stab of fear lancing through her. From the edge of her line of vision, Evers turned toward her. The pale blond stranger, who'd been standing by, observing in silence, shifted closer to her. Did she imagine the instant protective wall emanating from the two men?

Caitlyn blinked, and when she raised her eyelids and focused, Marcy stood at ease, smiling at her. Had she imagined what had happened?

"Forgive Catey. It's not every day she meets a famous person." Marcy stared pointedly at him. "Hey, listen, can you kind of keep an eye on her? I want to talk to a guy over there. He's your music tech, isn't he? If I can't have you, then he's next on my list. Catey, let me know when you want to leave, okay?"

Still unsure of what she'd just witnessed, Caitlyn nodded while Marcy pivoted and melted into the crowd. She'd known Marcy since junior high. There wasn't a mean bone in her body, yet what Caitlyn sensed and saw coming from her friend frightened her. Was Marcy jealous of her? No, she would never leave Caitlyn with him if that were true.

"Are you all right?" The question came from the stranger. He had remained silent, concern lining his features.

Caitlyn smiled and nodded. "Yes and thanks."

Shay frowned. "Did Lance send you a pass for tonight?"

"No." Her hair fluttered across her cheek as she shook her head. "I came with Marcy Richards."

The frown deepened. He looked even more handsome wearing such a dark expression.

"Marcy?" He repeated curiosity evident in his gaze.

Caitlyn kept her tone even, but on the inside, she cringed with embarrassment. "The blonde. The one who asked you to keep an eye on me."

His right brow rose, and he glanced in the direction where Marcy had disappeared. "You're not like her, are you?"

Caitlyn's back stiffened. "And what exactly does that mean? Marcy may be a little forward, but she's a great friend, and no, she and I are complete opposites. She's one of a kind."

"I meant no offense." He faced her, a wide grin spreading across his lips. He leaned close, his voice lowered to a conspiratorial whisper. "Are you spying on me? A little undercover work before the interview?"

Guilt rushed through her and heated her cheeks. She hoped he wouldn't notice the added tint to her face. "No, I'm not. I wanted to observe you unobserved. That's all." Her tone came out rigid and formal.

"Ah." He straightened and clasped his hands behind his back, staring at her. "I see you've met Rhys. He's my gardener."

Surprised, she looked at the tall blond man. "You're a gardener?"

"I have a magical thumb." Rhys held up his right thumb. His eyes lit with flashing blue glints. She relaxed and smiled at him.

"Do you always bring your gardener with you on tour?" she asked Shay.

Before he answered, Rhys spoke up, "No. I came to search for a rare and exquisite flower. Shay was kind enough to offer me a way home."

"Did you find it?" Caitlyn wondered, her curiosity piqued.

"Yes. As a matter of fact, I did, with a little help from Shay."

Glancing at Evers, she remarked, "My, what a paragon of kindness."

"Paragon." Shay slowly repeated the word, as though savoring the feel of it on his tongue. "I like it. Did you hear her, Rhys? I'm a paragon of kindness." He tilted his head and lowered his voice. "I've been telling him ever since our childhood what a good fellow I am. He doesn't believe me."

His words brought an unbidden smile to Caitlyn's lips. "Childhood friends?"

"Like brothers." He nodded and winked at Rhys. The gardener's mouth lifted with a one-sided smile that seemed to contain no humor. Interesting. "Rhys always pulled me into one scrape or another. Of course, he helped me a great amount too. I was happy to assist him with this matter."

Filing this bit of information away, she asked "So, you like plants?"

"You're not interviewing me, are you?"

"No. Do you see a tablet? A mic? I'm not here officially."

His gaze lingered on her a moment longer. The next second, the devastating white smile that had wowed most breathing females flashed. The area around them lightened. When he spoke, her heartbeat sped up and her breath stopped midway to her lungs. "I love plants. All kinds. I suppose you could say it's my hobby."

"What's your favorite?" The words came out breathless.

She hadn't wanted them to sound that husky, almost sexy. A strange tension came over her muscles. The sudden flare of desire caught her off guard. In danger of becoming one of those mindless women who swooned at the mention of his name, she tried to convince herself his smile didn't affect her. No, it wouldn't. Not her.

"Any kind. Want to know what Rhys's favorite is?"

"I don't believe Ms. Reiley cares to know," Rhys interrupted. The tightness in his voice took her aback. Shay called them friends but the other man's behavior pointed to something else.

"Oh, but I would. What's your favorite?" Caitlyn asked, relieved to turn her attention from Evers.

The superstar never gave Rhys a chance to reply. He took her arm to bring her attention back to him. The warmth of his hand through her sleeve's thin gauze blazed a trail along her nerve endings straight to the base of her belly.

"It's the blackthorn tree. Have you ever seen one?" As he spoke, her thighs squeezed tight.

"No," she whispered.

The waves of heat coming from his hand continued to send messages through her body. A rush of warmth pooled between her legs and the muscles at the junction of her thighs trembled. His gaze captured and refused to release hers. She attempted to shake her head but failed. Every part of her body flared with awareness, centered on him. The lyrical words he spoke poured over her, inflaming a need in her. Oh, she needed to breathe.

Deep and hypnotic, Shay's voice held her in its grip. "It's black. The twisted trunk and limbs are covered with thorns, hence the name. It's one of the few trees that bloom in the spring before the leaves. The fruit, if eaten too early, is bitter and vile."

Momentary silence, followed by his gaze cutting to Rhys, made a chill race up Caitlyn's spine. The tension between the two men grew stronger. Shay looked back at her and continued.

"Ah, such a wonderful tree to grow and to nurture. The blooms are a stark contrast to the tree. Waxy and white, they cover the branches. The tree can reach up to ten feet in height, though most people only allow them to grow to four or six feet."

He paused, and she shifted closer, trapped by the light in his strange and beautiful eyes.

"There are legends about the tree. One tells how a demon is imprisoned within the tree, sentenced for eternity in its trunk."

Caitlyn tried to swallow, to breathe. She grew lightheaded waiting for him to finish the story, but instead, he dropped his hand and grinned. "By the way, I love pansies."

The torturous build-up of tension eased from her limbs and left her muscles tingling.

Rhys cleared his throat. "We leave in an hour. I need to return to my hotel and retrieve my bags." He shifted his cool attention to Caitlyn. "Ms. Reiley, a true pleasure to meet you. Perhaps I'll see you once more during your stay in Wales."

She nodded, her smile stiff, but she remained intrigued. Rhys had reminded Shay of his trip as though informing a wayward child of their departure. "I hope so, too."

He bowed his head and strode across the room. Caitlyn watched him reach the elevator. A nagging thought told her Evers deliberately tried to hurt his friend's feelings, and he'd used his charismatic abilities to drive his point home.

After Rhys entered the elevator, she decided to try her hunch. "You did that on purpose. You like playing games with people, don't you?"

"Did what?"

Oh, no, he didn't just try to fluff her off. She had eyes and ears. What was he playing at? "You were pushing him. You wanted a reaction from him. Why would you be so mean? Isn't he your friend?"

"I like limits, Ms. Reiley. I like to push them. Do you?" Shay lifted a brow at her. Without taking his gaze off her, he raised a finger and motioned for an attendant to bring the wine tray.

"From what you said, you've known each other all your lives. That'd make you close, like you said, brothers. Why would you do something like that?"

"Do you ever talk to your friend about her behavior? Don't you wonder what it would be like to see how far you can go with someone or something?" He removed two glasses from the tray and nodded toward a nearby doorway. "This conversation needs more privacy. Shall we?"

"Of course," she said with a slight nod. Good, she needed to question him. All her previous impressions of him disappeared in light of the real man. He had behaved so strangely to a man he'd declared to be a close friend. She hoped to find out why. And this would give her a chance to relieve some of the tension he'd forced her emotions to run through since she met him.

They wove through the crowd, avoiding any major stops. When they reached the door, she glanced at the wine glasses in his hands for a second before opening it. He nodded thanks, and motioned for her to precede him. No one occupied the office with a sitting area. When the door breezed shut, they were alone, cut off from everyone.

Shay moved toward the sitting area. Stopping in front of the sofa, he faced her, still holding the glasses. Neutral in tone, the sofa and end chairs contrasted with his stark white and black attire, making him appear larger and dangerous.

Caitlyn studied him as he waited in front of the sofa. When he remained silent, she stepped to the closest chair and sank to the edge. He handed her a glass before sitting on the sofa and propping his feet on the table. He twirled the bowl of the fluted glass between his palms as he watched her.

"Now, Ms. Reiley, are you upset with me?"

The need to melt under his deep, relaxing tone came over her again. Fighting to maintain a hold on her senses, she took a gulp of wine. Warmth spread through her belly, helping compose her enough to speak.

Calmer, she responded. "I'm not sure. I assume you hate blackthorn trees."

"You assume correctly."

"And yet, they're his favorite."

"Correct again."

"So why did you describe the tree in such a dark, malicious way? I had the impression you were trying to make him angry or worse--hurt him." She leaned forward, staring hard. "Tell me why? Do you hate him?"

"I told you. I like to discover other people's limits. I know his limit, and I push it to see if he can take it. As humans, we all do it in one way or another. This is my way. What is your way, Caitlyn Reiley?" He raised his glass and saluted her before he took a sip.

His callous manner took her by surprise. Heat flooded her face and she struggled to maintain her even breathing as her anger flared. His charm had peeled off to reveal a cold-hearted man. Her attraction to him faded. "My friends are important to me. I wouldn't hurt them."

"Hmm." The very simple noise in his throat indicated a far more complicated thought roamed through his mind. "Well, it seems I've found one of your limits. But I'm thinking there are more. On the outside, you seem as you appear. Calm, cool, almost cold and analytical. But underneath, I can sense someone different."

He studied her far closer than before, his nostrils flaring a bit, and his gaze delved deeper than the surface of her body. He saw into her soul. The idea both intrigued and frightened her. "For instance, I think you would have me believe you aren't affected by me at all."

Her eyes widened with his unexpected comment. She started to deny it, but he continued. "I think you want me to believe that you, of all the women out there," he made an easy motion toward the larger, still crowded room, "are here only to observe me before you interview me.

Does that explain why you sit so far away? You're afraid if you come closer I'll see your interest is deeper, darker and a little less professional."

The finely-shaped lips curled into a seductive smile that forced her lungs to stop working. The uncanny way he guessed the truth about her spurred an instinctive need to return to the safety of the other room. She gripped the arms of the chair to remain sitting.

"But I can see there is still a professional side to this interview. And now I am led to wonder, what would you do to keep your place in this interview?"

Chapter 8

His question stunned her for a second before shock drove her to her feet. She set the glass on the table a little harder than she'd intended. The glass clanked on the wood. The burgundy sloshed on the mirrored surface. "There are some things I would never do."

She turned, intent on leaving the insufferable man behind, but the sound of slow clapping stopped her. She glanced over her shoulder. He stood, his feet planted solid on the floor. White teeth flashed in his tanned face.

Her gaze narrowed. "You said all this on purpose. Testing my limit."

Fury drenched her in fire. She didn't like his games. And she didn't like the rules he'd set. Did he think he could say and do whatever he pleased without any consequences?

Without another thought, she stepped toward him, hand raised, determined to slap the grin off his face. One second she swung with all her anger and frustration, the next, he'd grasped her hand. He tugged, and she landed against his chest. His free arm banded her waist, holding her still. Her gaze locked with his, and her rage turned to liquid heat. The depth of the desire surging through her amazed her. Confused, she silently tried to deny what her body screamed.

"Sweet Caitlyn, push the limits in your heart and free the magic in your soul," he murmured before his lips touched hers. Soft, tender, a gentle brush of skin over skin.

He raised his head, and she moaned. "What are you doing to me?"

"Calming you," he whispered. "If I release you, will you promise not to slap me?"

She nodded and tried to shake off the lethargy gripping her. "I promise."

With his help, she eased down onto the sofa. He sat next to her. Swallowing, she frowned at him. "Are you a hypnotist?"

Shay chuckled low, shook his head and shifted to face her. "Afraid not. I'm a simple illusionist."

He reached out and slipped the hair from her cheek with one hand, while with the other, he clasped her fingers on the sofa between them. "Feel better?"

After a deep breath, she nodded. "Are you going to tell me the reason behind what you just did?"

"I had to know how far you could be pushed." He stared at her fingers, brushing the pad of his thumb over the knuckles. "Do you understand what door you're opening with this interview?"

Frowning, she shook her head. "What do you mean?"

"Once it's known I asked you to interview me, all the sleazy reporters and photographers will crawl out of their holes and bombard you. I was nice. They won't be. They'll start rumors, swear I asked for you because we're lovers, demand to know my sexual preferences and who knows what else they'll come up with. Are you ready for it? Can you deal with it?" His gaze held hers, and her heart twisted at the deep concern in his eyes.

"I'm not normally defensive," she said with a small smile. "So much has happened today with the news of the interview, I suppose my nerves are overstretched. Don't worry about me. I can take care of myself." She squeezed his hand for a second.

He raised an eyebrow. "Can you? They'll pick you to the bone, Caitlyn. You're moving into the big league. It's not fun. They'll find out everything about you. Even some things that aren't true."

She opened her mouth to argue his point, but stopped. She'd never considered the negative changes this assignment would create in her future. Was she ready for them? Professionally--yes--but would her confidence and personal life withstand the publicity?

Refusing to consider defeat, she lifted her chin and said, "I'm not passing this up. I understand how crazy it's going to get, but the opportunity is too good to ignore. My future career depends on this interview. This is my chance for a spot at a major network. The only way I won't do the interview is if you change your mind, and I'm hoping you won't."

His gaze lingered on her for several seconds before he nodded. The light in the room seemed brighter, centralized on him as he issued soft, mesmerizing words. "Let darkness and light guard that no one intercede. From this moment on, your fate has been decreed."

Caitlyn frowned at his sing-song rhyme. It sounded medieval and out of place, but he was serious. His pupils had dilated to twin black pools.

While she stared into them, she swore low chimes tinkled and the room filled with the rich, earthy aroma of wildflowers.

She shook her head and smiled as she asked, "What does that mean?"

His grin flashed. "Nothing. I'm a fan of ancient manuscripts. Always thought I would impress the ladies with my eloquent and poetic phrases, but it didn't work out. You're the only one in a long time that hasn't looked at me like I'm nuts."

"If you do it very often, I'll think the worst. Might even call the men in the white coats to come pick you up." She couldn't stop smiling at him.

His eccentricities were minor compared to his overall charm. And as long as she kept the interview, it'd be nothing to overlook his poetic phrases and rambles. Just additional information she needed to help uncover the real man beneath the performer's facade.

His gentle behavior fueled her curiosity. She needed to survive the next two weeks without falling in love with him. Now, after meeting him, seeing him face-to-face, talking to him, she stood on the edge of the unknown feeling called love. He wound his net tighter around her emotions, binding her to him.

"Well, Caitlyn, I've enjoyed your company, but time is running out. I have a plane to catch. Rhys will have my head if I make him wait." He stood, unfolding his lean body from the sofa and pulled her with him.

Their bodies brushed, and her breath caught. She reacted to him like a school girl with her first crush. No, this was like a bee attracted to rich nectar. She couldn't remember the last time she had fresh honey. The memory of the sticky and sweet flavor had her mouth watering. So appealing. Just like Shay Evers.

With her heart pounding against her chest and legs weakening, her one thought was to press against him. She forced her body to stiffen and step to the side, glad to put distance between them. "Until tomorrow. Have a safe flight."

"You, too. I'm looking forward to seeing you again."

His gaze on her face sent warmth through her. He escorted her to the door. She aimed a pasted-on smile in his direction. Once through, she didn't look back. She needed to leave, now. Reaching the elevator as she pulled her cellphone from her pocket, she punched in Marcy's number. After three rings, her friend answered, her voice husky and low.

Caitlyn didn't give her a chance to say anything past the greeting. "Where are you?"

"On my way to my apartment. Why? Where are you?"

Static crackled over the receiver.

"You left me?" Caitlyn raised her brows, staring hard at the lighted elevator button.

"Why not? Last time I looked, you were with Evers right before you two disappeared. I figured you were in very capable hands. Well, how was it?" The question held a definite twinge of heat, jealousy evident. The reason behind the wicked look Marcy had given her was so obvious now.

"Nothing happened," Caitlyn muttered. "We talked, that's all. Listen, I'm going to get a cab and go home. Try to stay out of trouble, okay?" She didn't wait for Marcy to reply. The doors whisked open, revealing her avenue of escape.

* * * *

Shay studied Caitlyn until the elevator doors shut. He considered his earlier assessment of her. Dull, plain? No, he'd been wrong. She possessed a vibrant aura along with exquisitely beautiful features and form. A fire burned beneath her cool, collected veneer. At his touch, the fire had flared to life.

This would help him, even though he found he wasn't prepared for it. His own reaction to her surprised him. Rhys's voice soothed him, but touching Caitlyn filled him with such peace. Temptation to hold her and never release her came over him.

He sighed. Impossible. Until she returned home to her family and solved the riddle, thus breaking the curse binding her magic, she didn't have a future. Neither did he.

Shaking his head, he motioned to tell one of his bodyguards he was ready to leave. Surrounded by the protective barrier supplied by the men, he exited the party through a private door and traveled down a secure elevator to the basement floor.

The limousine waited at the end of a ramp sloping up from the basement. To avoid lingering fans waiting to mob him, Shay sprinted toward the vehicle. His guards kept up and one passed him, and when he reached the limousine, opened the back door.

Shay ducked through the opening and stiffened as he settled in the seat. Rhys sat where he had earlier, calmly waiting. Shay refused to break the mounting silence.

"She is like her mother," Rhys commented, his tone soft and contemplative. Shay shot a glance at him. The tender expression on Rhys's face hardened the second he turned to him. "Well, what do you think?"

Shay lowered his gaze. The silence grew for several moments while he wrestled with an answer. He'd learned patience in the last twenty-four years. Patience and silence had been constant companions, so the lengthy seconds did not weigh on him.

"I believe there is hope," he finally murmured. "She's not as shielded by the curse as I assumed."

"Excellent. So you shouldn't have any problem enthralling her so she will feel comfortable when she returns to the Sidhe," Rhys said. "I don't want her to believe she is insane. She must be kept calm through all this."

Shay shook his head. "It's not so simple. I didn't sense any belief in her. I can't guarantee she will accept the magic in her. She's been too long in this world." He sensed his friend's gaze as he waited for a response.

"You are a muse," Rhys said. "A court muse. Your magic is joined with Caitlyn's because of your part in her kidnapping. If you do not think you are capable of helping her, then you will return to your prison. Do you wish this?"

The hard tone in his words entered every pore and cell of Shay's body, making his joints hurt and his flesh sting. "No. I don't. You should be prepared if my powers don't work. It has been long since my true abilities were released, and even now I have held much back because I fear I cannot control them."

"Cease. What you cannot control, I will aid with. The one thing in which I have confidence in is your power. Gwyneth understood this also. 'Tis why she chose you to help her," Rhys added, his expression hard and unforgiving. "Enough of the past. When will you attempt to reach Caitlyn?"

Shay turned and stared out the window. The landscape sped by without him seeing it, a blur of dull greens and blacks with the brighter lights reflecting off metal. "Tonight. When we are on the plane."

"Will the distance affect you?"

"No. I touched her, and I placed a spell on her which will keep her from changing her mind about coming to me. No matter what happens tonight," Shay replied with a smile.

He didn't know all the details of how he would go to her, but he had to try. Perhaps through the television, radio. Any form of electric equipment would work, as long as it brought him into her mind. Once her consciousness focused on him, he would call her to him, and his mission would start.

Chapter 9

Caitlyn inserted Shay Evers's newest DVD into her player. She didn't want to watch the video after seeing him in person, but needed to for reference. Tonight's show gave her some insight on how he worked, but she needed more. Remote in hand, she moved to the burgundy-colored sofa and sat, curling her legs under her. The soft fleece material of her pajamas soothed her skin, warming her against the loft apartment's constant chill.

Two hours after leaving the party, exhaustion still gripped her. After arriving home, she'd taken a long hot soak in the tub, but it had done little to relieve the tension running through her body. She closed her eyes and inhaled deeply. Releasing the air in slow degree, she reminded herself once more how much she wanted to do this interview.

All of the magazine covers, televisions, and billboards with his face on them were nothing but coincidences. Just as if she'd bought a red car, and *boom!*, all of a sudden there was a red car on every street corner. As famous as he was, it was normal to see all those things a lot. They hadn't increased in numbers since this morning. She was just more aware of them after receiving this assignment.

Meeting Shay tonight had thrown off her usual equilibrium. He had baited her on purpose in order to test her. That meant he doubted she was ready for the publicity ahead of her. She cared little for the method he used, but at least she knew he wasn't a total jerk.

Soft guitar notes drifted from the television. Caitlyn focused on the picture and smiled. She liked this song. Calmness drifted over her, saturating her mind and relieving aching muscles.

On the television screen, Evers strode toward the camera. When he began to perform his illusion, she felt as though she were a part of the act. Her pulse quickened, and she shifted on the sofa, so focused on the man performing, her apartment faded from her awareness, until nothing existed but Shay.

The act ended. She sat on the edge of the sofa with her fingertips pressed against her lips. She jerked upright and stood. What had just happened? The entire performance was lost to her. As she strained to remember the video's details, she could only see Shay and his penetrating gaze.

"This is nuts," she muttered, heading to the kitchen. A tall glass of ice water would definitely cool the sudden heat stifling her senses.

Feeling a little better, she returned to the sofa with her drink and settled down again to finish viewing the DVD.

After an hour, numbness started in the tips of her toes and moved up her body. The longer she watched the DVD, her eyelids drooped, heavy with sleep. She slid a throw pillow beneath her head and stretched out, fighting to stay awake. She accepted defeat, removed her glasses and shut her eyes.

* * * *

Caitlyn opened her eyes. Her exhaustion had evaporated. Still lying with her head on the pillow, she gazed about. Deep purple midnight surrounded her. Stars twinkled everywhere. Sitting up, she blinked at their brilliance.

"I'm dreaming," she whispered. "But it's so real."

She lifted her hand and dusty sparkles followed the movement, leaving behind a trail like a shooting star. Such a strange dream. Instead of fear bubbling inside her at the unknown surroundings, the glittering darkness encircled her. It embraced her with a soothing ambiance. She felt secure in the twinkling silence.

Footsteps moved toward her, and from the purple blackness before her, Shay Evers appeared. Her heart skipped a beat. Blood pounded in her veins. The slow long-legged stride so unique to him brought him to her side. He knelt and smiled.

"Hello, Caitlyn." Amethyst eyes shone with an inner light.

She smiled, joy overriding everything else. "I'm dreaming."

He grinned wider. He lifted a hand and laid it over her heart. "Are you? A sweet dream?"

"Oh yes," she sighed, leaning forward. Her fingers itched to touch him and see if he was real. She reached out and laid her palm flat on his chest where his shirt gaped open and found solid warmth. "Oh."

A low chuckle brought her gaze to his, and her breath caught at the gentle glow in his eyes. "Do you like?"

She shifted to her knees. With a slow caress toward his jaw, she brushed her thumb across the satiny flesh of his full bottom lip and sighed once more. "Yes."

They came together as one and touched lips--soft, tender, their breaths exchanged for an instant. "Close your eyes and look to your heart." The accent flavoring his voice was stronger than she remembered. Beautiful and lyrical, she listened to each layer of it. "Look deep, past all barriers, to the center. Find what you've lost and you will be free."

"Only if you stay with me," she whispered against his mouth and slid her fingers into his hair to hold him.

His hands encircled her throat, his thumbs under her chin, tilting her head. She captured his lips and deepened the kiss, opening her mouth and crossing the threshold of his with a gentle probe of her tongue. He tasted of cinnamon, her favorite spice. She moaned as heat climbed from the soles of her feet to inflame her body.

"I'm dreaming, and I never want this to end," she whispered when the kiss ended, arching her back as his lips moved over her jaw to her neck. Warm breath slid across her skin.

An angry voice broke through her lustful haze.

"Shay."

The voice reminded her of Rhys's. He repeated Shay's name twice. Caitlyn opened her eyes, gasping. Her loft apartment sprawled about her.

She looked around in an attempt to explain what had occurred. Nothing helped as she sat there, stunned at her loss of memory over the last few moments.

The clock on the DVD player told her a little over an hour had passed since she'd sat down, yet it seemed longer. She tried to understand what her dream meant, but found no logical reason why Evers walked through her mind. The whole incident had been so real. Her fingertips tingled from the feel of his skin and her lips throbbed from the touch of his.

Heat raced to her face. The confines of her apartment threatened to smother her. She needed cool air. She stood and stumbled to the terrace door. One tug down on the handle opened the door, and she stepped out into the cold night. Two steps more and she grasped the banister. The metal chilled her palms as she curled her fingers about it.

She pulled in several deep breaths, trying to wash away the heat accumulated from her dream. Imagination, she thought. Meeting him tonight was messing with her mind. She was positive the concerned way he'd spoken to her at the party, and his kiss, triggered his appearance in her sleep.

The depth of desire Shay had stirred in her brought the blood to her face and warm tingling throughout her body. She had wanted him in a way she'd never wanted another man. Didn't think she'd ever want a man. The slow throbbing between her legs brought a moan to her lips. She squeezed her eyes shut, fighting to regain control.

All the other men in her life were either father figures or business associates. There had never been time for any type of relationship. Until now, she hadn't realized she possessed an ounce of passion. But if her reaction to the dream was any sign, well, she definitely had an overabundance of the emotion.

Several minutes passed before calmness came to her. Her gaze wandered over the building's facade across the street. She searched for something, anything to distract her thoughts. Her foster mother had often made her count to not only control her temper but also to help her focus. She concentrated on the building in front of her. Following a line of windows, she counted the frames to the bottom floor.

It didn't help.

She didn't care for the location of her apartment but her foster parents, Bill and Annie Reynolds, had sold it to her for an excellent price. They were good to her, and she missed seeing their loving faces every day. Both had died instantly in an automobile crash a couple of years ago.

Since counting was useless, she wondered what advice Annie would give her about Shay. Caitlyn smiled, imaging her foster mother's gentle, caring voice warning her to be careful around strangers. Annie had warned they might take advantage of her. At the memory of her foster parents, Caitlyn relaxed, rested her forearms on the banister and looked up at the sky. No stars tonight. The ever-present haze over Los Angeles prevented the light from shining through.

Yes, she needed to be careful around Evers. She had to keep that in mind during the interview. Determination pulled back her shoulders. She would succeed and move forward with her life. She'd promised Bill and Annie that they didn't need to worry about her. She intended to fulfill her promise.

Faint music floated on the night air, bringing her gaze to the street corner. There, a man leaned against the lamppost. Dark hair fell around his broad shoulder; his slim build was hidden under a black overcoat. The sight of him shot a tingle through her stomach. Something about him seemed familiar.

Loose-limbed, he moved away from the corner to a sleek black sports car parked at the curb. He strode around the front of the car, opened the door and slipped in. The engine ignited, and the car took off.

Her gaze stayed riveted on the vehicle until it disappeared down the street. She sagged once it sped out of sight.

Rest. She needed rest. Her imagination was running away with her. The man reminded her of Shay with his shape and the way he moved, but that didn't mean the stranger with the car was the illusionist. Right now, Evers was on board his jet, hours away from here, heading for Wales. There wasn't any way he was still in Los Angeles, much less outside her apartment. Besides, he didn't know where she lived.

Determined to unwind before Kramer arrived, she headed inside and grabbed the remote. She glanced at the television and froze.

On the screen, Shay Evers sat behind the wheel of a black sports car. The door opened, and he stepped out wearing a long dark coat. He stared at the camera for a second, then he grinned and winked.

The remote fell from her numb fingers, and she was unable to stop staring at the screen as the edges of the room narrowed under the onslaught of darkness.

Chapter 10

"Don't play games with her."

Shay shifted and opened his eyes. He stretched his legs and propped his feet on the seat across from him in an attempt to keep his body relaxed. Damn Rhys. He knew what Shay had been doing, and he had the gall to interrupt. Determined not to let the older man sense his tension, he rolled his head against the seat.

Caitlyn.

Guilt seared him. He glanced at Rhys. The tall blond radiated anger as he continued to speak, pacing back and forth in the plane's luxurious interior.

"First the tale about the tree, and now you're seducing her along with frightening her. Do not make the mistake of pushing me too far, my boy. I could cause the thorns to grow inward on you. I don't believe you would care for that." His tone sent a chill down Shay's back. Deadly sincerity edged each word.

"You forget whose help you need," Shay murmured. Exhausted from the constant pouring of magic into his music and illusions, he didn't need the added distraction of Rhys's demands. "Do your worst, it doesn't matter. You can't hurt me any more than I already hurt. Just remember, you need me. How else are you going to bring her home?"

Rhys crossed the distance between them in a second, gripped the sides of Shay's chair and leaned in close. In that second, he realized he'd pushed him too far this time.

The older man spoke through clenched teeth. "My worst? You could not imagine my worst. You stole my daughter. My child. Your sentence is light compared to what I truly wished to enforce, but Myrielle insisted you were repentant for your part in Caitlyn's kidnapping. I never believed it was true. You may have fooled my wife, but I have no doubt you were aware of your actions."

"How many times do I have to tell you, I didn't know what Gwyneth was going to do--"

Rhys cut him off with a foul curse. "*Liar. Enough.* No matter what you say, I will never believe you. I trusted you like a brother, but you betrayed me."

He straightened, his features cooling into the royal mask he often wore, and took a step backward. "Right now, I have ordered you to perform the simple task of opening Caitlyn's magic enough to allow her entry into our home dimension. This does not include frightening her, nor does it give you the right to seduce her. You take the chance of closing her heart completely, and we will never reach her. Do you wish that?"

Shay eyed his old friend. The pain still remained in his blue gaze. Rhys would never forgive him, and the agony caused by the loss of such a lasting friendship coursed through Shay. The older man had been the same as a brother to him.

"No. I want to bring her home, even if it means I will spend eternity within the confines of the blackthorn. I have to do this as penance for my conscience."

"I suggest you open her awareness slowly. The dream was all right until you allowed her to kiss you. I don't want her falling in love with you. Her heart will be broken once she is delivered from the curse. Also, the game you played afterward was foolish and dangerous. Don't make that mistake again."

Shay refused to respond. Caitlyn wasn't a fool. He had sensed a realistic attitude in her, and this added strength to her disbelief. A little mental anguish on her part would be worthwhile if she was to believe in magic. Her system needed jarring, either through fear or seduction, which emotion it took didn't matter to him as long as her power was awakened. It was obvious Rhys would never agree to him seducing her, yet the older man didn't seem to understand there were cracks in the spell surrounding her. He doubted Rhys would change his mind if he told him.

He glanced at his watch. Two weeks. All the time she had left in this and every other world. He had to make headway with her so she could cope once she returned to her home dimension in the Sidhe.

Time. He needed more time, yet there was no more. Unless he found a better way to reveal the magic in her, she would die. The spell the bitch had placed on the newborn had a limit to it. If Caitlyn didn't return to the Sidhe and solve a riddle by her twenty-fifth birthday, she would fade into oblivion. He refused to allow that to happen. He silently went through a windstorm of melodies and lyrics in an effort to find a surer way to save her.

Shay cut a glance at the blond who now sat at the other end of the plane. Rhys had told him not to allow her to fall in love with him. Perhaps, passion was the key to unlock the magic in her heart. He allowed the conscious level of his mind to speed through his music, while his darker consciousness planned a method of seducing Caitlyn. He just hoped he didn't fall under the same spell he wove for her.

* * * *

Hammering vibrated in Caitlyn's head. She forced a crack in her eyelids and stared at the fabric strands in the area rug under her sofa. The pounding increased in volume and someone shouted her name.

Disoriented, groaning, she rose up on one arm and shook her head, trying to clear her mind. Was her foster father building something again?

The noise continued. She glanced at the door. In a second, the present snapped into place. Kramer beat on her door, not Bill Reynolds, her last foster father, but her boss. The clock on the DVD player displayed three thirty. She was late. Legs trembling, she stood and crossed the room to fight with the bolts and lock. Constraints gone, the door opened without a sound.

"You overslept." Kramer's frowning face wavered in front of her for a bare second. She blinked to clear her vision and stepped out of the way to let her boss enter.

"Sorry," she muttered. "I couldn't sleep earlier. I must have dozed off. Give me a few minutes to get ready."

"Hurry up. The plane's ready to leave at four thirty. You don't want to screw this up by being late. It's a good thing I told Blake to meet us there. That'll save some time." Kramer propelled her away from the door. He shut it before heading into the kitchen, while she climbed to her bedroom loft.

The stairs swam before her eyes. She gripped the handrail and forced her body up, too tired to race to the second floor like usual.

A suitcase lay open on the full size bed in the same spot she'd left it last night. Only a few minor items and she could close the lid. The deep green linen pantsuit she decided last night to wear lay next to the suitcase.

She looked around the room. She fought to weave through the sleep-induced haze in her mind, trying to understand what had happened last night. Her memory after she'd sat down to watch the DVD no longer came to her. The time prior to her waking up remained a void, much like dreamless sleep.

The sight of her dark trench coat draped over the back of a nearby chair stopped her. Memories flooded through her.

Shay Evers.

In an instant, the image of his tall figure dressed in the dark overcoat appeared. He grinned. And the memory of his touch, the kiss--heat rushed to her face.

Had she imagined the man or had it been nothing but a dream? She rubbed her temple with trembling fingers. What was happening to her? Doubts poured through her. Was this interview really a good idea?

"Hurry up, Reiley." Kramer's commanding voice held a steely note.

She couldn't let him down, let the station down. Everyone there needed the financial and emotional boost this interview promised. No one, especially Kramer, would ever understand about a small problem like her unstable sanity.

It was just her imagination. She repeated the word under her breath while she dressed and finished packing. Calmer now, she grabbed the coat and suitcase. She refused to believe the events of the night before. She wouldn't allow anything to affect her decision to continue with the interview. Head up and jaw clenched, she hurried down the stairs.

"You ready?" Kramer stood on the other side of the counter separating the living area from the kitchen. Steam escaped the cup he cradled in his hand.

"Just about. Pour me one, will you? I have to grab my computer and extra thumb drives."

Relieved her voice didn't reveal any signs of the tension occupying her thoughts, Caitlyn set the bag next to the door. She glanced at the television and hesitated. She wasn't sure if she should take the DVDs with her. They were supposed to help her understand Shay as an illusionist. Most artists allowed their emotions and inner desires to seep through their work, which was why she'd tried to watch one last night. Her throat constricted with unease at the idea of viewing them again.

She needed to watch and listen to them without a repeat of last night. This needed to stop. All of it was her imagination. She steeled her muscles and strode to the player, pressed the button, removed the DVD, and snatched the other two off the player.

"Here you go," Kramer spoke from behind her.

She pivoted. The angry glower in his eyes forced her to take step back, her body stiffened in defense. He had every right to be upset at her for not being ready, but the look on his face along with the glare in his eyes sent stronger, threatening messages.

"Thanks." She held out the DVDs with one hand while she took the coffee in her other. "Would you put these in my carry-on? I'll watch them on the flight over."

"Sure. I turned the pot off and rinsed it. Finish and let's go." He turned away and headed to the door.

Caitlyn studied him for a second, confounded with his abrupt actions and words. She shook her head. A sip from the cup perked her up a little. She had to stop this sudden paranoia. Kramer was Kramer. He was as abrupt as always.

After one last check around the apartment, she drained the cup and hurried to the door, her laptop case hanging from its strap over her shoulder. She breezed past Kramer and waited for him to step out. She inserted and turned her key in the lock.

No looking back. This interview provided her ticket to the big time, and she wouldn't allow her insecurities to stand in her way. She followed Kramer to the elevator, determined to fight the new and sudden emotions flooding her.

On the way to the airport, she stared at the scenery flying by with blind eyes. A road leading to the private planes veered to the right past the main entrance. Kramer accelerated on the stretch from the gate to the hanger with a huge E stenciled on the door. He screeched to a halt just past the open doors. The internal lights reflected off the chrome and white paint on the plane.

"There it is. Not bad, huh?" He threw the shift into park and opened his door. "You're traveling first class, Reiley."

She stared at the sleek jet. Hanger lights cast illuminating shades across the plane's sides, giving it the appearance of silvery flames shooting away from the wings and sides.

She sat still, hand gripping the car's door handle. This was it. All she had to do was pull the handle. The door would open. She'd get out, go to the plane. Get in. The skin on her forehead and her palms dampened. Shay Evers waited at the end of this flight. He caused her uneasiness, and yet, he was her chance for advancement. Her chin lifted. She wanted this.

A quick tap on the window jerked her from her thoughts. Blake Myers, her photographer, opened the door and squatted in the opening.

"Moving too fast? We'll be in Wales in no time on that baby."

His familiar grin brought her a measure of calmness. She didn't try to hide the slight tremble in her voice. "Much too fast. I think I'm losing it."

"No. Just nerves. That's all. Don't worry, sugar, I'll be with you the whole way. I won't let the boogie man eat you."

Caitlyn smiled. Blake thought in terms of Shay Evers, but what would he say if she told him about what happened during the night?

"I'll hold you to that promise." She let him help her out of the car and followed him to the stairs leading into the jet.

"This is it, Reiley," Kramer said from behind her. "Call me when you arrive. Here, take this." He handed her a white plastic bag containing a cellphone and accessories. Reaching inside, she removed the phone while he continued. "It has full coverage. Don't worry about the charges."

"Right," Caitlyn said. The phone was solid in her hand, a firm reminder of what she needed to accomplish. "Well, guess we'd better go. The plane won't wait."

She climbed the steps and entered the open hatch. A low gasp escaped from her as she stared around at the rich interior. With Shay's wealth, she shouldn't have been surprised, but she'd never flown on such luxurious plane. Was that a wet bar over there? Yes, the bar seats matched the passenger ones. The natural hue of the beige leather seats, positioned on cream colored carpet, eased her rattled nerves. Two occupants sitting close to the cockpit turned to face her. Caitlyn's eyes widened when she looked at one of them.

Marcy stood and met her in the aisle. With a confused expression on her face, she asked. "What are you doing here?"

Caitlyn stared, speechless.

"Catey. Hey, are you home or what?" Marcy waved a hand in front of her eyes.

She blinked. "The interview. Remember? I told you I had an important interview."

Her friend's eyes rounded, and her mouth fell open. "The interview is with Evers?"

Caitlyn fidgeted.

"You never said a word last night. Why didn't you tell me?"

"Because I didn't want you to become all excited. Something might have happened to cause the deal to fall through." Caitlyn brushed past and set her small bag on the floor near one of the other seats. "What are you doing here?"

"Dafydd asked me to go with him."

Caitlyn frowned.

"Shay's music tech. Hello--the one I went home with last night. I thought, what the heck? I called my boss, woke him and told him I quit," Marcy said with a wicked grin.

"Why did you quit? You liked that job." Caitlyn wasn't really surprised by her friend's actions. She flitted from one position to the next like a butterfly among flowers. The woman didn't know the meaning of job security.

"Waitress jobs are a dime a dozen. I'm not worried," Marcy said. "I'll find something else when I get back."

"When are you going to settle down? You can't keep going through life without a solid purpose." At times, she felt older and more mature than her friend even though they were the same age.

Marcy's expression froze. After a second, she grinned. "I don't have any intention of growing up. It's what keeps me young. Come on, Catey, lighten up. You must be really stressed over this interview. Is that what you and Evers were talking about last night?"

Caitlyn sighed. Marcy was impossible. She saw only what she wanted to see. Good times were important to her and to heck with the future. "Yes, among other things."

A restless movement from the front caught her attention. "Uh, your guy seems impatient. Go keep him company. I need to start taking notes on the interview. We'll talk about all this later."

Marcy glanced over her shoulder. Caitlyn followed her gaze to look at the good-looking blond stretched out in his seat with a foot tapping the seat back. Marcy squeezed her forearm. "Sure. Don't get too weighed down by this assignment. I'd hate to lose my best friend because she can't handle a man like Shay Evers."

Caitlyn's brows shot up. "What's that supposed to mean? You make it sound like I'm going to die or something."

"No, not that. He just seems like someone who isn't showing his true face. I don't know, call it a gut instinct. Be careful around him. There's more to him than he's letting on." Dafydd called to her. Marcy groaned. "Come over in a little while and I'll introduce you, but hands off. This one is all mine," she said, twirling around and grinning at the music tech.

Her remarks concerning Evers swirled in her mind. The truth rang out in Marcy's comments. There was more to him than what everyone knew, and Caitlyn intended to find out what that something was.

Chapter 11

An hour after arriving in Wales, Marcy's perfume still clung to Caitlyn's clothes. Each time she moved, the lingering odor would come to life and remind her of her friend. She smiled. Marcy's face had been radiant as she and Dafydd whizzed away from the airport in his compact car.

Now Caitlyn sat on the back seat of the sedan Evers sent to bring her to his home. The Welsh countryside sped by in a whirl of green, rolling hills gradually rising to rugged, towering ridges. Mountains, carpeted with fir and hardwood trees, loomed on either side of the road. Caitlyn swung her gaze from the scenery to glance at Blake. Slumped next to her, he worked readying a camera.

"Hey, what do you think about Evers?" Her voice sounded loud but steady in the silent vehicle.

Blake glanced at her. "What about him?"

"Is he real? Can he actually perform magical feats or are all his acts just that--acts?" She shifted in her seat, trying to find a comfortable position. Her body ached, exhausted from the late night, long flight and now the drive to Evers's home.

"Don't know. Won't know until we finish with the interview."

Blake shot a look in the driver's direction. He slid his gaze back to Caitlyn. She realized what he implied. They weren't alone. No use in talking about Evers in front of his employee. The driver was, no doubt, instructed to report to Shay. This obligated him to tell his employer what had happened on the drive to the castle. She gave a slight nod to acknowledge Blake's silent message.

He grinned and continued. "You wanna know the first thing I'm gonna do when we get to his place? Soak in a hot bath, then catch some zees. I'm bushed."

She agreed with a slight smile. Blake focused on his equipment, and she turned to the window, sighing.

For the rest of the drive, she mulled over last night's memories, trying to differentiate between what was real and what was her imagination. The incident with the sports car had to be coincidental. Any other explanation bordered on Evers possessing true magical powers and that was impossible.

The black sedan swung onto a paved driveway that followed the slope of the mountain. The car rounded a bend and the illusionist's home came into view. Kramer was right. The tall multilayered building was a castle. Stone walls rose from the side of a ridge. Three turrets reached for the ocean-blue sky. The sight reminded her of a nursery rhyme from her childhood, about a princess trapped in a magical castle.

The vehicle sped up the drive, and Caitlyn noticed the abundance of thriving plants decorating the lawns and bordering the drive. Beds of bright blooms banded the base of the building. Despite the cold weather, verdant vines climbed the white stone walls of the three-story structure. The gables, a forest green, gleamed under the bright sunlight. She smiled at the beauty of the place.

Once the sedan pulled to a stop, two men exited the polished double-door entrance. The older of the two hurried to open her door. Dressed in dark slacks and matching jacket with a white shirt under, he nodded and murmured a greeting to her.

"Mr. Shay is awaiting your arrival, miss. I'll see that your luggage is taken to your rooms, after which, I will lead you to him." With another nod, he went to join the younger man at the trunk.

Caitlyn smiled and studied the front of the castle as she slid from the car. A large stained-glass oval centered above the passageway caught her attention. Chiseled glass sparkled in the early afternoon sunlight. Brilliant colors blurred and didn't reveal the image in the glass from the outside of the building. Curious, she made a mental note to study the piece once she'd entered.

Her gaze wandered past the lacquered double-door entry to the flowering vines climbing the white stone façade and along the beds embracing the front of the castle. Pansies appeared to wave their colorful petals in welcome. A warm aura of happiness at her arrival reached out to her from the vibrant plants.

Unable to resist, she moved toward the nearest bed and murmured, "Hello, pretty ones. How are you today?"

Several buds opened in a wondrous splendor of purple and yellow. She'd never seen flowers bloom like that. The world she lived in consisted of mostly concrete and steel, she never paid much attention to the green stuff around the city and most of the ones she tried to grow ended up dying from over-watering. She smiled, a trill of excitement and joy beating in her heart. Realization of what happened struck her. She stiffened and leaned closer to study the plants. Had they responded to her voice? Maybe this was just a coincidence. She shook her head and hurried to the door where Blake waited.

She approached the entry and imagined a wonderful scene of Evers carrying her over the threshold. Her wedding dress and train, dazzling white amid the greenery flanking the door, brushed against the three steps leading inside. She blinked the picture away and moved up the steps. Her imagination ran wild today. That's all there was to it. She was here to do a job, not fall in love.

The older man rejoined them and led the way inside. He continued past the open foyer, but Caitlyn stopped on the mosaic tile covering the floor to look up at the stained glass oval above the entrance. The image of leaves encircling a golden crown formed in green, blue, yellow, and purple sent slivers of color to shower the foyer with a rainbow of light. Such a glorious sight brought another smile to her face.

Unbidden, a sense of joy welled inside her from just looking at the window. Peace mingled with the happiness for the first time in as far as she could remember. The window was at least eight feet wide and four feet high--the beauty of the tints with the light shining through took her breath. Clearer from this side, the crown and the leaves entwined about it glinted in the light from the chandelier. Who had Shay hired to design and install the masterpiece of stained glass?

She glanced at the man, she assumed was the butler, and nodded toward the window. "Who did the work on that?"

He glanced at the cut glass for a second. "Locals, miss. They're powerfully talented. Now, this way please. Master Shay is expecting you."

She studied the man. The way he phrased the talent of the artisans struck her as odd. Maybe it was just the way the locals spoke. She nodded to him to lead the way.

With Blake close by her side, she followed the man down the cavernous foyer toward the back of Evers's home. They walked deeper into the heart of the house. Rich tapestries and heavy medieval furnishings occupied the entrance and hallways. Gleaming armor with razor edged weapons stood guard along the route. The scent of aged burnished wood, faded flowers and something indubitably masculine filled her senses. Shadowed nooks popped up every few feet along the wide corridors. She squinted to peer into the dimness. All the wonderful treasures she witnessed so far made her hunger for what else might be hidden in the recesses.

After several minutes and many twists and turns, she heard voices ahead of them. She glanced at Blake. He cocked a brow at her.

Through an arched mahogany doorway, a sprawling room, bordered on the opposite side by multi-paned windows and open French doors, came into view. Leaves and twigs lay scattered across the flagstone floor in wild abandon, blown inside through the open doors. The beamed ceiling gave a rustic look to the off-white plaster walls.

Two sets of leather sofas with matching chairs flanked the stone fireplace directly across from the French doors, and just to the right of one sofa stood the man behind her journey to Wales.

Evers stood with a group of four men behind the well-padded sofa. Her breath caught in her throat and refused to move. She stopped in the doorway and studied Shay for a moment, confident he hadn't noticed her yet.

With his hip against the furniture and balanced on one foot with the other flat on the opposite knee, he laughed with the men. Feet bare, he wore old, faded jeans with blown-out knees. A white open-collar shirt bagged about his body, its tail covering his hips and the tops of his thighs.

He shifted, placing both feet on the ground. With his hands tucked into his back pockets and his eyes alight with laughter, he leaned over and commented to the man nearest to him. The servant who led them to the room cleared his throat. Evers glanced toward them with a shy twist of his lips.

Caitlyn answered with one of her own. She liked this smile so much better than the devastating grin he'd made famous. This one with the sexy curl of his lips brightened his amethyst gaze. Warmth sprouted in the area of her heart.

He padded across the area rug covered with pagan Celtic symbols. When he reached her, he hunched his shoulders, tilted his head and grinned. "Hello."

His strange shyness amazed and captivated Caitlyn. He hadn't been timid in Los Angeles, but now he possessed a bashful, boyish manner. Perhaps, it was because he was home and comfortable.

She smiled. "So this is where you live. My boss, Mike Kramer, told me it was a faery tale castle but I thought he was joking. He wasn't. You have a beautiful place."

"Thanks. You should have seen it when I first bought it. All falling apart. It's amazing what a little work can do. The house is over a hundred years old, built by an industrialist in the last century. They were real big in constructing huge homes. A lot of them considered themselves lords over the less fortunate. Didn't last long, though."

He stopped and turned, holding out his hand toward Blake. "You must be Caitlyn's photographer."

"Yes, sir. Blake Myers. This place is fine. A photo hog's heaven." Blake clasped Shay's hand. The photographer, an awed expression on his face, turned to glance around him. "Have you ever thought about doing a home magazine spread?"

Shay shook his head and chuckled with a quick wink at Caitlyn. "The man appreciates beauty. But please, come in. You must be exhausted. It's a long flight." He grasped her arm with gentle fingers and escorted her into the room.

The shrill voice of a woman came from the opposite side of the room interrupting any introduction he'd been about to make. "Master Shay, how many times do I have to tell ye? When ye come in, close the doors behind ye. Look at the mess ye've made."

An elderly woman stood near the French doors, a broom in her hands and a wrinkled frown marring her features. Shay detoured, turning toward her. Caitlyn trailed behind, her arm still captured by him.

"I'm sorry, Grazelda. I forgot again." Features contrite, he bent to look into the woman's wizened face.

She sniffed. "It's bad enough ye have Master Rhys bringing all those plants into this house, but it makes it harder to keep clean if ye leave the doors open." The old woman shook her head, glaring at the leaves scattered across the flagstones. "I simply don't know what I'm going to do with ye, young sir."

Shay plucked the broom from Grazelda's aged hands and started sweeping with long, strong strokes. "Here, give that to me. You keep Ms. Reiley company. She's the reporter I told you about. From Los Angeles."

"Ah, Ms. Reiley." Grazelda stared at Caitlyn, curiosity reflected on her face. She nodded as though satisfied with what she saw. Her hair, pulled into a braided crown about her head, bounced. "I believe Mr. Shay told me yer name was Caitlyn. Yes?"

"Yes, it is."

"Ah, such a lovely name. Do ye know the meaning of it?"

"I remember looking it up once, but I don't recall the meaning," Caitlyn hedged. She didn't care about her name. Her interest lay in what Shay was doing.

The leaves and wind fought with the broom. He stopped for a second, glanced from the leaves to outside. He reached for the doors and shut them one at a time. Working quickly, he gathered the rebellious foliage into a large pile.

Next, he bent and scooped up a bunch, cracked the door and tried to stuff the debris through the small gap. The breeze appeared determined to keep the leaves inside, with more flying back indoors than those that went out. Caitlyn bit the inside of her cheek to keep from laughing.

Grazelda leaned closer and spoke low. "Caitlyn means pure beauty, and ye certainly live up to yer name, young lady. It's about time he brought a young lovely home. Poor dear has little interest in finding a wife."

Caitlyn's eyes widened at the mention of a wife, and she turned her full attention to the old woman. "I'm interviewing him, not marrying him."

"Of course not, dearie, but I can still hope." A toothless grin brightened the elderly woman's face. Caitlyn shook her head, wanting to make it clear to the woman she had no intention of becoming involved with Evers.

She looked over at Shay in time to see him turn from a large ornate urn next to the closed door. He grinned at the housekeeper and handed her the broom. "There now, all cleaned up. I'll show Caitlyn to her room."

"Oh well, sure. Poor dear, she's probably worn to the bone, coming from so far away." The old woman nodded and ambled toward the door on the far side of the room.

Caitlyn crossed her arms and tilted her head, looking hard at Shay. "Where did you put those leaves?"

He shifted from one foot to the other. A slow grin appeared. "I'll throw them out later."

A laugh bubbled up and escaped her. His smile widened, and he glanced at the urn. With his voice deliberately higher, he spoke in a squeaky feminine voice. "Come on along, dearie. Time for ye to settle in."

"And Blake?"

He reverted to his normal tone, his gaze aimed at Blake standing near the doorway.

"Fred will show him where to go, but you..." He winked at her. "You receive special treatment."

Caitlyn's heart pounded hard over the last part. Heat circulated to the insides of her thighs. "Do I?"

"Sure. I know who to cozy up to so this interview goes smoothly." He took her arm and tugged her out the door and down the hall. He instructed the man who had guided them to show Blake to his room.

Shay pulled her with him through the house to the foyer. This time, she noticed the repetition of intricate Celtic designs. They dominated the decorations and architecture in the castle. Once they reached the entrance, he led her up the stairs to the second floor. She saw the same patterns she'd noticed below.

They continued through hallways and rooms to reach the back of the house. He stopped in front of a door and twisted the knob. The door swung open, revealing a sitting room done in pale blue.

"Oh, it's so pretty."

"I thought you might like a view to the gardens." He breezed by and strode to the windows. He opened one and leaned out, inhaling the fresh air.

She followed and stood to one side. Sunlight poured over him, revealing glints of red in the thick mass of hair tumbling past his shoulders. He turned sideways, studying her. "So do you like it?"

With a smile, she nodded. "Yes, I do. It's lovely."

"Good. Well, I'd better go and let you rest. When you're ready to come down again, there's some stairs at the end of this hall. They'll take you to the kitchen. Someone should be there. Odds are, they'll know where I am if you should need me."

She raised a brow. "Is this room above where we were a minute ago?"

He grinned, shrugging. "I wanted to show you the house."

Caitlyn laughed and slowly shook her head. He amazed her with his charm. He had just led her through the entire house then back again on the second floor. All they needed to have done was go to the back staircase to reach the room a lot quicker.

He started to turn away, but for a moment, seemed to hesitate. She held her breath and waited for him to speak. He remained silent, pivoted, then headed to the door.

"When did you want to begin the interview?" She called after him.

He answered over his shoulder. "In the morning. That'll give you and Blake a chance to recuperate from the flight."

Before she could answer, the door closed behind him. Caitlyn chewed on her bottom lip. He'd acted like he wanted to say something, but changed his mind.

She leaned out the window and shut her eyes, inhaling the crisp cool air. Peace and joy entered her. The air held a chilly bite to it, but the sky was clear and the sun warm. She opened her eyes and glanced around the rolling gardens below her window.

A man working with a shovel about five hundred feet from the house caught her eye. He looked familiar. He straightened, removed the floppy hat from his head, and swiped the moisture from his brow. Rhys. No mistaking that golden hair. She opened her mouth to call to him, but stopped. Shay came into view several feet from Rhys. He spoke to the gardener, turned to leave, but froze as Rhys's right hand slashed down. Even from a distance, his anger was visible.

Shay, head lowered, stood listening to whatever the older man said. He nodded once before he strode away toward the forest bordering the gardens.

Her investigative instinct sprang to life. What had Shay done to make the older man chew him out? Rhys returned to his flower bed.

Exhausted, but still keyed up from the plane ride and long drive, Caitlyn decided to follow Shay, determined to discover more about the illusionist. She managed to make her way back to the den area in the rear of the house. No one was about, so she slipped through the French doors. She stopped and inhaled the wonderful aroma of flowers. All sorts of floral scents permeated the air. Smiling, she walked down the path in the direction Shay disappeared.

Several yards from the house, the path took a sharp right bend and sloped downward. Trees grew tall and solid along either side of the path. She slipped once and had to grab the nearest tree. The moist bark scraped her palm. She pulled her hand away and wiped at the dark lined marks in the scratches.

Further down the path, the slope of the land leveled. A small clearing appeared to her left and a large hangar-sized barn stood toward the back of the area. Two panel trucks were backed to the open doors. Men, laughing and talking, moved to and from the trucks into the building. They unloaded Shay's equipment for his performances.

Caitlyn grinned, knowing she'd find him there. Without considering what he might think, she hurried to the building. Some of the men stopped and stared at her in curiosity, but others frowned like she intruded on them. She waved and continued forward to enter the three-story high hangar. She stopped, allowing her eyes to become adjusted to the dim light.

"Caitlyn?"

She pivoted to see Shay striding toward her from a side row of crates and boxes stacked neatly on the right.

"Hi. I couldn't rest so I thought I'd explore a little."

The puzzled expression relaxed and he smiled. "Of course, though it might be a little dangerous roaming about in here."

"I'll be careful."

He nodded and asked, "Would you like a tour?"

"Sure, but if you're busy, I'll look on my own."

"Oh no. I'm not doing anything in particular." He held out his hand, palm up, to her. "Come on. Let's go back here. We'll be out of the way."

He guided her to the aisle he had just come from and they entered a wide corridor stretching the length of the building. Each side was bracketed by crates and tall boxes.

As they walked down the row, Caitlyn saw the mirror from his act in Los Angeles standing at the end. Uncovered, the lacquered wood picked up the small bit of light and gleamed. She motioned toward the piece. "That was a great performance, the one you did with the mirror."

"Want to take a closer look?" Shay asked, lengthening his steps and tugging her behind him.

She had no choice but to follow. Once at the end of the aisle, he stopped, standing to one side so she had a better view. An uneasy feeling nudged her, and she couldn't look into the glass. Shay reached over and brushed the back of his fingers across her cheek.

"Do you believe in magic, lovely Caitlyn?"

She glanced at him and gave a slight laugh. "No."

"What if I tell you that after your stay here, you will definitely believe in it?"

"I'd say you were crazy." She swatted his hand away. "Listen, maybe you can fool other people. Make them think magic is real, but your tactics won't work on me. So give it up."

One side of his beautiful mouth twitched. "Nope, can't do that."

She frowned. He was playing with her. "Why not?"

"Because." He grabbed her hand and lifted it closer to his chest. "I feel a great magical aura deep in your soul. This magic will awaken soon."

Caitlyn rolled her eyes. She wasn't a magical guinea pig. He leaned toward her. A wonderful cinnamon aroma floated about her. Her mouth watered, and her knees weakened. He winked at her, and her heart missed a beat. "Guess what this mirror really is?"

Breathless from the way he affected her, she found coherent words hard to form. She fought against the reactions coursing through her body and managed to murmur, "Sorry, don't know."

His smile lingered, and his eyes brightened. "This is a mirror which reflects the truth. When a person gazes into the glass, the image projected is who the person truly is."

His improbable explanation caused a measure of sanity to return. She tilted her head. "So, it's not a gateway."

He laughed low, warm breath touching the bare skin of her neck. "Sorry, that was just part of my act. This isn't."

Not understanding, she frowned. "But it's the same mirror."

"Look again." Evers released a deep throaty chuckle. Her skin prickled. Wildflowers and fresh grass engulfed her mind and reminded her of a sunny spring day. Her confusion deepened the longer she stared at him, wondering about the sudden surge of floral aroma. Maybe he still carried the scents from the garden on his hair and clothes.

She glanced at the wood on the mirror and failed to see any difference in this design from the one of his performance the previous night. The deep mahogany framing the glass gleamed in the small amount of light. Carved Celtic figures roamed across the arch. Spiraling wooden pillars encased the sides, holding the glass in place. The designs appeared the same.

With her gaze angled at him, she questioned, "So you're saying that if I look in this mirror and I'm fat then it'll show me as being thin. Right?"

"Sort of," he said and leaned even closer to her. His chest brushed against her shoulder. "Are you ready, Caitlyn? Do you wish to see your true self?"

The pupils in his eyes dilated until they filled the white. She had never witnessed a person's eyes do that. Why did his? She tried to remember if they were this way when she first saw him at the entrance. The light in the hangar wasn't dim enough to make the black centers expand until the amethyst banded the black with only a small ring. She sighed, wanting to finish this game he played with her.

"Sure, why not?"

Caitlyn allowed him to move her so she was in front of the glass. He stepped away from her and stood on the side of the tall frame. She lifted her gaze to the peak of the mirror, estimating the frame to be at least ten feet from top to bottom and five feet from side to side.

He leaned toward her, but did not step away from the mirror. Lifting his hand, he pointed toward the reflective surface. "Look. See who you are and accept it."

In the shiny glass, dark hair entwined with twigs and leaves flowed around his crown and over his shoulders. She moved her head to the left a fraction, but his face remained hidden by the cascade of his hair.

Her heart pounded. Fear sliced through her. He played with her mind. She accepted the fact, but she didn't care for it. Had to be an act. Fake.

"Are you frightened? There's no need. Look into the mirror." His words held a hypnotic tone.

Each breath she pulled in became shallower, and her eyelids drooped. Numbness raced up her body as she fought to control her muscles. The area about them darkened. Silence filled the hangar.

"I don't want to," she whispered.

"Why not?"

"Because it's fake."

"Then you have nothing to fear. Show me your strength. Look." Again, he pointed toward the glass.

Struggling to draw air into her lungs, Caitlyn glanced at her reflection and froze.

A dress created from starlight draped her slim form from shoulders to feet as her hair, free from its brushed neatness, flowed, longer and thicker, in a mass of waves haloing her body. The dull olive green of her eyes had changed to brilliant emerald. They stared back at her minus her glasses, below a gold band sparkling with starlight which rested on her brow. A silver pendant, flickering with frozen flames, lay on her chest, its dainty chain encircling her throat.

Disbelief forced a gasp to escape. She wanted to say this was false, yet something stirred in her, a memory of a woman leaning over her, smiling, speaking to her. A feeling of intense love filtered through her. Caitlyn tried to pull the image closer, clearer, but failed.

His voice whispering her name came to her through the muddled haze of her thoughts. She tore her gaze from the mirror and looked at him. He grinned at her, but his eyes, the pupils normal once more, held a watchful glint.

Unable to comprehend what had happened, she answered with a small smile. She hoped to avoid explaining what she'd really seen, so commented, "So I am fat."

His mouth tilted up on one side. "You're perfect."

Laughing, trying to control a round of shivers racing along her back, she moved away from him and the mirror. "Now, I know you are crazy. Well, it's growing late and all of sudden jet lag has caught up to me. I'm going to lie down for a while. Maybe take a nap."

She turned, refusing to look at him again.

"Rest well, Caitlyn. I'll see you later." The soft tones in his voice reminded her of her dream. With her heart racing, she had trouble pulling in a breath.

With a nod, she made her weakened legs hurry down the aisle and out of the hangar. She kept walking until she reached her room. Going to the window, she stared down at the gardens. She tried to logically decipher how Evers had succeeded in changing her appearance the way he had with the mirror. Twisting her thoughts this way and that, she found no answer to help her understand how he managed to accomplish something so impossible. He toyed with her emotions, pushing her limit. He had to be, yet she couldn't understand how. Or why.

After several minutes, she stepped away from the window and wandered around the room. She touched a few of the dainty porcelain figurines adorning the mantel and small tables. Mythical figures danced in the paintings she didn't recognize on the walls. They were probably from Celtic lore. A doorway on the right caught her attention, so she made her way over to it and turned the knob. A gasp escaped before she could stop it.

The entire bedroom centered around the king-sized, canopied bed on the far wall. Caitlyn glided across the room to feel the beautiful blue spread. Silk. Nice, luxurious, so out of the ordinary for her. Unable to resist, she ran her hand back and forth over the covers, enjoying the soft material.

She hated to mess the bed, but with exhaustion kicking in, she lay on top of the mattress and pulled a pillow under her head. She removed her glasses and placed them on the bedside table next to a phone. As she shifted into a more comfortable position, she closed her eyes, ready for some much needed rest. Within moments, sleep enfolded her in gentle arms and whisked her away.

Chapter 12

Twigs snapped and leaves crackled with each running step Shay took. He ignored the cool damp forest surrounding him. He leapt over a fallen log and landed on one foot. With slow precision, he set the other one down. Balanced on the balls of his feet, he stilled all motion and listened. The forest was alive with creatures seen and unseen.

"Myrielle. Where are you?" He whispered, and searched the foliage under the towering fir trees. He didn't see or sense anything. Where was she?

"Why, here I am."

The soft answer came from in front of him. Shay relaxed, planting both feet solidly on the damp earth.

"Happy I am to see you, sweet Shay."

Lights twinkled and glinted in a spot not six feet ahead of him. Myrielle, Queen to the Tylwyth Teg, had come.

A woman stepped from within the lights. Long black hair floated about her and mingled with the thin cloth of her gold and lavender colored gown. Eyes, deep emerald green, sparkled with unsuppressed joy. Shay's breath caught in his chest as he gazed upon the beauty of her face. A gold band, glittering with the magic of starlight, encircled her brow.

"Why have you summoned me, my muse? If you wish to tell me the news of Caitlyn, you are much too late. Rhys came early this morn and celebrated with me. My daughter has been found and soon will she return from whence she came."

"Your joy may not be lasting. You know this as well as I, my queen. Caitlyn must solve the riddle if she is to remain alive." Shay didn't stop the words. Myrielle knew just as well as he what risks were involved in saving Caitlyn.

"Well I know this, but just to have the child of my body returned to me is enough for now. So many years have passed. I cannot stop the hope that if this is possible, then the solving of the riddle is also possible." She glided nearer and raised a hand. A gentle touch on the crown of Shay's head sent waves of peace through his heart.

"I ask once more. Why have you sent for me?"

The sweet smile she bestowed on him made him want to weep for all the wrong he had bestowed upon her. She had come to him years before to tell him that she believed he had truly been innocent in Caitlyn's kidnapping. He realized somehow that Myrielle had discovered some clue or spoken with someone who verified he had been deceived the same as she and Rhys. He'd never asked her. She never volunteered her reasons for forgiveness. And now, here he stood about to demand more from her.

"Call your mate off me. Tell him to leave me be, where Caitlyn is concerned. She must learn to believe in our world before she can accept who she is. Rhys threatens and rants about not wanting me to frighten her. It is through her fear that I will succeed." Shay stepped to one side, averting his gaze.

He would not look into Myrielle's eyes. She would see into his mind and know there was more to his request than what he wished her to know. What would she do if she realized he intended to seduce her daughter? He could not even begin to imagine what her ire would entail.

"He told me what you have done. You caused her to faint with fright. Do you think this is good for her?"

A slight breeze brought the sweet scent of wildflowers to him. The forest, very much aware of the one standing within its boundary, came to life with the clatter and rhythm of animals and plants rejoicing in the splendor of having their queen visit them. High above the two of them, branches separated and allowed rays of sunshine to fall across the forest floor and onto Myrielle.

"You are much loved, my lady," he murmured, in awe of how nature reveled in Myrielle's presence.

"As were you. I will do as you ask. In turn, I would that you do not hurt Caitlyn. She is fragile, living as she has all these years. I fear for her now even more than I did at her kidnapping. Gwyneth is still alive, and I know she watches. She will not like that you have found Caitlyn. Beware for my daughter and for yourself, my Shay. Gwyneth cares not who is harmed while she waits for the fulfillment of her curse."

He turned and bowed low, extending a leg to show his homage to his queen. His right hand covered his heart and his eyes remained shut. When he opened them and straightened, Myrielle no longer graced him with her presence. The sunlight faded and coldness crept from the forest to enfold him.

He swallowed and hoped he'd succeed with his plan.

* * * *

A soft breeze tickled Caitlyn's face. She brushed a hand across her cheek. Her eyes drifted half-open, and she smiled at the beautiful glowing light in front of her. So pretty. A sense of peace washed over her. She wanted to feel this way forever.

She stretched, enjoying the luxurious texture of the covers against her skin. Arms under her, she pushed up and leaned back, breathing deep. She smiled, enjoying the strange feelings of happiness within her.

Opening her eyes, she looked around the room. A deep midnight blue void spread far and wide, stars sparkling about her. Excitement accelerated her heartbeat. She dreamed again. Her dream.

She slid her legs over the bed's edge and stood. For a moment, she listened for approaching footsteps. No sound came to her. She pursed her lips and wondered why he wasn't here with her. This was her dream, and she wanted him. With slumped shoulders, she sat on the mattress.

A whisper reached her. Hope flared in her heart. Her name, spoken softly, came to her on the breeze. She leapt up, searching for him. Once more, wind washed over her. This time it brought not only the whisper, but a wildflower scent.

Taking a step, she stumbled over the hem of her dress. She ran a hand down the front, staring at the gown made from starlight. The same dress from the mirror. Yes, she needed this dress while she dreamed. She needed--

Grasping the skirt, she hurried forward, determined to find him. There, straight ahead, a beacon shone bright. She laughed out loud, eager to see him. Ripples in the void circled her feet and flowed from her with each running step.

She blinked. In a second, she stood motionless in front of a tree. Tall and slender, the black bark glistened in the starlight. White flowers, their petals thick and waxy, covered the branches and limbs. She frowned, disappointed Shay wasn't there. She looked around but still she couldn't see him.

"Caitlyn."

His deep voice came from the tree. She leaned nearer, raising a hand to touch him, but when he continued, hesitated, "Do you trust me?"

A smile quivered at the corners of her mouth. "This is my dream. You should ask if you trust me."

"Do you believe in me?"

She raised her chin and stared at the tree, her smile widening. "I do in this place. Come to me. I want you here with me. Come now."

The tree blurred, mingling black with white. Shay stepped forward. Caitlyn tilted her head back and laughed.

He traced one finger across her collar bone. She released a shaky gasp, and gazed at him through half-lowered lids. "This is my dream."

Unable to resist, she caressed his cheeks, sliding her fingers through his silky hair and pulling him closer. She grazed his lips with hers. Inhaling his clean scent, she sealed their mouths, dipping into his with her tongue, savoring the cinnamon flavor she found there.

Gentle hands glided past her shoulders, down her back, and tugged her hips snug against his. She moaned, heat pooling between her thighs.

Slanting her head, he held her still for a moment, breaking away to mutter against her lips, "This is your dream. Do you wish it to continue?"

"Yes," she murmured, groaning softly.

"Open your heart, and find what you lost. The magic is yours. I know you will find it. Open your heart," he said. He covered her mouth and delved deep while his hands spread wide over her hips, holding her firm against the solid ridge pressed to her belly.

"I don't know how to," she cried as she twisted her face away and gasped for breath. The warmth increased, adding to the throbbing need in her lower region.

He kissed and sucked in slow spirals over her jaw and down her neck. "You must believe...believe...believe..."

Caitlyn jerked. She sat up and stared wildly around her. The beautiful guest room swayed, then came into blurred focus. Hands trembling, she swiped her brow, trying to calm her reaction to the dream. The fire in her veins continued for several moments. She waited for her blood to cool and wondered why she'd dreamed of Shay. She wasn't interested in him. The interview was the important factor in her life. Once her assignment ended, she would never see him again.

Another dream, that's all it'd been. Even as she thought that, in the same motion she'd made in the dream, she slid her legs over the side of the bed. She picked up her glasses from the bedside table. After she slipped them on, she stumbled to the other door in the room. The bathroom shone with startling brightness, and she inhaled the fresh floral fragrance from the air freshener the servants had used after they'd cleaned. With a twist of her wrist, cold water gushed from the faucet. Two handfuls helped bring her from the heated daze.

Too tired. That's the only reason behind the dream. She'd pushed her body and mind too far the last couple of days. When her mental and physical exhaustion disappeared, the dreams would vanish.

The phone on the bedside table buzzed twice. She hurried over and grabbed the receiver. "Hello."

A masculine voice came from the other end. "Ms. Reiley, would you care for supper in your room or do you wish to dine downstairs this evening?"

"What time is it?"

"Five thirty, miss."

She didn't care to see the object of her weird dreams just yet. She needed time to come to terms with them. "I'll dine here this evening.

"Very well, miss. A tray will be brought up shortly," the strange man answered.

A dial tone sounded over the line. Caitlyn set the phone on the hook and faced the room. The drapes were closed. Her bags were stacked against the entrance.

Someone had entered her room while she slept. She hoped it was the servants. *Please, tell me it wasn't Shay.* The idea of having to face him brought heat to her cheeks. The dream reappeared in her mind. No one knew about what had happened, and no one would ever find out.

Chapter 13

Shay reclined, pressing his back against an ancient oak. His eyes remained closed while he savored the memory of Caitlyn's kiss. She thought she'd dreamed. Good, he wanted her to believe that until their last day in this dimension.

Evening shadows widened and spread over the forest. He winced at the idea of returning to the castle. Dread filled him. The dangerous game he played to awaken her magic threatened to backfire on him. He must stay focused. When he'd met her in the void, the rampant desire rushing through his veins made him forget his purpose.

So sweet, so tender, her taste lingered in his mind. He shook his head. He must not allow this to affect him. Making love and charming women had, over his lifetime, been an unattached frivolous activity for him. A means to release sexual tension. Yet, with her, he hungered for more. So much more.

He groaned, pushed down with one hand on the damp moss-coated soil and stood. At least Rhys had not bothered him. He hoped the older man had no idea what had occurred moments earlier.

Shay stretched, relieving some of the tension from the knotted muscles between his shoulder blades. After two slaps against the seat of his jeans, he meandered through the darkening woods. The castle loomed ahead, its turrets and towers reminding him of a place in Los Angeles. The amusement park with its faery tale castle. He chuckled. If the humans only knew. The power behind Tylwyth Teg magic was greater than they realized. Much stronger than a child's story.

The words and notes from the music he performed in this dimension did not come from him but from the suggestions he sent to the songwriters who worked for him. Performing his true music made him capable of mighty destruction as well as great healing, depending on how he chose to use it.

He halted at the forest's edge. Standing with his feet apart and hands stuffed in his pockets, he surveyed the landscape. The gardens stretched out before him. The peaceful evening enfolded him in its embrace. A lazy tranquility took control of his body and mind for a few moments. Dusk gathered and the plants darkened. A slight wind whirled past him, bringing with it a pungent smell. Shay froze as he scanned the gloom behind him.

Wolves. Their strong scent worried him. Magic brought them here. Local beasts were long gone, yet he well-recalled the wet, musky odor. A thousand years before, several had attacked him. But for Rhys, they would have torn him apart. To this day, he still remembered the rank, sour aroma of wild wolf.

Twigs snapped nearby on his right. Easing from the tree, he leapt back into the forest. Fear no longer controlled him where the wolves were concerned. He had nothing to fear. His life would mean absolutely zero after he helped Caitlyn. He couldn't die before though. Rhys and Myrielle would never find a way to help her. Caitlyn, whether she knew or not, needed his help to return home. Reaching up, he grasped a branch and swung onto a low limb. He squatted among the leaves, waiting.

Bushes rustled. A burst of movement erupted from a thicket to his right. Four rangy wolves loped forward. They stopped at the edge of the woods and sniffed at the spot where he had stood only moments before. He waited for them to find him.

Their yellow gazes whipped up and met his. With vicious snarls and fangs flashing, the wolves sprang against the side of the tree. He grinned and released a shrill, sharp whistle. There was still too much daylight out. He didn't want to chance a human witnessing his power. There were other ways of dealing with this problem.

Deep, low howls poured from the back of the castle. Gray streaks flashed across the garden. Three wolfhounds' long legs ate the distance between the building and the forest. Unerringly, they bounded forward. The wolves, driven by instinct, fled with their tails tucked.

Shay laughed. Soon, Gwyneth would stop sending her minions. He wanted her to come in person. The desire to crush her throat between his hands burned in him. She must be worried, to try to kill him so soon.

He jumped down and called the hounds to him. Rubbing their necks and sides, he spoke low, praising them for their worthiness. "Come, boys. Time to go home."

Turning, he stepped from the black shadow of the forest onto the cool grass. He strode forward, the hounds prancing at his side. Without realizing, his glanced at Caitlin's windows. She stood there, staring at him, her hair trailing over her shoulder. He halted, returning her stare. So beautiful, so sweet, so not for him. Raising a hand he saluted her, and continued to the back entrance. He needed a stiff bracer of brandy.

Chapter 14

After a dreamless night, Caitlyn rose early. She dressed and hurried down the back staircase. A short hallway led to a swinging door. She gave the wood a gentle push, and the door swung open into the room beyond.

The kitchen, wide and spacious, appeared on the other side. A long rectangular table sat in the center. To her surprise, Shay sat at the far end, facing her.

He held a filled spoon midway to his mouth. One brow cocked at her, then he grinned before he popped the rounded end of the spoon between his lips. Images from her previous dream raced through her mind of what those lips did to her. Heat flared in her face.

She wished the real man wasn't more attractive than the one in her dream. The white cotton shirt clung to his wide shoulders. His hair curled in wild abandon about his head. As he looked at her, his amethyst eyes deepened in hue. She tried to steady her accelerated breathing.

With slow steps, she moved to his right side and sat. "Good morning," she murmured, embarrassed by her memories.

"It's a beautiful one." He took another bite, chewed and swallowed. "We'll get started as soon as you eat. What would you like?"

She shrugged. "Toast and juice?"

Right now, she didn't care what she ate. Excitement started to overshadow her self-consciousness.

"That's all?" The dark brow arched up again. "No wonder you're so thin. Maybe, while you're here I can fatten you up." He grinned and winked. He called over his shoulder for Fred. The man who'd taken her and Blake through the house appeared at another open doorway.

"Ms. Reiley wishes toast and juice," Shay informed him.

Fred nodded, went to the stove and lifted a covered platter. He placed it on the table. When he removed the cover, she saw a full breakfast of eggs, bacon, and toast on a plate. He took the plate and set it in front of her.

Shay spoke between bites. "Eat, Caitlyn. You need your strength for this interview."

She eyed the plate before glancing at his bowl. Curious, she studied the thick mixture. "What's that?" she asked, nodding toward it.

"Custard."

So, Shay had a sweet tooth. This surprised her. He was lean and appeared in the best of shape. She tore a corner off a slice of toast and ate it. Fred set a glass of orange juice by her plate. She glanced up at him and smiled. The older man bowed his head and ambled out the door.

"Do you have a sweet tooth?" She dipped a fork into the fluffy eggs and tasted them. Delicious.

He chuckled. "A tiny bit of one. Of course, I consider this dessert. I've already had the full works. Even managed to stuff some sweet oats down. Grazelda cooks the best sweet oats in the world."

She smiled and tucked into her meal. After the first taste, she realized she was hungrier than she'd thought. She ate fast, and when she finished, Grazelda bustled in and shooed them out so she could clean the dishes.

Shay led her to the back sitting room where she'd first seen him yesterday. He produced a tablet and pen from a cabinet and handed them to her. Seated across from him on the sofa, she opened it to the first page.

"What part of Wales are you from?" Caitlyn glanced down at the blank sheet, pen poised, waiting for him to answer.

"Here and there."

"No, I mean where were you born?" She released a low laugh, angling a glance at him over the rim of her glasses.

"To the east." He grinned at her and winked.

"East Wales?"

"No. Further." He shook his head.

"You weren't born in Wales?" She frowned, wondering about his short abrupt answers.

"No."

"Then where in the east? England, Russia?"

"No. Further."

Her temper, never a tolerant aspect of her personality, started to rise. "Look, Evers, I don't like playing games. Can't you answer my questions in a normal civilized manner?"

"Of course. All right, I will tell you. I was born far away in a distant galaxy. I am an elf of the Tylwyth Teg clan. A muse of the royal court." He finished speaking, giving her a firm nod.

Caitlyn stiffened. Her temper flared and she bit out, "What kind of drugs do you take?"

His eyes widened, and a twitch started at the corner of his mouth. "None that I'm aware of."

She stood and glared at him, "If this is how you intend to treat this interview, I don't think we need to go any further. Good day, Mr. Evers. I'll see about scheduling a flight out in the morning."

He leapt up and held his hand out, staying her. "Wait. Sit down."

The sincere expression on his face gave her a reason to resume her seat. Once she settled, he continued. "Which do you think sounds better? That I am an elf from a distant magical planet or my parents, alcoholics, savagely beat me when I was a child? That I ran away from home at twelve and lived on the streets until I was discovered because of the quickness of my hands in doing card tricks? I much prefer the first explanation than the reality of what happened to me. If I believe I am an elf, then what's the harm in it?"

Her heart constricted. His early life had been no better than hers. An image of her mother and father, their clothes soiled and wrinkled and smelling of stale whiskey and the remnants of dope, flashed through her mind. The laughter on their aged faces switched in a blink to livid rage, and she saw her mother's swinging fist. Caitlyn flinched. If they were truly two of a kind, he had desired his parent's love but had never received it. The alcohol and drugs were much more important.

She spoke softly, "Where are they now? Your parents?"

"Don't know. I never went back to find out," he said. "Enough. Ask me another question, and I'll decide whether to be honest." He grinned at her.

Caitlyn smiled and shook her head. One thing about this interview, Evers would keep it interesting.

They spent the rest of the morning verbally sparring. During a short break, Fred brought them a tray of tea and biscuits. After they ate, she tried to stifle a yawn.

Shay leaned forward. A worried frown creased his brow. "You're tired? Was your room all right? Were you comfortable?"

Caitlyn waved a hand, averted her eyes and mumbled, "Everything's fine. I was tired before I arrived. I guess I haven't caught up on my sleep yet. Sorry."

"Maybe you didn't sleep long enough. Would you like to finish later? I don't mind," he said.

She raised her gaze and stared into his worried eyes. Her breath stuck somewhere between her lungs and her lips. Desire flared. She wanted to reach out and brush away the lines on his forehead.

"I've been dreaming a lot lately." Oh, god, she couldn't believe she'd said that. Why had she told him that?

"Dreaming?" He tilted his head, a grin forming on his sculptured lips. "What about? Was I in your dream?"

Fire burned her cheeks, and she squeaked, "No."

She cleared her throat and put strength in her voice. "You were not in my dream. Listen, maybe I do need a little nap..."

Shay stood and moved to sit next to her, staring at her with a serious expression.

"Caitlyn, you're not a very good liar."

"I am not--"

Leaning closer, he spoke low. The deep tone vibrated over her nerve endings. "Yes, you are. I can tell. You dreamed about me. What happened? Damn, I wish I could have been there. Come on, Caitlyn, spill the beans. Sing like a canary."

A laugh bubbled from her. Her embarrassment ebbed. "Dream on, Evers. You'll have to show up in another one to know for sure."

"Aw, tell me. I swear I don't gossip," he said, shifting closer. He reached out, cupping her jaw in his palm. "What happened?" Flames scorched her skin where his hand rested. She tried to breathe. He moved nearer, his gaze focused on her mouth.

A gust of wind ruffled the pages on her tablet. Caitlyn glanced toward the French doors leading to the garden outside. Rhys stood in the opening, his eyes hooded, staring at them. Shay released her face and eased away, and she missed the warmth of his touch.

"Excuse me. The shipment you've been waiting for has arrived. I thought you might like to inspect it." The blond man's face remained expressionless.

Tension radiated between the two men. Curious and hoping to delve deeper into the conflict bubbling under the surface between the two of them, she started to question Shay, but he got to his feet.

"Of course. Caitlyn, I'm sorry, but I must go." Without meeting her gaze, he crossed the room and brushed by Rhys. The gardener nodded to her, turned and followed him.

Caitlyn stared at the closed door for several minutes. Something major was definitely wrong with Shay and Rhys's relationship. The harder she thought, the harder it was to fit the fragments of their odd behavior together. Rhys couldn't still be upset about Shay's little snip at the party in Los Angeles, could he? Maybe they'd had words on the flight home. If not, then the friendly way they acted toward each other in LA was fake.

The hostility she sensed coming from Rhys toward Shay had not started in the last two days. This type of animosity tended to grow with passing years. They had claimed to be friends since Shay was a child. What had happened in the past which dug such a rift between them? She didn't know, but she would find out.

Sighing, she closed the tablet. The idea of a short nap tempted her. A disturbing thought tiptoed through her mind, but she quickly pushed it away. She was not starting to like sleeping better than she liked being awake.

No, she just needed a little rest, and if she dreamed...well, she couldn't help that. After all, a person couldn't control her dreams. Rising, she headed for her room.

Chapter 15

A cold breeze ruffled Shay's hair. He gritted his teeth. Behind him by several feet, Rhys's aura shoved him forward with each step.

The bastard possessed perfect timing. One kiss was all he wanted, one, but as soon as he made headway with her, Rhys had to interrupt. Again, damn it.

The gardener's shed came into view. Without stopping, Shay threw open the door and stepped inside. Pivoting, he barely saw the well-aimed fist looming before his eyes. Caught off guard, he crashed against the work table on the far side of the room, tilting it on its back legs. Tools and clay pots scattered across the one-room building.

"If you touch her again, I will see you dead." Rhys towered over him, fury contorting his handsome features.

Shay straightened and swiped at the side of his mouth. Blood streaked the back of his hand. He glared at Rhys. "Good. Kill me now. Be done with it."

"You are unfit to lick her shoes." The flesh on Rhys's face flared a crimson hue. One hand rose, but he became still, his gaze boring into Shay's. The older man inhaled a deep breath. His coloring faded to normal.

When he spoke, his voice was calmer. "No, I don't believe I will. Not now, at least. She is opening to you. I can sense it. But, I have come to the realization that the years you were imprisoned have affected your memory. 'Tis why I am watching you. Let me remind you once more. Your task is to open her mind to magic. Not once did I grant permission for you to seduce my daughter. Am I making myself clear?"

Shay shifted, anger still controlling his thoughts. "I don't care about what you want."

"You will. I swear on my lady, you will," Rhys bit back.

Before Shay could open his mouth to speak, his feet burned. Roots emerged from his flesh. The ground trembled and cracked.

"No," he shouted, reaching out and grabbing the other man by his shirtfront. The flesh covering Shay's body tightened and split. Twigs sprouting leaves sprang from the fissures. Pain flooded his body. Gasping, he managed to rasp out, "She...needs...me. You...know it."

Rhys smiled, the twist of his lips more mocking than amused. He stepped back, tugging his shirt free. "Perhaps, but then, perhaps not. She is here, and that is more than what I had hoped. You will consider your actions for the remainder of this day. Mayhap, by the morn, you will see the folly of disobeying me." He pivoted and left, silently shutting the door. The lock rattled.

Unable to move, Shay stood suspended in a half-flesh, half-tree form. He tried to straighten his back but pain bolted through him. He stared at his outstretched arms. Blood seeped from his torn skin.

Birds trilled outside the small window, and Shay struggled to breathe. Bitter hatred boiled for not only the witch who'd caused this but for his own part in Caitlyn's taking. Gwyneth had caused his suffering but he had helped her. *Gwyneth.* He would make her desire death the same way he wanted freedom. In the end, they would both have their just desserts.

Sunlight moved across the room with the passage of time. The door creaked open. A shadow fell across the floor. With the door hiding the identity of the intruder, he couldn't see who was about to enter. Worry shot through him. *Please, not Caitlyn.* The idea of her seeing him in this condition overrode all his suffering. He had wanted to frighten her but not like this. She'd be driven over the edge and be lost to him forever.

A titillating laugh reached his ears. Worry and pain forgotten, he centered on the sound. So familiar, yet, he couldn't recall from when and where. The door clicked shut. An arm, slender and graceful, came into view followed by a feminine shape. She stepped closer. How did he know her? With a finger, the stranger traced a path down his cheek.

"Aw, poor Shay," she murmured.

His heart missed a beat.

Gwyneth. Yet, not her. The once glorious golden hair was now a deep chestnut. Shorter, the ends brushed the top of her shoulders. Still slender, the witch wore casual khaki slacks and a mud brown fleece pullover. She tilted her body and gazed up into his eyes. Her irises were clear blue, the pupils dilated. The same as he remembered.

Damn Rhys and his anger--with Gwyneth before him, Shay was unable to exact revenge. Rhys had left him in this unprotected state. The older man had to suspect she would appear.

"I had no idea he makes you suffer so. Does it hurt?" she cooed.

The fingers brushing lightly across his cheek drifted to his right arm. She glanced at it. Those same delicate fingers peeled the skin further apart. Shay groaned, intense agony searing through his arm.

Even as she stayed in his sight, she left him and wandered about the room, wiping the blood from her fingers against her slacks. After a few seconds, she returned. She held a grass blade. When she passed by a patch of sunlight coming from a small window, the blade flickered. Fearful anticipation coursed through Shay's veins.

Dammit. Where was Rhys? He had to feel her presence.

She pointed the sharp tip of the blade at his chest. "I wonder, sweet, how much blood you have left in your body? Or did it turn to sawdust? Um, let's see."

Slicing into an unmarred section of skin, she cut a shallow furrow into his flesh. Shay gusted out a breath. Droplets of spit flew from his mouth, some landing on her cheek. She laughed.

"So, you do bleed." Giggling wickedly, Gwyneth proceeded to make another incision on the top of his right thigh. Once she finished, she flipped the blade and placed it under his jaw, pressing against his throat. "Send her away. Have mercy on her. Let her simply fade away. If you don't, I'll kill her now. You can't watch her every second. I'll find an opportunity. I will have my revenge."

From outside, footsteps approached. Gwyneth lowered the blade and retreated several steps. Tilting her head, she listened. The steps drew nearer, and the door handle rattled. She raised the blade and swung at him.

Pain seared Shay's shoulder. The door was flung wide. Rhys stood inside the threshold. Gwyneth barreled past the older man. He grunted and fell against the door. Off balance for a breath, Rhys met his gaze. The other man's gaze shifted and caught on the gardening blade. The cutting edge glinted in the sunlight above where it protruded from his shoulder. Rhys swung about and leapt out the door.

Shay listened to his blood drip, land with tiny splashes at his feet. Several minutes dragged by before Rhys returned. Crossing the room, he winced and took hold of the handle. He jerked it free as he muttered an incantation to release Shay from his transformation spell.

The enchantment dissolved from his body. His legs folded under him, and he gulped air as he collapsed. Rhys knelt next to him, studying the slices. He probed the stab wound and asked, "Gwyneth?"

His rough tone belied his true feelings. Shay searched the older man's emotionless features. Yes, there in the lines bracketing his mouth, the strength of his frustration and anger lingered. Rhys was always more dangerous when calm. A shiver of unease shook him. He'd had enough of his punishment, along with the bitch who was too cowardly to fight fairly.

Shay's strength ebbed, and he lowered his head. His chin bumped against his chest. "She intends to see Caitlyn dead. She'll kill anyone who gets in her way."

Rhys lifted Shay's left arm and pulled it around his shoulders. "Come, you need a bit of magic to heal you."

"Is that why you returned? You realized she'd come here?" Shay bit his lip as Rhys helped him stand. The pain cleared some of the haze in his mind.

"I suspected she might. Caitlyn's too close to home for Gwyneth to feel secure."

Shay glanced at him. "I should choke you for leaving me like that. If you suspected, did it not occur to you that she might want me dead too?"

"No, it didn't. I thought she would go after Caitlyn, not you. Curious, though. Why would she want to hurt you? Did she give you the answer to the riddle when she took Caitlyn?"

Rhys half-carried him out the door and to the back of the shed. The forest, closer at this spot, greeted them as they entered it. Branches swayed, their leaves fluttering where no breeze existed. Even the grass shifted to draw closer to their liege. Flowers bloomed in his footsteps.

Shay swung to face Rhys. A small smile lifted the older man's lips. "You, my king, are as much loved as the queen."

"Of course, I am. They are well tended. In return, they adore me."

"I've never noticed before. Was it always so, or have I forgotten?" Shay frowned.

He fought for each breath. Had the blade punctured his lung? Heaviness pressed on his chest. Blackness edged his vision. His tired mind wandered. He searched for the queen. His eyelids drooped. Blood flowed from his wounds and left a trail behind them. With each step, he heard the slight splash as another life-giving drop fell and struck the leaves covering the forest floor.

Rhys stopped and eased him down on the ground with his back against a tree trunk.

Myrielle spoke as though from far away. "Oh my dear, what has happened?"

Blackness continued to creep closer, blinding him. "Rhys, go to Caitlyn. Keep her safe until I return. Must keep her...safe." He had difficulty speaking. Weakness gripped him.. Tired of fighting against the beckoning darkness, he allowed it to carry him away.

Chapter 16

Caitlyn sat up straight in the bed. Something had awakened her. She wasn't sure what. Fumbling around on the bedside table, she searched for her glasses. Finding the elusive pair, she slipped them on. She switched on the lamp next to the bed. A quick glance around the room revealed nothing out of place. The clock on the mantle read eleven o'clock. Still exhausted and suffering from jet lag, she'd overslept.

She shut her eyes and, for a moment, an image appeared behind her eyelids. Her eyes shot open. The image remained. Filled with pain, Shay's face paled while blood poured from his body.

She whispered his name.

Heart pounding, she struggled against the covers. Her legs tangled within the sheets. A need to see him increased with each passing second.

Something was wrong. Very wrong. She knew it.

One foot hit the floor, and she had to tug twice to release the other. She had to find him. Make sure he was all right. Racing across the room, she came to an abrupt stop.

Rhys. If he hurt Shay...

She frowned and stopped, hoping to calm her frantic pulse. She was acting like she cared about him. Like she... No, she wouldn't finish that thought. She'd had a nightmare. That was it. No, wait--she was awake when she saw him. Perhaps the image was a fragment left over from her dream. A dream she didn't remember having?

As quick as it started, her disquiet lessened. Her heart slowed to a normal beat. Her reasoning made her uneasy while worry for Shay still nagged at her. She would find him to see if what she envisioned was true.

The darkened, silent hallway bothered her. She squinted in the dimness, trying to see a switch plate or control. Her stomach growled. She rubbed the spot. Why had no one called her about dinner? Concern deepened.

Something wasn't right, and she intended to find out what was causing her to feel this way.

Battling the building anxiety, she moved with caution the few feet across the hall to the rear staircase. She'd never realized there was darkness, and then there was a deeper dark. Before her, the black opening to the staircase beckoned her forward. She hesitated a moment. She stepped onto the landing and narrowed her gaze, fumbling along the walls, searching for the light switch. She found nothing but painted wood along both sides.

Now, this was great.

Feeling her way, she found the banister and placed her foot on the first step. One by one, she maneuvered down the stairs.

She thought about Marcy and grinned. She could just hear her friend. *'News reporter found dead in famous illusionist's kitchen after tumble down back staircase'.*

Feeling a little better, she went down two more steps. When she reached the first landing, relief raced through her. The enclosed space was warmer, and the air thicker than upstairs. An old musty scent surrounded her.

"Almost there." Hearing her voice gave her a little comfort. Where was everyone? The silence hung heavy in the air about her. What about Blake? Was he in his room or somewhere else in the immense spaces of the castle?

Four steps and at last, she reached the bottom. She sighed. Searching for the door leading into the kitchen, she found it and twisted the knob, shoving until it swung open.

On silent feet, she moved through the short hallway, able to see with the light coming from where the swinging door stood propped open. She reached the threshold and stopped. The only light in the room came from the hood over the stainless oven on the opposite wall. The table was occupied.

With his back to her, Shay's long hair spread over his shoulders. His right arm moved from the table to his face. Relief flooded her, and she found herself sagging against the doorjamb. Thank goodness, he was all right. She whispered his name.

The muscles in his back stiffened. He glanced over his shoulder at her. The twin amethyst pools of his eyes glimmered in the dim light.

"Caitlyn. You're still up." The reassuring sound of his voice washed over her. "I thought you were asleep by now."

"No. I just woke up," she said, moving closer to the table. Pulling out the chair next to him, she eased down, gaze glued to his face. "Are you all right?"

A slight frown puckered his brow. His stare drilled into hers as if he searched for the reason behind her question. Caitlyn had a sinking sensation her vision held a measure of reality.

He slowly nodded. "I'm fine. Why do you ask?"

"I had an impression something was wrong--with you," she said, placing her folded hands on the table top. "You were in pain and..."

Hearing the words spoken out loud forced her to stop. Was she crazy? She sounded that way to her ears. He appeared healthy. With no apparent injuries in sight, she watched his movements for any signs of damage.

"And?" He prompted.

She shook her head, glancing away. "It's nothing."

The warmth of his hand covered hers, sending heated streams through her body. With a gentle look in his gaze, he squeezed. "Tell me."

"I thought there--I saw blood..." She cut a quick glance in his direction to assess his reaction.

The slight widening of his eyes didn't tell her anything. His gaze dropped to the table and he shook his head. "No, I'm not hurt."

She remained expressionless. A strong feeling washed over her that he lied. But why would he? He was too quiet, subdued even. The charismatic illusionist no longer sat next to her. She didn't recognize this man. "I thought maybe you and Rhys had fought."

His brows shot up. "What makes you think that?"

"I saw you two yesterday in the garden. He didn't look happy. And then this afternoon when he interrupted us, he seemed angry. Why? Did you do something to upset him?"

He studied her for a second. "I suppose you can say that. I've been promising to help him with some things, and I keep putting him off. He doesn't like to wait."

"Oh, so that's what you did this evening. You helped Rhys."

"Yes. He had me rooted to the ground in the gardener's shed among all the potting supplies."

"It was nice of you to help him. He's not angry anymore?" Please let him tell her the truth. She had to know.

Shay shook his head and ensnared her in his gaze, refusing to release her from the burning purple depths. Finally, he lowered his gaze to the bowl in front of him.

The silence started to affect her the longer she stared at him. He looked at her. She jerked at the impact. "This impression you had about me. It frightened you?"

"A little," she said, shrugging and sliding her hands from beneath his. "I suppose it's my imagination. New place, I guess."

"That's probably so. After all, you're not psychic." The corners of his mouth twitched.

For a second, she observed him. This was the Shay she was familiar with--teasing and full of life. The quiet, contemplative man from a few moments ago was the stranger. She wasn't sure she cared for the subdued man. That man carried deep secrets and unseen scars. He reminded her of her past with its painful memories.

These were the types of facts she needed for the interview. Yet, at that moment, she dared not delve deeper into his soul. She would discover the inner man at another time. Not now.

"No, I'm not." She smiled in return. Glancing around, she found the porcelain bowl on the table. Strawberries sat soaking in rich cream. Her smile widened. "So, is that one of your vices?"

The famous grin flashed as he looked down. "I suppose you could say that. For some reason, I can't get enough of them. What about you? What's your vice?"

"Strawberries." She lifted a brow. "Are you going to share?"

"By all means, take as many as you like," he murmured, sliding the bowl closer to her.

Caitlyn chose a plump, deep red one. Sweet and tart, the juices escaped to drip down her chin. "Mmm, this is good."

Shay chuckled and leaned nearer. "Here, let me clean that up." He brushed a napkin over her chin.

She watched him through half-lowered lids. The smooth and lightly tanned skin of his face showed laugh lines radiating from the corners of his eyes. She studied his features, looking along the slim ridge of his nose and stopping at his berry-stained lips.

She forgot to breathe.

Memories rose unbidden. Her nipples hardened. When she shifted in the chair, they rubbed against her shirt, sending pangs shooting to her toes. Heat built in a throbbing rhythm at the junction between her thighs. When she looked up, he watched her with fierce intensity.

Their gazes held for several moments before his shifted to the strawberries and he released a soft chuckle. "Here, take the rest. I think I'll retire. Sleep well, Caitlyn, and enjoy your sweet dreams."

With that, he stood and strode to the door leading outside.

So much for him retiring. She contemplated the closed portal, trying to ignore the messages her body sent her. Sticking her finger in the cream, she stirred then licked the sugary juice from the tip.

What was wrong with her? She had a job to do, and it did not include lusting after the person she needed to interview. She repeated in her mind his parting words.

Sleep well, Caitlyn, and enjoy your sweet dreams.

The general comment brought forth a memory of what he'd asked in her dream. The words 'sweet dream' were common. Of course, she didn't use them. She never dreamed. Never, that was, until she'd met Shay Evers.

A nagging thought rose. She denied it but it remained. What if he really was an elf? Did he have the capabilities to come to her in her dreams? The night visions were so real. She shook her head. No, that was impossible. She didn't believe in magic. All this analyzing wasn't helping her.

She glanced at the door. Where had he gone? Curious, she decided a walk through the gardens might help her relax enough to go back to sleep. If she happened to see him, maybe she could watch without him knowing.

Her mind made up, she finished off the strawberries and drained the cream in several swallows. Taking her time, she washed the bowl and wiped the table. A jacket hung on a peg next to the door. She tugged it from the peg and slipped it on, hoping no one minded if she borrowed the battered coat.

The door opened on silent hinges, revealing a moonlit wonderland. Bluish-gray light covered the plants and grass. The stone-covered path glowed white. She looked toward the horizon, then lifted higher in search of the full moon. Silver clouds floated in the midnight blue sky. Stars twinkled, their light battling with the bright moon.

Caitlyn smiled. Living in Los Angeles, she had never had the opportunity to see the night skies in such a clear, open place. Strange, that she'd never thought about what the stars and moon looked like, but here it seemed appropriate.

Did Shay request this night's beauty just for her? A low laugh escaped her. She tugged the jacket closer, moving with slow steps down the path. Peaceful silence enfolded her in loving arms.

Stopping here and there, she admired the plants along the way. They appeared silver- tipped in the moonlight. Coming to a fork in the path, she stopped and glanced in both directions. The one to the left led toward the forest. She shook her head. No, not that way. With a sigh, she headed to the right.

The path climbed a low hill. She reached the top and halted. Looking down at the sight before her, she clasped her hands to her chest in awe. This was one of the most spectacular views she'd ever seen. An irregular lake reflected the night sky on its surface.

"So beautiful," she whispered, unable to tear her gaze away. She sat on the dew-covered grass. In this rare, different world of beauty and silence, peace wrapped around her.

Chapter 17

Shay hung within the shadows of the forest, his gaze captured by Caitlyn. She sat, hugging her knees, her chin resting on the top of them. His fingers itched to remove the hairpins securing the long dark strands. He wanted to touch and comb through the silky tendrils.

He chewed on his bottom lip, allowing pain to seep into his heated thoughts. She needed his guidance to open her heart to magic.

His focus had wavered too much the last few days. Gwyneth's action this afternoon highlighted the fact Caitlyn's life depended on him.

Sending a silent blessing to his queen, he touched the tender spot on his left shoulder. With the medicine and her healing touch, the wound had started to heal. Still too sore to stand much pressure, by tomorrow the slice would disappear.

He frowned. Gwyneth had managed to come too close to Caitlyn. She had slipped by their defenses and attacked him too easily. He ground his teeth. Never again. He wouldn't allow her another opportunity.

Caitlyn worried him also. Surprised to see her in the kitchen tonight, he hadn't known what to say when she asked if he was all right. She had had an impression.

He clenched his fists.

Dammit, she'd had a vision. Myrielle possessed the same ability. He should be happy, but why had her power shone through now? After all these years of searching, and now she had begun to show abilities inherited from her parents. He'd believed the spell Gwyneth placed on her had been stronger. A nagging thought warned him that Gwyneth's magic was involved in this. If so, she wanted to play with Caitlyn's mind, possibly drive her insane. He'd have to keep a closer watch on Caitlyn.

A howl came from deep inside the forest. He straightened and glanced over his shoulder. The animals were on the move. He brought his gaze around to the solitary figure on the crest of the hill. She released her knees and leaned back with her arms at her side, hands pressed flat on the ground. Either she hadn't heard the wolves or she believed this place safe from wild beasts.

Danger drew closer. He eased out of the shadows and approached her on silent feet. Worry filled him the nearer he came to her. She appeared so fragile and small, sitting there, staring up at the star-filled sky.

"Do you often wander about the grounds at night?" she asked.

He stopped and studied her. How had she known he was the one walking toward her? "I enjoy the quiet moments the night offers. And you? What brings you out here?"

"I wanted to spy on you." The honesty in her answer surprised him.

Behind the glass lenses, her emerald gaze shifted toward him. He swallowed hard. "Did you see me do something wrong? Catch me in a scandalous act?"

Her laugh washed over him. His lips twitched, but he stopped the smile threatening to appear.

"No. I was distracted. It's so beautiful here. And peaceful. A long way from the hectic motion of Los Angeles. I never realized there were places like this until tonight." She patted the ground next to her. "Come, sit down. Talk to me. Tell me about this place and your magic. I want to know everything."

He swallowed once more. Temptation beckoned him. He wanted to, but the wolves drew dangerously near. Struggling to maintain control, he shook his head. "No, it's late. Time to go in." He held out his hand.

She studied his face for a moment. With a smile, she placed her hand in his. A lustful fire scorched him. The slight widening of her eyes and the way her breath caught told him she'd experienced something similar. She reacted often like this when they touched. Once more, temptation rose. This time, though, he relaxed the hold on his need.

Tugging her forward, he wrapped his arms around her waist, dipping his face. His lips covered hers in a searing kiss. Another slight catch in her breath caused his control to slip further.

He allowed her freedom when they were in the void, but here he controlled the kiss. She opened to him, sighing into his mouth. With a groan, he delved deep into the warm recesses past her lips. She tasted of strawberries and cream, and he feasted on her.

A howl, closer to the gardens, echoed in the forest. Shay tore away from her. She panted and moaned, reaching to pull him to her.

"No. Caitlyn, we have to return to the castle. Now." He wrapped his fingers about her wrist, turned and tugged her behind him.

"Shay?"

He glanced over his shoulder. She seemed to be in a world of her own, with nothing but him in her focus. Her gaze pleaded with him, but he shook his head. He had to protect her from the danger bearing down on them.

He sensed her assumption of his refusal followed by her embarrassment a second before she jerked her arm free. Her eyes glistened in the moonlight. He spoke her name, but she hurried down the hill toward the castle.

Shoulders slumped, he watched until she reached the kitchen door and disappeared inside. Pivoting, he strode in the direction of the howls. The expression on her face remained with him. He'd hurt her. Even as he felt relief that she was safe, guilt ate at him. His hand shook as he swiped at his brow.

The wolves drew nearer. Their paws crunched the dry leaves on the forest floor. Shay reached behind his waist and pulled an elfin blade free. He needed to release some of his frustration. He hurried toward the trees, increasing his speed with each step.

They met at the edge of the tree line. Three against one. Shay slashed the braver of the wolves across the neck and shoulder. A screaming yelp erupted from the beast a moment before it dropped to the ground. The last two snarled and hurled their rangy bodies at him. He kicked out, knocking the one coming in from the left clear, while he gutted the other one.

With two wolves writhing in dying spasms, the third wolf fled. Shay growled and gave chase. Leaping over fallen logs, breaking past low limbs and through thickets, he lost track of the beast on the edge of his land.

He squatted under an oak, his palm flat on the bark. He searched the area. Nothing stirred. The animal had gone to ground. It was not wounded, so it would return. When it did, he'd kill it, just like he had the other two. Gwyneth would soon find out who she dealt with.

* * * *

Caitlyn stared at her reflection in the bathroom mirror. Sharp pangs shot through her stomach. How could she have believed he'd want her? Look at her. Unattractive and certainly not desirable. At least, every other man she'd dated in the past had thought so. Some had even told her.

Marcy's gorgeous features popped into her mind. Even her friend wanted Shay Evers, but he had reacted with disinterest. What signs had he shown to prove he wanted her? Sure, he'd kissed her but how many other women had he done the same with? He hadn't shown any signs he cared for her, Caitlyn Reiley. None.

Tonight, nature's ambiance made her forget her real purpose here. She'd assumed the nice way he'd treated her was an invitation, when all it had been was a part of his courteous behavior.

She twisted the knobs on the sink. Water gushed out, tumbling over her hands. She scooped the clear liquid and splashed her face. Her hands trembled. She held them up, trying to stop the shaking. The look in his eyes when she had said his name haunted her.

Pity had shone from his gaze. Under the surface of her dismay, fury brewed. No one had pitied her in a long time, and she loathed the idea Shay Evers would do so now.

If she was the crying type, she'd burst into tears, but she wasn't. Tears never helped. She turned the water off, grabbed a hand towel, and marched to the bed. Twisting the terry cloth into a knot, she slumped on the mattress. Weariness washed over her, and she lay back, closing her eyes. Images of Shay whirled through her mind.

The kiss they shared tonight was so different than the ones in her dreams. She'd initiated those. Tonight, this one belonged to him. He'd fueled the fire and left her scorched in the aftermath. She gasped, pressing the heels of her hands into her eye sockets, hoping to erase him from her memory.

Rolling onto her side, she pulled her legs onto the mattress. By slow degrees, her body relaxed and she dozed. Waking several times during the night, she burned for him to come to her in her sleep. Each time she closed her eyes, she hoped to find him, but he remained absent.

Chapter 18

Dawn arrived too soon. Blurry-eyed, she stumbled from the bed, showered, and dressed in casual slacks and a soft green sweater. She made her way downstairs, hoping not to see him too soon. The castle belonged to him. No way to avoid him for the rest of her stay. Her job revolved around him.

She reached the door at the end of the staircase and cracked it open. More than one voice came from the kitchen. Shay's wasn't one of them. Thankful, she followed the hallway and entered the room.

Rhys sat at the end of the table, facing her. He raised his head, smiled and greeted her. She nodded in return. Grazelda stood at the stove, stirring something in a pot. A delicious aroma rose with the steam. The old woman glanced in her direction and motioned for her to join them.

"Ah, good morning to ye, dearie. Come, come, sit yerself down. I was preparing a few sweet oats. Would ye care for some?" She waved the spoon in the table's general direction. Caitlyn smiled. She liked Shay's housekeeper.

"Good morning, Grazelda. How are you today?" She took a seat next to Rhys.

"Couldn't be better, dearie, and ye? Did ye rest well last night?"

Before she could answer, Shay called a greeting from the doorway leading to the gardens. At the sight of him, Caitlyn forgot her embarrassment.

His cheeks were flushed, his wind-blown hair flowed past his shoulders and his eyes twinkled with mischief. He caught her gaze and held it for a moment. In a flash, last night rushed forward. He'd given life to her dreams but smashed them to pieces. She stiffened her resolve, broke eye contact with him and tried to appear unaffected.

"Good morning, Caitlyn. Rhys, how are you this glorious morn? Grazelda. Looks to be another sunny day." He breezed into the room, rounded the table and wrapped his arm about the old woman's shoulders for a quick hug.

"Oh, go on with you. There's rain coming today. My old bones feel it," the elderly woman warned.

"Do you think it'll rain, Rhys? There's not a cloud in the sky. It's a perfect day." Shay grinned. He stepped around the end of the table and leaned against the counter directly in front of her.

Her back tightened at his deliberate maneuver to put his body in her direct line of vision. Rhys stood, retrieved a cup, and poured Caitlyn some tea. Glad for the distraction, she kept her gaze on him, admiring the gardener's graceful movements.

The scrape of the chair next to her against the stone floor made her gasp. Turning her head, she came face-to-face with Shay. When had he moved? He'd turned the chair so the back was to the table, and he straddled the seat. When he spoke, his voice fell soft and close to her ear. "Did you sleep well?"

She jerked her head away from him. "No, as a matter of fact, I didn't. I think it's the strange place syndrome. I'll rest better tonight. I hope." Her voice held a chill to it. Good, let him know up front she wasn't playing games anymore. She'd come to do a job, not have an affair that he obviously did not want.

"Perhaps--"

She cut him off. "When did you want to continue the interview? That is why I'm here. We need to start filming. Do you have time today?"

He raised a brow. "Sorry, not today. I have other obligations. Perhaps Rhys can show you around the place. Give you a tour. Would you like that?"

No, she wouldn't. She wanted to finish this interview and leave. Instead, she said, "That's fine."

Turning, she smiled at Rhys and caught him frowning at Shay. Sudden realization came to her. He seemed to be matchmaking for her and Rhys. This thought fueled her anger and prompted her to question Rhys, "You don't mind, do you? If you have other plans, I'm sure I can wander about the place alone."

The gardener glanced at her. "No, I have nothing pressing. Let me take care of something first. By the time I return, you should be finished with breakfast. I'll give you the tour of the castle and gardens. They are extensive, so you might consider comfortable shoes."

Without waiting for her answer, he disappeared through the door. Mindful of Grazelda, Caitlyn sipped her tea, refusing to look at Shay.

Tea was not her favorite morning beverage, but at the moment she didn't care. Her body relaxed. She took a chance and said, "You're up early this morning."

"I'm an early riser," he replied, setting his chin on his forearms where they crossed over the chair's back.

She wanted to know if he was able to sleep last night. A part of her needed to know he suffered a little. "Were you up late?"

"All night. I wandered through the gardens and into the woods. I returned to find your photographer in the screening room watching a movie." He raised his head, angled it to one side as he paused. "There's something I need to tell you."

Relief flowed through her. He had not been able to sleep last night--his words verified it.

"Yes?"

His eyes focused on a spot over her right shoulder. "I don't want you walking about the grounds alone anymore. Make sure someone is with you."

"Why?" She raised the cup and sipped a little of the steaming tea.

"There were wolves about last night. That's why I wanted you to go inside. You might have been harmed," he said.

Understanding, but unable to accept what he had told her, she eyed him. So he hadn't broken off his kiss because he didn't want her.

She frowned, doubting his comment. "Aren't wolves gone from Great Britain? I recall reading that there weren't any wild wolves here. Do you expect me to believe you?"

"You can't believe unless you see with your own eyes, can you, Caitlyn?" He narrowed his eyes and raised his left hand.

He held it with the palm facing her, then turned so she saw the back of it. With no more than ten inches between her eyes and his hand, he bent his wrist and flipped his palm facing up. In the center lay a dew-sprinkled white rose. The petals were crisp and pristine. Her heart skipped a beat. So close, and she had not seen how he'd managed to hide the rose.

His mouth tilted upward on one side. "One day, you will believe without seeing. Magic is real, and so are the wolves. I killed two last night. Their carcasses are in the shed. Have Rhys show them to you, and then perhaps, you'll believe."

With those words, he stood and walked out, whistling a cheery tune. The strong scent of green grass and fresh air wafted from the air he stirred when he passed behind her. She inhaled, and a smile formed on her lips.

"He's a good one, that he is," Grazelda commented, setting a bowl filled with sweet oats in front of Caitlyn.

She thanked the older woman and started to respond, but Rhys came through the door. The three of them visited, discussing unimportant matters while Caitlyn ate. After she finished, they helped the old woman clean the dishes from the meal.

Holding the door leading into the main part of the house for her, Rhys glanced at her loafers and smiled. "Do you think those will be fine for a bit of walking?"

"We won't be running, so they'll be okay," she said, slipping by him. She hoped the impression she had of Shay trying to throw Rhys and her together was wrong. She liked the tall slender gardener, but she felt no attraction for him.

They spent the remainder of the morning going through the house. Caitlyn found the place amazing. One thing that it did not have surprised her.

"Where's the gym?" She glanced up at Rhys as they made their way toward the kitchen for lunch.

"There's not one."

"Why not? I assumed Shay kept in shape by working out. Most stars do. Does he go to a local gym or a spa? I assumed he had a trainer." Most of the celebrities she read about usually had their own trainer.

"He doesn't need a gym. Shay stays active walking. Sometimes, he'll run. I recruit him to help me in the gardens when he doesn't have anything pressing to attend to. All of that keeps him healthy and strong." Rhys smiled at her.

"Are you married?" The question escaped before Caitlyn thought. She had to know. Though older than her by at least a decade, she didn't want the gardener to think she was attracted to him.

He chuckled and stopped in the doorway leading to the grand ballroom. The sprawling room captured her attention, and she forgot for a moment the question she'd asked.

Frescos on the walls depicted magical creatures frolicking through a forest. Across the walls, unicorns and tall slender elves strolled and played among woodland creatures. She studied the detailed designs of the paintings. Braids twined within the elves' hair revealed the pointed tips of their ears.

Four double doors opened at the far side of the room onto a side terrace. Golden cloth hung from circle brackets and was caught at the doors' corners to flow down the sides of the frames. The room captivated her. She leaned to look further inside and noticed a grand piano sitting on the far end, as though waiting for someone to arrive and produce music befitting this place.

After surveying the ballroom, she realized several minutes had passed and she glanced at Rhys. He watched her, arms crossed over his chest and a slight smile on his lips.

"I am married to the most beautiful woman in the universe," he said. "You remind me of her."

Caitlyn straightened and faced him. "Do I? How?"

He studied her for a moment. "Your hair and eyes are the same color. I believe, though, it's your smile that reminds me the most."

Without thinking, she smiled at him.

"Yes, your smile is like hers."

"Where is she?"

"Our home is not far from here. Perhaps, one day you will meet her. She doesn't come here often. She worries she will distract me." He held out a hand in the direction they were going and Caitlyn turned and walked with him.

"Would she?"

A low chuckle came from the gardener. "Oh, yes. My wife knows me very well."

Relieved, she questioned him about where he lived and his beautiful wife. His quiet answers carried the happiness that radiated from his gaze as he spoke of his home and love. They both enjoyed gardening.

She listened as they continued toward the back of the house.

"We'll have a bite to eat and after I'll show you the gardens," Rhys said.

She smiled and nodded, enjoying the tour and the companionship he offered. He helped to soothe her ragged emotions. The interview had turned her world into mire, where she continued to sink deeper and deeper. This time with him helped to stabilize her feelings and clear her thoughts.

Once lunch was over, they strolled through the gardens. The place glowed with such splendor last night, but now, in the light of day, the glorious colors of winter plants astounded her. She questioned Rhys on how he achieved so many flowers when the icy chill of winter should have killed them. He laughed and commented about his magical thumb again. She remembered that he'd said the same thing in Los Angeles. Back then, she thought he'd been teasing, but now, seeing the extent of his abilities, she knew he had spoken the truth. He did have a magical thumb.

They came to the top of the hill where she and Shay had shared the heated kiss. She and Rhys stopped and gazed down on the lake's shimmering beauty and the grounds surrounding it. The breeze passed over her and with it she heard music.

She glanced at Rhys. "Do you hear music?"

"It's Shay. He's practicing in the pavilion," he said. Raising an arm, he pointed to the opposite side of the lake. "There, across the lake."

She peered across the lake and saw the Greek-styled pavilion. Eight white columns held up a domed roof. Several people stood inside and more moved around outside.

"Do you want to go? Shay won't mind," Rhys said. He took her arm and led her down the hill onto the path circling the shore.

"Are you sure? I'd hate to interrupt him."

"Of course, I'm sure. If my eyes aren't deceiving me, I believe your photographer is there also. He's snapping pictures."

She glanced in the direction Rhys noted and saw Blake. He squatted several feet to one side and in front of where Shay stood in the opening of the pavilion. The nearer they came, the louder the noise of his camera's shutter whined and fluttered just below the sound of the music. A video camera hung from its strap on his shoulder.

Caitlyn experienced a guilty pang. Treated with noticeable special care, she had almost forgotten about Blake. She knew the workaholic photographer well. He'd been busy performing his job while she'd allowed strange dreams and heated desire for the interview's subject to distract her.

As they approached the group, she saw Marcy. Her friend stood to one side of the pavilion. Dafydd, Shay's music tech, worked on a computer, punching keys with a flurry of movements.

"He's trying out a few new songs for his show. What do you think?" Rhys leaned close so she could hear him over the instruments and Shay's vocals.

The music and lyrics flowed through her. Shay lifted his gaze and locked it with hers, giving her the impression he sang only to her. He held out his hand. Caitlyn didn't hesitate. She walked closer and climbed the four steps leading into the pavilion. The warmth of his hand wrapped about hers brought a smile to her lips.

The music faded, and he grinned at her. "What do you think?"

"I liked it." Her heartbeat sped up. Trying to hide the sudden flare of heat in her body, she slipped her hand from his. "Are you planning to use this song for your next show?"

"Perhaps. I haven't decided." He smiled, and from the glint in his eyes, she wondered if he suspected how he affected her.

The musicians started another song. A strange cracking noise reached her above the music. She looked toward the ceiling, and stared at the sight of all the faeries and nymphs painted there. Shay shifted nearer to her.

In the center of the painted scene, a thin line formed. Slowly, the line increased until it fractured open. What was happening up there? She opened her mouth to tell Shay but the jagged ends of a huge limb tore through the gap and shot down, straight at them.

Her scream was cut off as he shoved her to the left, out of the way. The limb hit the ground where she'd been standing. It teetered for a second, then tilted toward them. The branch fell over, striking him in the shoulder before rolling away and crashing onto the ground in front of the pavilion.

Chapter 19

Marcy shouted her name. Unable to respond to her friend's cry, Caitlyn kept her gaze locked with Shay's. His eyes widened for a second before his knees gave way, and he slumped to the stone floor.

Grabbing him around the waist, she knelt in front of him, trying to hold him up. Aware of the voices surrounding them, she held him, his head cradled to her neck.

She whispered his name. Fear solidified as a lump in her throat. He groaned and raised his head. "It's all right. Just stunned me."

His breath came in short gasps. She sat and helped him rest his head in her lap. The white shirt he wore flattened against his chest. A crimson flower bloomed on the shoulder the limb struck.

She raised her eyes, searching for someone to help. Rhys appeared in front of her. "He's hurt. He's bleeding."

"Let me see." He lifted the collar to Shay's shirt. "It's only a gash. Shay, come on. Let's get you back to the castle. I'll call the doctor to tend to you. Can you stand?"

Marcy pressed against Caitlyn's side. "Oh, Catey, I saw the whole thing. You were almost killed."

Distracted, Caitlyn failed to hear what Shay answered Rhys. He allowed his friend to help him to stand. Freed from his warmth, a chill entered her body. Marcy's arm encircled her shoulders, but she still shivered.

He'd come so close to death. Suddenly, she couldn't imagine living in this world without him. Sharp painful twinges sliced through her middle. She brushed Marcy's arms away. "I'm okay. Rhys, I'm coming with you."

They moved at a slow pace to the castle. Rhys stopped a few times to give Shay time to rest for a moment before they continued. Closer to the house, Caitlyn ran ahead and opened the door for them. She followed behind until they came to Shay's room.

Once inside, she moved to the bed and jerked the covers back. He eased onto the mattress. Lying flat with his head cushioned with a pillow, he lifted his unhurt arm and covered his eyes.

"Maybe we should take him to a hospital. He might have a broken shoulder or even his collar bone," she said, tearing her gaze away from Shay. His face expressionless, Rhys stood on the other side of the bed watching the illusionist.

"We'll see what the doctor says. If he thinks Shay needs a hospital, we'll take him. Not before," Rhys replied.

"Why not? He's hurt." She experienced an instant surge of anger.

"Caitlyn."

At Shay's soft whisper, she twisted toward him. "I'll be all right. It just stunned me. Listen, I can't go to a hospital. The paparazzi will have a field day with it."

Reality reared its head. Of course, he wouldn't go to the public facility for medical attention. The news would be broadcast around the world. Rumors would start and grow to outlandish proportions. Once more, she'd allowed her growing emotions for him to cloud her professional perspective.

"You're right," she said, stepping away from the bed. "I'll leave you with Rhys." Shooting a glance at the blond man, she continued. "Let me know what the doctor says."

"Yes, of course."

She pivoted and walked to the door. She hesitated, but then stiffened her back and left, pulling the door shut behind her. He didn't need her. She would have insisted they take him to the emergency room for a checkup, but he'd never allow that. He was Shay Evers, the superstar.

Her short stay in this isolated place had caused her to forget that bit of information. She hadn't even called Kramer and let him know what was happening. She had deliberately ignored the missed calls and refused to return them, worried her boss would hear in her words her growing feelings for her assignment.

Somewhere along the line, her objective had changed. She searched her memory for some clue as to when this had occurred. Perhaps the first night she'd met him, or maybe after she had arrived in Wales. She didn't know how, but she had allowed this man to become important to her.

Without paying attention to where she was going, she just walked, lost in the memories of what had happened. Once she became aware of her surroundings, she saw she had returned to the pavilion. Everyone was gone except for Blake.

He called out a greeting to her. She moved toward him, determined to discover how this accident had occurred. Skirting the limb, she stopped near the spot where Dafydd and Marcy had been when the limb had fallen.

"Did you film it?" She asked Blake.

"Yes. I think that accident was the strangest I've ever seen." He opened the viewer on the video camera and pressed a button. "Here, you watch and tell me what you think."

The film blurred as it reversed. After a few moments, it reached a spot just before the accident. He pressed Stop, then Play. Music and voices came over the speaker. Marcy's laugh came through louder than the rest. Strange, Caitlyn didn't remember Marcy laughing but she'd been so caught under Shay's spell, no one else had mattered.

The scene played out, but even at the camera's angle, she saw nothing to make the limb fall. The tree limb was above the dome. It broke and fell through the ceiling. Was this simply a freak accident?

Her heart missed a beat once she saw the expression on her face as she helped Shay sit and laid his head in her lap. Fear and anguish covered her face. And there was another emotion that flickered over her features as she looked down at him. Concerned adoration.

She shook her head in denial. Uncomfortable, she shifted away and walked to the limb, refusing to admit what she'd seen. All her secret feelings had surfaced in those few seconds. She felt bare, open for everyone to see.

Blake snapped the viewer into place and said, "Well?"

"I don't know. It was an accident. Something like this will probably never happen again," she murmured. Squatting next to the limb, she studied the splintered ends. The branch was at least eight inches in diameter. She continued to study it as she sought a reason for it to break. The wind hadn't been gusting, and the wood didn't show any signs of disease. Yet, it had snapped.

"The weight might have done it," Blake remarked. He moved to her side and stared at the splintered piece of wood.

"I doubt it. The wood looks healthy. It shouldn't have fallen." She sat on the top step of the pavilion. "I just don't understand. If Shay hadn't pushed me out of the way, it would have hit me, not him."

She sensed Blake's gaze on her, but didn't return the look. When he spoke, she realized how stupid her comment had been. "So what are you saying? Nature has it out for you?"

Slumping, she pinched her nose just below her glasses. "No, I'm just saying that it would have been me, not him. He saved my life."

"You're not one of those people who believe you owe him now, are ya? Hey, it happened. Just a freak accident. That's all," Blake said. He squeezed her shoulder. "I'm going back to the house. You gonna be okay out here?"

She nodded and watched him stroll around the lake and up the hill. He stopped at the top. Marcy came into view from the other side. They spoke to each other. Blake pointed in her direction. Marcy nodded and headed toward the pavilion.

Caitlyn's shoulders slumped. She didn't want to see her friend right now. She wanted solitude for a little while. She needed to sort through the roller coaster ride she'd been on the last few days.

Marcy's blond hair bounced as she marched toward her. A determined glint shone in her friend's eyes. "Are you all right?"

Caitlyn nodded.

With her hands on her hips, Marcy stopped in front of her. "That scared the hell out of me. I saw the whole thing. If Evers hadn't pushed you, you might be dead right now. God, Catey, I swear I saw our entire friendship pass before my eyes."

Surprised at the anger and concern on Marcy's face, so opposite of the carefree, happiness normally on her features, Caitlyn laughed. All her nervous tension oozed from her muscles. Leave it to Marcy to help her relax. She should have found her friend first instead of coming out here.

"It's not funny," Marcy muttered, plopping down next to her.

"I know. I just can't help it. Shay's hurt because he saved me," Caitlyn murmured, sobering with that thought. "I'm wound up tight and didn't even know it until you showed up and brought me some normalcy."

"No prob. That's what friends are for. I don't know what I'd do if I ever lost you. You are my best friend, even though I don't act like it sometimes. No matter what I do, you're always there for me. You don't look down your nose at me. I guess I never realized that until today." Marcy wrapped her arm around Caitlyn's shoulders and squeezed. She leaned over and her head against the side of Caitlyn's.

Touched by her friend's words, Caitlyn patted Marcy's cheek. They sat in silence for a few minutes. A shout from the hill caught their attention. Dafydd waved his arm, calling Marcy's name. He motioned for her to come.

She sighed. "I guess I need to go." Standing, she stretched her arms above her head. She straightened and grinned at Caitlyn. "You know, I never thought I'd see the day I would cater to a man. I'll call later to check on you. Love ya."

Caitlyn nodded and smiled. As her friend hurried to meet Dafydd, she wished she had Marcy's easy go lucky attitude. Thinking about her blond friend, she stood and wandered along the lake's edge.

The wind picked up, and clouds roiled over the horizon. Grazelda was correct. A storm approached. Not wanting to get caught in the weather, Caitlyn hurried back to the castle.

Chapter 20

Shay grimaced. A vile odor came from the black pot on his bedside table. His stomach cramped, threatening to rebel. "Grazelda, take that from here. It more than sickens me."

"Nonsense, young sir. The poultice will ease yer pain and take the swelling down in no time." Her lined face puckered in a fierce frown. "Now, turn yerself over and let me apply it as it should be."

He shifted onto his left side and a groan escaped. His right shoulder throbbed, while sharp pains shot through his upper body with the slightest movement.

"Hurry with you, old woman." He gasped at the first touch of the heated remedy. "It's hot."

"As it should be. Now hush ye, or I'll place a sleeping spell on ye. Do ye wish that, my fine sir?" Grazelda said, spreading the thick concoction over his aching shoulder. "Oooh, yer skin, 'tis as black as soot, it is. Ye took the full strike from that limb. Are ye crazed? 'Twould've killed a normal human. Good thing for ye that ye've Tylwyth Teg blood flowing through yer veins."

She touched a more sensitive spot. He bit down on his bottom lip, trying to fight the pain. Waves of dizziness blurred his sight. Darkness edged his vision. "Hurry. I don't want to pass out."

"Ye need to. The rest will help heal ye. I'm almost done, then we'll get ye comfortable for the night," she said, her touch gentler than before.

Rhys paced next to the bed. His deep voice remained low when he spoke. "'Twas magic that caused this. Gwyneth was close. Did you sense her before you were struck?"

"I told you, I didn't sense anything. I saw the look on Caitlyn's face and that caused me to shove her. I know she saw something. The limb fell so fast, I didn't have time to look up." Shay panted as he tried to control the pain. He concentrated on the carved Celtic curves and interlocking designs flowing over the headboard of his bed. He tried to think past the agony but failed.

"Done now. Mind ye stay on that side tonight. Let this one heal without yer weight on it. Come, sire, let the poor dear rest for a bit," the old woman said.

Exhausted, riddled with pain, Shay clenched his teeth as Grazelda rose from the bed. She and Rhys moved away from the bed to the doorway. Shay heard the low murmur of them talking but couldn't make out what they said. It took him a moment to realize they had left.

The gentle crackling of the fire lulled him. His eyelids drooped lower and his breathing smoothed out. Even as he teetered on the edge of sleep, he heard soft steps approaching the bed.

"Shay?"

Caitlyn's faint whisper sent currents of electricity through his skin. He forced his eyelids open. Long dark hair framed her face as she knelt on the floor beside his bed. He smiled.

"Hello."

A softening of her face melted his heart. "Are you okay?"

"No. I hurt like hell. I suppose I'll live, though," he muttered.

She smiled wider and wrinkled her nose. "I hate to say this, but you smell. Really bad."

"It's an acquired scent. Stick around, you'll become used to it." He shifted his legs and regretted it. White-tipped flames scorched through him. Another groan escaped.

"Maybe I should leave so you can rest," she said, a frown furrowing her brow. "You need quiet and here I am, disturbing you. I'm sorry."

"Don't go. It hurts only when I move. I swear I'll be still." He patted the bedcovers next to him. "Lie down with me. Talk to me. Tell me about yourself. Your childhood--everything."

She tilted her head and studied him. With careful movements, she lay down next to him. Their faces were on the same level, eye-to-eye.

"Why do you wear those glasses?" His curiosity needed assuaging. They looked like plain reading glasses without any magnification to them. If that were true, then why would she wear them?

"I can't see without them." She brushed a piece of his hair that fell across his cheek behind his ear. Her gaze caught and held on something at the side of his head.

He smiled and asked, "What's wrong?"

She released a stuttering breath before whispering, "Your ear has a point on the tip."

He chuckled and regretted doing so. "Of course it's pointed. I am an elf. You're the one who chooses not to believe me."

"Are you sure it's not a birth defect?"

He bit his lip to keep from laughing out loud. Birth defect. She was amazing. "Caitlyn, you're wanting me to suffer, aren't you?"

She stiffened, and he sensed the tension growing in her body. Her answer was precise and cool. "People don't have pointed ears."

"Not everyone is the same. Have you ever looked at your ears? Are you certain they aren't pointed?"

A muscle in her jaw tightened. He had gotten to her. "They're not. I'm normal, you aren't."

He smiled wider. "That's what makes me special."

"Shay. I'm trying to be serious. Why do you have pointed ears?" She traced a path over the edge of his ear. Heat, not from his shoulder, started to circulate through him.

"I don't know. I was born that way. Now, let's talk about you."

"No, not tonight. You need to rest. I shouldn't even be here, but I just needed to make sure you were all right." She released a soft sigh. Her gaze met his and stayed. "I'm a reporter doing an interview, yet, I feel as though I'm in limbo. My focus is gone and..."

"And you don't know which way to turn?" He prompted.

She glanced down. "Yes."

"I suppose that's my fault. I have a way of causing some people to lose their focus. Don't worry, I'll see you through this." He swallowed, then whispered, "I swear on my mother's heart."

Her eyes widened. "Even though she hurt you, you still love her?"

"She was my mother, how can I do anything else?" he muttered. His pain caused him to say things he shouldn't. She would catch him. It made the chance of losing her greater. But the need to make her trust him overrode his caution. The soft smile curving her lips made him relax.

"You're a good man, Shay Evers. That, or you're the biggest con artist around. Either way, I intend to discover all your secrets. Now, sleep, so you can heal. Rhys said the doctor wants you to have complete bed rest for a couple of days. I'll come back in the morning." She slid off the bed but lingered, gazing at him.

Drowsiness came over him. A dulled sense of excitement rushed through him. He sensed her powers working. Her desire for him to slumber projected to him and forced him to do as she wished. He smiled as he battled to keep his eyes open.

"I wish you would stay. Just a while longer."

"Go to sleep," she ordered.

The last thing he remembered was the satisfied expression on her face.

* * * *

Caitlyn remained by the bed and watched him nap for several minutes. His personality didn't need the added attraction of his looks, but combined with it, he was devastatingly gorgeous. She had met many handsome men. Most acted like jerks, but Shay consisted of more than a pretty face.

If he covered his face with a brown paper bag, people would still love him. The beauty of his face only added a nice cover to the package. Sort of like a comfortable bed made with silk and lace. It was the comfort offered that made her want to lie down with him, not the spread and pillows. They just added to the picture.

She smiled and bent, brushing her lips against his brow. She inhaled and almost choked. This close to the poultice coating his right shoulder and side, she cringed at the odor struck her full force. Pivoting, she headed for the door with a smile.

In the hallway, she turned to go to her room. Blake stood in front of her. She jumped and gasped. She'd almost run into him.

"Hey, easy," he said, grasping her upper arms.

"You scared the life out of me. What are you doing?" Caitlyn glared at him, swatting his hands away.

"I wanted to see how he's doing." He jerked his head toward the door to Shay's room.

"He's resting," she said. "He let Grazelda put some nasty stuff on his shoulder. I'd love to be here if the doctor shows up again and smells it. It stinks."

Blake chuckled. "Hey, have you called Kramer? I talked to him this morning, and he was fuming because he hadn't heard from you."

Her shoulders slumped. "I can imagine. I was about to call him. Listen, let me know if Shay has problems. I know you'll be wandering around. I'll be in my room."

Blake nodded.

She grinned. "Wish me luck. I'm going to need it with Kramer." With that, she left him and made her way to her room.

There wasn't any need to put off contacting her boss. Her job balanced on this interview. She hoped Shay's influence kept her in good standing with the station until after the interview was finished here.

Chapter 21

The library doors beckoned her to enter. With her laptop case slung over her shoulder, she gazed at the Celtic designs engraved on the doors. Everywhere in this castle, she found these patterns repeated on furniture, doors, even walls. What was it about Shay and these motifs? They seemed like an obsession.

She gripped the brass twig-shaped door handle and twisted. The solid wooden slab swung open on silent hinges. She bit her bottom lip. So far, she'd seen only three people working inside the castle: Grazelda, Fred and a younger man she'd seen but hadn't met. Yet, the castle stayed so clean and in perfect condition. She hadn't noticed dust or dirt anywhere, except for the leaves scattered across the floor that first day after Shay forgot to shut the door. How did three people manage to keep the place so clean? She never saw anyone working, yet her rooms were spotless each time she returned to them.

After leaving the pavilion this earlier today, she'd spent the rest of the afternoon and early evening in her room. While talking to Kramer, she'd developed a sudden awareness that things weren't what they appeared. As she'd listened to him plotting what course to take with the interview, she'd gone to the bathroom for a drink of water. She'd spilled a little on the counter. Kramer, impatient, had ordered her to take a couple of notes. Leaving the puddle of water, she'd returned to the small writing desk set up for her on the far side of the room next to the door leading into the sitting room.

No one had entered while she'd worked there. Sometime later, when she hung up with Kramer, she went to wipe up the spill. Her heart had pounded when she saw that not only was the water gone, but the glass had been washed, dried and turned upside down in its original place.

If she believed in helpful phantoms, she would have run screaming, headed back to Los Angeles in a blink of an eye. If she believed in magic she would have done the same, but she didn't. She had to find out what was going on.

She remembered Shay saying he'd had this castle refurbished. Her thoughts centered on secret passageways. After what happened in the bathroom, she'd searched for one, but didn't find any latch leading into a hidden hallway.

She'd gone to the kitchen and found his entire household eating supper. During the meal, she'd discovered where everyone planned to spend the evening. The time seemed right for her to snoop. Odds were a blueprint existed, possibly somewhere in the library. At least, she hoped so. She would start searching here. If she didn't find what she wanted, she would go to the nearest courthouse to find out about Shay's home.

The room spread out before her. Two stories of wall-to-wall books faced her. She turned in a circle, trying to decide where to start her search. A mahogany desk positioned to face the room sat before three sets of French doors. White lace curtains poured down from rods over the doors to pool on the wood floor.

Curious, she strode across the room and touched the lace. The silken feel, the beauty and intricacy of the weave left her puzzled. Where had Shay found this type of lace? Although she was not familiar with cloth and materials, she knew intuitively this was not made by a manufacturer. Birds perched in trees abounding with deep green leaves and white flowers with golden centers in the design.

She stepped back and studied them. Once more, the pattern paralleled others in the castle. Tension built between her shoulder blades. She had to find out what made Shay decorate his home like this.

The need for this information pressed in on her. How she wished to see deep into his mind. Sure, he'd give her a pat answer for the interview but she wanted to go deeper, to the true reasons behind his need to surround himself with these types of patterns. With some insight into that side of him, maybe she'd be able to understand him better. It would be nice, as an extra bonus, to discover the truth behind those fantastical illusions.

She faced the desk. The deep tones of the wood relaxed her a bit. With her hand pressed to her right shoulder, she massaged the rigid muscle. Throbbing started behind her eyes.

The surface of the desk shone bright with wax. As she drew nearer, she noticed her reflection on the surface. Setting her laptop on the floor, she pulled the huge leather chair out, sat and leaned back. A smile formed on her lips. She brought her feet up and placed them on the clean desktop. Smudges appeared where the back of her heels pressed into the surface.

Placing her feet on the floor, she sat forward and stared, waiting for the smudges to disappear. After five minutes her eyes started to water. Nothing happened. She sighed. Well, so much for thinking there was a supernatural force at work.

Idly, she fiddled with a desk drawer. The drawer slid out. Oh, shoot, she hadn't meant to open the thing. Unable to stop, she looked into the opening. A leather-bound book lay in the bottom. She glanced at the door, listening. Once sure she wouldn't be disturbed, she lifted out the book.

Stained a deep burgundy, the leather covering the book rivaled the desktop's gleam. A golden Celtic knot was centered on the front. Caitlyn remembered Shay telling her he read many old manuscripts. This was probably one of them.

Careful of the edges, she opened the book's cover. The title page whirled and blurred a moment with foreign words. She blinked several times. Finally, she squinted at the letters and they came into focus. One more blink and she was able to see without a major struggle.

A book about the Tylwyth Teg? So this is where Shay got his ideas about elves and magic. Of course, he had researched and found this book, a mask to hide behind to help with his mysterious and magical image. How would people react if he announced his elfin origins on camera, during their interview? She chuckled. They'd think, like she had yesterday, he was either insane or on some sort of drug.

Lost in thought, she turned a page. The first chapter stared up at her. A dragon hovered menacingly above the section title. The dragon's eyes were painted a flaming red and its gleaming teeth were like daggers. Wide jaws spread in the semblance of a grin. She wrinkled her brow.

Ignoring the toothy creature, she started to read, absorbing every word. When she became aware of her surroundings again, a nagging soreness pressed across her shoulders. She glanced around the room until her gaze landed on an ornate clock on the other side of the room. Midnight. She had lost track of time while she read.

Stifling a yawn, she mentally marked the page number and shut the book. Carefully, she laid it back inside the drawer. She got to her feet and stretched, working the kinks out of her stiffened limbs. Drowsy, she moved to the door to retire for the night.

* * * *

A thunder clap startled Shay awake. He lay quiet for several minutes, listening to the raging storm outside the stone walls of the castle. The light from the fireplace cast shadows in the corners, but he didn't sense any danger.

Secure in his bed, warmth curled around him. He felt much better now than he had earlier. A smile twitched his lips. Grazelda's frowning features came to mind as he remembered how she'd come to check on him and found he had managed to shower the disgusting plaster off his shoulder.

The pain of removing the smelly concoction had been worth it. Shifting in the clean sheets, he heard footsteps approach and stop at his door. Instantly tense, he waited. The door opened, and his night visitor moved nearer, into the dim light. At Caitlyn's soft whisper calling his name, he wanted to shout with relief.

"I'm awake," he responded.

"You shouldn't be," she said, sitting on the mattress next to him. "I was about to go to bed, but I started worrying that you might not have eaten. Have you?"

"Earlier. I'm not hungry now."

"Are you sure? I can make you a sandwich. Would you like that?" She started to rise, but he brushed his fingers over her hand.

"No. I would like you to lie with me," he said. By the slight widening of her eyes, he knew he'd surprised her. "You ran off earlier. Please, just for a little while."

"It's late. If I do, I might fall asleep. What will Grazelda say in the morning when she finds me in your bed?" White teeth flashed in a breathtaking smile. Every day, he noticed her beauty breaking past the plain physical surface. He knew now her dull outer coating was part of the curse, the projection of a lie.

"She'd whoop for joy and dance a jig. I've never invited a woman to join me here. Grazelda worries about that. Come, let's give her something to liven her day. From the sound of the weather for tomorrow, she'll be bothered with her old bones, so this might help take her mind off them."

He cocked a brow. One important characteristic he'd observed about Caitlyn was her sincerity in wanting to help others.

"Sorry, won't work. Next thing we'll know, rumors will spread around that we're lovers and we're not," she said as she shook her head.

She'd slipped away. Thinking fast, he spoke as she tensed to stand. "What if I need something during the night? It hurts to move. Aren't you worried I might fall off the bed? I'm dying here, Caitlyn. Don't you care?"

She laughed out loud.

He tried to look hurt, but she slid off the mattress and leaned over and kissed his forehead. Emerald eyes glinted in the firelight, and her skin glowed with a new tawny radiance that had been absent before her arrival in Wales.

"You're not dying, and I'm not staying. Go to sleep, Shay. You'll heal faster. I'll come by in the morning." She straightened and stepped away.

He wouldn't change her mind. Her father's stubbornness ran strong in her. "Goodnight, Caitlyn. Sleep tight and enjoy your dreams."

She tilted her head a moment, her eyes narrowing. Then she smiled and murmured, "Good night." Once the door closed behind her, he sighed and relaxed his muscles. He'd not realized how uptight he'd become until after she'd left.

Chapter 22

Several minutes passed as he patiently waited for her to reach her room and go to bed. Careful of his shoulder, he slid up and sat, putting all his weight on his uninjured side.

With the forces of nature whirling in a powerful vortex, the time was right for him to go to her. Twisting with care, he laid his palm flat on the wall behind the bed. He searched with his mind through the castle until he reached her room.

In the deep shadows across from her door, he sensed someone squatting, staring at her room. A chuckle escaped him, and Rhys's eyes snapped open.

Their minds connected. The king used his forceful pitch to speak to Shay. "Go to sleep. I will keep watch this night. She is well protected."

While Rhys spoke to him, Shay checked the guards the king had posted. Vines, thick and impenetrable, covered every window in Caitlyn's room. Even the plants within the bower stood at attention, watching, ready to call to Rhys should an invader cross the barriers. In the gardens below, several warriors, hidden from human eyes by the weather and plants, watched.

Returning to where Rhys squatted in the shadows, he mentally spoke. *"The storm is strong. I intend to go to her. This night, she will return home for the first time in twenty-four years. 'Twill make it easier on her when she arrives from this dimension."*

A lengthy silence followed his announcement. During the minutes that ticked by, connected to his liege, he experienced the myriad of emotions flowing through Rhys. He'd never fully realized how deeply the loss of his daughter had affected the other man.

Fear, joy and worry raced through him. At last, acceptance reached him. Rhys's soft tone reassured Shay he wanted this to happen. *"Are you strong enough? Your shoulder will not cause you problems, will it?"*

"No. I'll be fine. I ask one thing from you. I wish to go alone. Swear to me you will not watch or interfere."

Again silence filled his head for a few moments. Shay felt Rhys weigh his request. Finally, he responded, *"Very well. You saved her today, and I will grant you this one boon but if you make one move to seduce her, your punishment will be much worse than the last time. Watch her well, my muse. The first sign of stress, return her immediately. Your word on this."*

"You have it." With his promise, Shay separated from Rhys. He removed his hand from the wall and relaxed on the mattress.

With slow deep breaths, he focused on Caitlyn. He sensed her sleeping in her room. Now was the time. Without considering his options too long, he leapt off the edge of reality and plunged into the world of her dreams.

* * * *

Caitlyn heard Shay calling her name. She brushed a hand over her head. Something tickled her cheek. Eyelids heavy with exhaustion, she forced them up. Sunbeams dotted with thousands of motes and small insects came into view. His face wobbled then came into focus. He knelt on the side of her bed, holding a fern leaf between his fingers.

"What are you doing here? You're hurt," she said. Battling the sluggishness pressing in on her, she sat up. Blinking several times, she wondered about how quickly the night passed.

"I'm unhurt here, in your dreams. Come. I would show you something special. Come," he said. A lean hand stretched toward her, and she stared at his palm.

"I'm dreaming. But this isn't like before."

Her glance took in her surroundings. No longer the midnight void, a covered balcony took its place. Marble columns fashioned into twined saplings braced the balcony's roof.

She swung her legs off the bed and sat up, admiring the plants and flowers swaying in the light breeze.

When she looked at Shay, he still knelt beside her. She smiled at him, and he returned her greeting with a devastatingly beautiful grin. Without thinking, she placed her hand in his and allowed him to help her stand. Layer upon layer of white silky lace flowed down her legs and spread in a wide flare about her.

Glancing down at the dress, she gasped in surprise at the wondrous beauty draping her form. Fitted over her arms and torso, the waist dipped into a point so that the dress clung to the tops of her hips. Low cut, the bodice scalloped over her shoulders and breasts and plunged in the center.

Silky layers started at her hips and flowed down her legs. For all the material in it, the dress was light and cool.

She met Shay's eyes and smiled. She liked this dress as much as the other one. A laugh bubbled when he lifted the hem and touched her ankle. He held a slipper in his other hand. The low-heeled shoe fit her to perfection.

"What are they made of?" she wondered, admiring her foot, twisting it for a better view.

"The finest webs in the world. Each spider spun stardust into their webs so their princess would have a fine pair of slippers. Do you like them?" He slid the second one on her other foot.

Instead of being upset about wearing spider webs, she studied them. How did they seem so sturdy yet so fragile? "Is there a mirror? I want to see." Excitement surged through her. She needed to see if she was as lovely now as she was before.

Shay stood and pointed behind him. She saw the looking glass and hurried to it. Yes, she looked just like the last time. Only the dress had changed. She still wore the crown and pendant. Amazed at the change, she felt new and vibrant.

A vine clinging to the side of the mirror inched toward her. Instead of feeling fear, she smiled, knowing the plant would not hurt her. When it entered the thick long strands covering her head, it moved through, lifting and separating until her hair was fashioned into a beautiful coiffure.

The vine secured her hair in place, allowing stray tendrils to escape. White flowers bloomed throughout her hair. The stem to the vine snapped and curled between her bare shoulder blades.

She twirled around in a flurry of white silk. "I can't believe how pretty this is. Do you like it, Shay?"

He kept his back to her. She stepped nearer. His hair seemed longer, and in the light of the sun, she noticed tiny braids shooting through the thick strands. Gold and silver threads were woven in the slender braids.

Moving to stand in front of him, she smiled at him. His eyes were closed, and she brushed the back of her hand over the side of his face. When his eyelids rose, his brilliant amethyst eyes locked with hers.

"Come, let us go. There is much to see." He caught her hand and tugged her toward an opening in the terrace's pedestal wall.

She laughed, grasping the long folds of her dress, and raced by his side. Sweeping gardens spread before them. Hurrying through the plants and sunshine, they stopped on the far edge. A vast expanse of breathtaking beauty stretched toward the horizon.

Buildings, carved from stone and marble, were positioned into the sides of three ridges that surrounded a three-tiered waterfall. At the base of the falls, rainbows danced across the smoothness of a small lake. Beyond the lake, meadows and forests flowed to the western horizon.

Caitlyn gasped, clasping her hands to her chest. The air, fresh and crisp, washed over her and filled her. She'd never known a place like this existed.

Birds flew and sang in the green trees abounding throughout the land. Small and large animals roamed about without fear. A large golden-brown bear lay along the short of the lake, while several children played close by. The animal merely watched, with its head resting on its front paws. A dark-haired girl ran up to the creature and climbed onto its back. The bear didn't even lift its head as the child reclined on top of it.

Glancing at the buildings, she noticed several people moving around. "Who are they?"

"They are your clansmen. Their blood is the same as yours and mine. They are the Tylwyth Teg." Shay stepped closer to the edge that dropped off the side of the gardens.

He pointed to the right. She saw a narrow trail winding down the side of the ridge. This time, she pulled him forward, her laughter echoing across the ravine. She wanted to see everything here, wanted to learn all there was, and deep inside, she wanted to stay here forever.

With Shay.

Chapter 23

As she and Shay walked, they came across several men and women along the trail. Their tall slender bodies were dressed in clothes that sparkled and shimmered. Long blond and dark hair covered their heads to fall about their shoulders and down their backs. Five-stranded braids on the sides of their heads were decorated with ribbons and tiny trinkets. Some of the men wore sleeveless tunics, and when they raised their arms to wave, Caitlyn noticed tattoos marking the flesh on the underside.

As they passed different groups, the people greeted them with cries of joy, pressing flowers into her arms until she carried a large, fragrant bouquet. Why were they reacting this way?

Roses, pansies, lilies and anemones bobbed as she hurried forward. Her dress flowed behind, brushing against Shay's legs. He followed her and didn't question whatever she wanted to do. Of course, this was her dream. Anything was possible.

At the trail's end, small wooden docks with carved white boats awaited them on the lake's calm water. Two men grinned and helped her aboard. She sat toward the front, then turned and smiled at Shay.

"Sit by me." She patted the place next to her.

Watching him cross to her, his balance perfect, brought a laugh from her. Dark hair caught in the slight breeze fluttered away from his face. Her heartbeat sped as her breath caught in her throat. Desire flooded through her with such a strong surge, her body heated with the need to touch him. Once he was seated next to her, she reached across him and tugged at the tie on the other side of the tunic he wore. Somewhere along the path, the cloth belt had come untied. A large amount of smooth skin presented a strong temptation. She watched the muscles in his belly tighten. So, he was more aware of her than he let on.

She pulled the two ends together, meeting his gaze and smiling. Still holding the tie, she tugged him closer, her lips close to his ear. "Let's fix this. I wouldn't want any other woman to see you. You belong to me, and I will not share you."

A low chuckle vibrated in his throat. "So you think to possess me, do you?"

"Completely. You're mine." She leaned in and brushed a quick kiss over his lips. The contact sent heat through her body, and she wished the watchful eyes would disappear.

"Calm your desire, we still have much to see." He bent and returned her kiss with a soft touch to her cheek. When he straightened, she pressed her head to his shoulder and smiled.

She didn't want this to end. The ride across the lake was peaceful. She trailed her fingers through the water and watched the crystal clear liquid dripping from her fingertips when she lifted her hand.

"Everything is so fresh and new. Why?" She tilted her head at Shay.

"This place has never been touched by humans. We value nature and in turn, she protects and shelters us," he said. He raised an arm, sweeping it in a wide arch. "All of this is protected by magic. Only when mankind is gone will we return to the land and restore what was lost."

"But you're human--"

"No, I am Tylwyth Teg," he said, cutting her off. "A light elf from the planet Vanir. We came here many centuries ago, hoping to begin a thriving colony, but the humans refused to let us live in peace."

"Why didn't you leave?"

His chest expanded with a deep breath, and his chin lifted as he answered, "We declined to. Well met in battle with the humans, a truce was called. Mankind will have the surface, and we will live in the Sidhe."

His voice rang out over the waters. He angled his head upward. Amethyst flames still flickered within his eyes when he glanced at her. "This is your home. 'Tis where you belong. You weren't meant to live in the human world."

"I must have eaten something really wild today. I don't want to talk about my ancestry. This is what I want to do." Pressing her palm to the back of his neck, she covered his lips with hers. Her tongue slid into the heated depths of his mouth and stroked his tongue. Cinnamon burst in her mouth, eliciting a moan from her.

Without breaking contact, she said, "You taste so good." To prove her point, she deepened the kiss, applying light suction to capture more of the heated spice.

Shay groaned.

She felt a bump and the boat stopped. He pulled away, and stood, balancing on the rim of the boat for a second before leaping to the dock's solid wood. Despite being disappointed, she took the hand he held out to her. Tugging her to him, he wrapped his arms around her and squeezed. "You are indeed a great joy to me. Come, love, we must hurry. There is much more I wish you to see."

The smile budding on her lips froze. He called her *love*. Was she? His love? What was he to her? A simmering emotion bubbled inside her. Her smile changed to a wide grin. Yes, in this place she was his love. When she took a step, flowers bloomed under her feet.

Shay stopped and glanced at her over his shoulder. He swallowed, and shook his head. "Still your heart, Caitlyn. What you wish cannot be."

She laughed and twirled ahead of him, her arms raised above her. "Still yourself. This is my dream and I can wish for what I want. And I intend to get what I want. Right now, I want to race you to the meadow. The flowers look so pretty from here."

Without waiting, she lifted her skirts and bolted ahead of him. His answering laughter followed her. A quick glimpse over her shoulder found him not far from her. In a second, he caught her hand and pulled her with him.

When they reached the meadow, Shay continued until they reached the center. Caitlyn twirled in a circle, taking in the sunshine, blue sky, green grass, wildflowers and the rich earth. Nature's wonderful odors greeted her. Dizzy, she fell backward. The meadow's plants rose to meet her, then laid her gently on the cushioned ground.

Shay passed her and lay end to end with the top of his head against hers. They stared at the fluffy clouds floating above. Contentment filled her.

After several peaceful minutes, she raised a hand and touched his hair. "Are you awake?"

"Mmm."

She rolled onto her stomach and stared at him. He laid, arms out, legs crossed and his eyes shut. Plucking a daisy, she twirled the stem between her fingers and tickled him under the nose. She stifled a giggle when his nose wrinkled and his mouth twitched. One amethyst eye cracked open.

In a fluid motion, he rolled over. Now face to face, she stared into his eyes and became lost. Together, they leaned forward and kissed. Sweet, painful desire blossomed.

"Make love to me. Now. I want to feel you over me and in me. Please Shay," she whispered.

He cupped her face in his palms, passing his thumbs over her cheeks. His eyelids drooped, and his gaze caught on her mouth. "You tempt me sorely but we cannot. I am not meant for you."

She stared at him through narrowed eyes. "I say you are. This is my dream. You can't refuse me."

"I have to. You don't really want me." Sadness pulled at his mouth. "Your dream will be over soon."

"Not until I say it is. Right now, I want you. Don't make me beg." She brushed a finger over his bottom lip. "I need you."

With a groan, he captured her lips. Pleasure throbbed at the base of her belly and increased as sharp pangs flashed in her middle as he touched her shoulder, sliding his fingers under her dress. The material slipped off and revealed the curve of her breast. He pulled away to stare at the bare skin.

Twisting until he lay next to her, he ran his hand down the side of her waist to her hip then lower, pulling the flowing skirts up. Her pulse quickened. He touched her inner thigh. She forgot to breathe.

His amethyst eyes rose and seized her with their burning depths. She panted, passion growing out of control. Wrapping her hand around his neck, she tugged him to her and devoured his lips and mouth with hot, wet kisses.

With the first touch of his lean fingers at her center, she arched her back as her legs spread. Her heels dug into the soil. Her low cry entered his mouth. Fluid rushed from her and coated his fingers. He slid a couple fingers inside her while his thumb rubbed against the pulsing nub.

Breaking free of his lips, she whispered his name.

He raised his head. Warm breath blew over her chest. She struggled to drag in air as she watched him nuzzle the edge of her dress until her breasts lay exposed to his dilated gaze. She moaned as the pressure grew from where his fingers caressed her. He licked between her breasts, a soft flick from his tongue. Electricity shot through her, the tingling racing along her skin. Deep inside, the coil of need tightened. Unable to control her reaction, a low whimper escaped.

Another swift flick on the swell of her breast, and she would explode. Eyes shut and no longer able to think, she let the pounding heat flow through her. This was Shay. He was touching her, making love to her. She wanted him. Only him.

The touch of his lips clasping, sucking her nipple sent her over the edge. White light exploded behind her lids, and her body squeezed the hard length of his fingers. Wave upon wave of exhilarating pleasure poured through her, between and down her legs. She reared back and cried out her delight.

Time stilled. She refused to open her eyes and face the world. Floating on wings of light, she had experienced heaven in the last few minutes and wanted it to last forever.

Shay rested his head on her shoulder. She threaded her fingers through his hair and inhaled deeply. The scent of wildflowers, the earth and the musky odor of her passion filled her senses. He brushed a light kiss on her collarbone.

His warm breath washed over her sensitive flesh as he murmured, "We must go. Time is short."

She hesitated. She wanted to stay, but this was only a dream. It would end, and she wanted to spend every second of it with him. When he rose and held out his hand, she grasped it and wouldn't let go once he pulled her up. With his assistance, she was able to fix her clothing so it appeared nothing had happened between them.

The need to tell him how she felt built inside her heart, but she refused to release it. This was a dream. Whatever she told him wouldn't matter here. He wasn't real.

Battling a wave of sadness, she smiled and pulled him to her for a swift kiss. "Lead on, handsome sir. I am yours to do with what you will."

A deep chuckle rumbled in his chest. "Then come, my princess. We will visit other places."

Laughing, he helped her straighten her dress before they raced across the meadow back the way they'd come. The sun drifted across the sky. He showed her everything in the wondrous place. Toward the end of the day, they walked hand in hand up the steep trail leading to her room. When they reached the gardens above, Caitlyn turned to face the magical land.

Movement from the forest caught her gaze. A solid white horse, a golden horn centered on its forehead, pranced from the trees. A dark-haired woman sat sidesaddle on the animal's back, her lavender dress billowing out behind.

Caitlyn's eyes widened. She grasped Shay's hand and squeezed. "Is that a unicorn?"

He laughed low. "Of course. What else would it be?"

"Who is she?" Her breathing accelerated, and her heart pounded.

As the woman rode nearer to the buildings, several of the men and women came out and greeted her. The men dropped to one knee and the women threw flower petals in her wake.

A trail of flowers bloomed on the path the woman traveled. Caitlyn gasped in amazement. She repeated her question, tearing her gaze away and focusing on Shay.

A gentle smile brightened his eyes. He knelt on the ledge and bowed his head, placing his hand over his heart in homage.

She looked back at the woman. The unicorn pranced in a circle below. Its rider raised her face toward them and smiled. For the first time since she started dreaming, Caitlyn didn't want to be here. Jealousy filled her.

"Who is she?"

He stood and brushed his thumb across her lips. "She is the Lady of the Forest. Our queen."

"What is she to you?" Caitlyn pushed his hand away and frowned at him.

He chuckled. "Do not fear that she has my heart. That was stolen many years ago, and I find that I have none left to offer."

"Even to me?" Her voice sounded hollow and empty. She tensed as she waited for his answer.

With his gaze locked on hers, he leaned nearer and touched her lips with his. "And who else would have it, but you?"

Joy filled and overflowed her heart. She grinned. "No one. You'd best remember that too."

Their laughter echoed across the ravine as they turned and raced to her room. The setting sun cast magenta and orange-red shades over the horizon.

Chapter 24

Caitlyn came awake in slow degrees as the gentle patter of the rain on the window's panes caught her attention. The chill in the air made her want to snuggle deeper under the wildflower scented covers. Dim morning light showed through her eyelids. She groaned. She wanted to go back to sleep and return to her dream.

A smile flitted over her lips. Her sweet, sweet dream. Tingling sensations traveled through her nerve endings.

The ringing of the house telephone on the bedside table forced her to sit up. Fumbling with the receiver, she mumbled a greeting.

"Catey?" Marcy's bright voice sounded over the line.

"Oh, hi." Caitlyn swiped a hand over her face as she braced her back against the headboard. The comfort the bed offered soon helped to lull her so she dozed off.

"Wake up!"

Hearing Marcy's enthusiastic order, Caitlyn glanced at the clock on the bedside table. Seven-thirty blazed across the digital face in bright red. She blew out a gust of breath, not happy at being awakened, when all she wanted to do was sleep.

"Why are you calling so early?" She adjusted the receiver against her ear and slid into the depths of the bed.

"I thought I'd swing by and pick you up. Let's go shopping. Shay will be down for a few days with his injury. So while he's unavailable, let's take in a few sights," Marcy said.

She was on a job assignment, and Marcy wanted to go shopping. No excuse would be good enough for Kramer. Already he was furious with her for not calling him several times a day. Now, her best friend wanted to go shopping.

Of course, Marcy did have a point. For the next couple of days, Shay wouldn't be able to do much of anything. Caitlyn might never get another opportunity to see the local area. Roaming around gave her a reason to research the castle's background. Maybe even find some information about secret passages. The need to discover how someone entered her room and cleaned the bathroom still bothered her.

And, there were the locals. What did they think about their famous neighbor? Kramer had to understand. Technically, this all revolved around her assignment.

"Okay," she muttered. For once, Marcy had given her time to consider and answer. They discussed what they would do, and Caitlyn hung up.

Yes, she needed to spend some time away from Shay. Over the past few days, she'd let him affect her emotions, waking and dreaming. Her feelings were torn, and she didn't know what to do about it.

Fleeting images from her dream came to mind. She gasped at what he had done to her. Her cheeks heated at the thought of seeing him after that dream. Struggling out of bed, she hurried to dress for the day.

Once she finished dressing in casual khakis and a natural yarn pullover sweater, she headed to the foyer. Halfway there, she stopped and glanced in the direction of Shay's room. Odds were he still slept. If he did, he would never know she had checked on him this morning.

She had to reassure herself he was fine before she left. After the dream last night, she had to see him even just for a moment. Determined, she hurried to his room. Standing in front of the door, she laid her ear against the wood. Silence came from the other side. She slowly twisted the handle and shoved the door open enough to slip through.

Her gaze glued to the bed, she inched forward. The second she found him in the dimness, a smile formed on her lips.

Sprawled on his stomach, the sheet twisted about his waist, he slept. With his mouth slightly open, his breath stirred a lock of hair spread on the mattress. The skin over his right shoulder appeared a darker purple-black than last night. The mark ran from the top to an inch below his shoulder blade. She winced at the ugly discoloration.

Caitlyn squatted by the bed near his head. One hand hung off the side, and she was tempted to move it but didn't, afraid to wake him up.

He was so handsome. She wished she didn't care so much, but she did. She admitted it. Every facet of Shay Evers pleased her, and she wasn't sure she liked the way this pleasure felt.

What she had felt in her dream was different. The words she had wanted to say to him had refused to come out. Now she realized why. The man in her dream was just that. A dream. Loving him wasn't real, but loving this flesh and blood man sleeping in front of her was true. She studied him. Out of the two, her fantasy lover lacked the vitality of the real life man.

She raised a hand to touch the dark hair on the back of his head. Her hand froze in midair. A sharp pain shot through her temples. She tried to take a deep breath, but the air stuck in her chest.

There, amid the dark strands, were hundreds of slender braids laced with gold and silver. She blinked several times, hoping the braids would disappear, that what she saw was just her imagination, but they remained.

Confused and afraid, she retreated to the door. Once in the hallway and after the door clicked shut, she couldn't walk away. She rested her forehead against the wood, breathing deeply, trying to calm the thunderous pounding in her chest.

Last night had been a dream. Or was it? She squeezed her eyes shut. Of course, it was a dream. Shay probably had the braids in his hair last night, and she just didn't notice. Yes, that explained it. During her dream, she must have remembered the braids in his hair.

Calmer, she stepped away from the door, turning to go downstairs. When she lifted her gaze, she found Rhys standing in front of her. She gasped, holding a hand up.

"Easy." He grabbed her hand and held it.

"You scared me. Don't you know it's dangerous to sneak up on people? You could get hurt. That is if the person you scared doesn't have a heart attack." She pulled her hand free and stepped back, frowning at the man.

A low chuckle rumbled from his chest. "I am sorry. I thought for certain you heard me walk up. Had I known you hadn't, I would have cleared my throat or made some other sound."

The light dancing in his blue eyes infected her, and she responded with a nervous laugh. "I'm sorry. I was so lost in my thoughts," she said then stopped. She stared at Rhys for a second before continuing, "I know this may sound strange, but does Shay have braids in his hair?"

The gardener returned her look, his face expressionless. When he spoke, his voice was low and calm. "I really haven't noticed. Why?"

"He has some in his hair now. I didn't notice them last night. I'm just curious why he would have them," she said, as she tried to keep her tone and words nonchalant.

"Are you sure you saw braids? Could it have just been the way the light shone on his hair?" He tilted his head.

She lowered her eyes. Was he right? All she had to do was return to Shay and find out, but she wasn't sure she wanted to. The braids might still be there, but they might be gone. Since assigned this interview, she found she doubted her sanity. "I don't know. Maybe so. Listen, I'm going to the village this morning. Could you look at his hair for me? When I come back, I'll check with you."

"Of course. One thing, though. What is so important about the braids?"

Because the man in her dream had braids, and now, so did Shay. "Just curious, that's all." She replied, stepping around the tall blond. "I've got to go. See ya."

A few minutes later, she was waiting in front of the entrance as Marcy drove up. She climbed into the compact car and shut the door. She glanced up at the house as the car turned to leave. Rhys stood, staring down at her from an upstairs window. Shay's room.

* * * *

"Wake up, fool."

Rhys's deep voice penetrated the thick fog in Shay's head. He cracked open one eye and glared at his sovereign. Rhys stepped away from the bed and sat in a nearby chair.

He studied Shay for several minutes. When he did not say anything else, Shay closed his eye. Just as he started to doze, Rhys barked another order for him to wake up.

"I'm tired. I want to sleep for a bit," Shay snapped. Throbbing pain radiated from his shoulder, and he dreaded having to move.

"Aye, much too tired to remove your glamour. She saw your braids this morning." The sharp tone in Rhys's voice increased the throbbing pain.

"What do you mean?" He squinted at Rhys.

"She came to check on you, and noticed the braids in your hair. I'm assuming they were there last night in her dream."

Shay shut his eyes and groaned. He was such an idiot. He should have known she would come. "Why is she awake so early?"

"She's going shopping in the village with her American friend. I'm sure that woman woke her up." Rhys stood and paced back and forth. "Caitlyn expects me to look at your hair and tell her if you have braids."

Shay glanced at him. "Tell her, yes, there are."

"Are you more of a fool than I thought?"

"No. If you tell her that there are none, she'll wonder at her sanity. If you tell her yes, she'll think she just didn't see them last night."

His king shook his head and strode to the window. He stared down at the driveway. Shay tensed, waiting for Rhys's reaction.

"Tell me what happened last night? How did she react?"

She came all over my hand. Shocked at the thought, he shut the memories off. He didn't want to take the chance Rhys would sense the impressions coming from him. "She did amazingly well. Much better than I expected."

"Tell me everything. Did Myrielle see her?" He moved back to the chair. The tender expression on his face stirred guilt in Shay.

"Yes. The whole of our clan greeted her. She crossed the lake in a boat, and we went to the meadows. She liked the flowers." He sat here, speaking to Caitlyn's father, the one who blamed him for the loss of his daughter, with a straight face. Especially after what he had done with her? He'd become a bastard after all these years?

A warm smile flitted over Rhys's face. "Did she?"

Shay nodded. He regretted it in the next instant. Sharp pains shot up his neck from his shoulder. Taking a shallow breath, he told Rhys most of what had happen. He deliberately left out the meadow part.

"Good. This is good." Rhys pushed to his feet and wandered back to the window. Feet apart, he stared out. "Perhaps she could come home sooner than we discussed. One week isn't enough time for her to solve the riddle."

"No. I intend to ask her to help me solve it before we leave. Her curiosity is strong. Hopefully, she will figure out the answer." Shay closed his eyes and rested his head against the headboard.

"Hopefully? No, she must solve it. Her very existence depends on the answer." Rhys paced back and forth, his heels clicking on the wooden plank floor.

Shay heard the irritation in his king's voice, and sensed the unbridled frustration. Hoping to calm him, he commented, "She's intelligent. The riddle won't be that difficult for her. Have a little faith. She is your daughter, after all."

Rhys strode to the foot of the bed and stopped. "It's not the difficulty of the riddle. Gwyneth had a purpose in making it simple. There is a trap in it. I feel it. I have no doubt she made sure the riddle had many secret meanings. The answer we believe it to be might not necessarily be the true one."

"Yes, but Caitlyn will know the right one. She must know it." Shay tried to speak with wholehearted conviction, but his words rang hollow between the two men. She would not succeed without his help. He fully intended to give it to her, regardless of the cost.

Chapter 25

Caitlyn sighed. As she watched the rain drizzle down the side of the car's window, she tried not to think about Shay. The trip to the village had done little to distract her. Marcy, disappointment evident in her voice, had suggested they leave and Caitlyn hadn't argued. Questions about Shay whirled in her, never leaving her alone.

Cold rain washed over the landscape, coating everything in a layer of water. It cleaned nature of any impurities. Why wasn't it possible for her to do the same with her thoughts? No matter what, she hadn't imagined the braids in Shay's hair. Once they arrived in the village, she'd questioned the local people about the illusionist. Their answers hadn't helped her discover anything new. Most were vague, and she soon realized they didn't know Shay very well. They dwelled in the same geographic location, but didn't live in the same world.

The local governmental office held some documents on the castle but none shed any light on whether the place had secret passages. She had grown more anxious with each passing moment. She wanted to find something new, something to explain all the strange events. Marcy must have sensed her unease. A mere hour or two into the day, she'd declared enough shopping and that she was ready to leave.

A hint of a smile played on Caitlyn's lips. Her friend knew her so well. Even now she felt Marcy's curiosity, but Caitlyn was determined to remain silent about what bothered her. Besides, there wasn't any real explanation, so telling her wouldn't help.

Marcy slowed down to take the turn onto Shay's property. "We're almost there. Caitlyn, what is wrong with you?"

Her smile widened, and she released a little laugh. Marcy never used her full name unless bothered. "You don't give up, do you?"

She turned and faced her friend. Marcy shot her a quick look and continued. "You're not acting normal. At least, not normal for you. You think I didn't see what you did in the village, but I did. You talked to some plants. I don't know about you, Catey, but in Los Angeles that's grounds for an extended rest in a loony bin."

Caitlyn laughed. Her friend frowned and gripped the steering wheel tighter. She opened her mouth to continue, but Caitlyn cut her off. "I'm sorry. Coming here, being away from the hustle of the big city has caused me to be more aware of what nature has to offer. The plants were pretty, and I couldn't help telling them that."

"That's not normal. Don't do it again. What do you think your boss would say if he knew about this? He'd pull you off this assignment quicker than you could blink." Marcy bobbed her head. "Do you want that to happen?"

Caitlyn leaned her head against the headrest and stared at her friend. "Don't worry about me. I'm fine."

"No, you're not, and I am worried. It's Shay, isn't it? He's doing this to you. Catey, maybe you should go home. I feel like I don't even know you anymore. You actually seem happy here."

Raising a brow, Caitlyn tilted her head. "You make that sound like a bad thing."

"I didn't mean it that way. It's just, this is not permanent. You shouldn't let yourself get carried away. Shay doesn't want you. He doesn't want anyone. Dafydd told me." Another quick up and down with her head, and Marcy shot her a glance.

Caitlyn sat up straight. "What did he tell you?"

Dread soaked through her skin. Dafydd knew Shay. She assumed he'd been with him for a while so he had to know a lot about Shay. She shouldn't allow Marcy's comment to affect her but she wanted her life to be like the dream.

"Oh, Catey, I didn't want to say anything, but I can see it in your eyes. You're falling for the guy, and he's not worth it." Marcy slapped the steering wheel with an open palm. "Dafydd told me Shay had a girlfriend a few years ago. She hurt him, and since then he's never had another one. It's like he's still stuck on her."

Marcy's words swirled through her mind. An image of Shay sitting at the kitchen table appeared. That brooding quiet man was a stranger to her. He had to be the one Marcy spoke about. The one so hurt by a woman, he refused to attach himself to someone else.

Caitlyn opened her mouth to speak, but a loud crashing noise on her side of the road stopped her. A boulder slid down the embankment and rolled toward them. Time slowed down as the large rock came closer.

Oh, shit, it was going to hit them! In the second she formed the thought, she looked straight ahead as calmness came over her.

Within seconds, the boulder impacted the front of the car and the back end swung around. Shattered glass rained down from the side window.

Marcy's scream echoed in the interior.

The rear fender struck the boulder as the vehicle veered, out of control. A gust of wind brought the rain through the broken glass. Unfettered by seat belts, her body swung toward Marcy. With the second impact, Caitlyn was tossed the opposite way. The door opened and unable to stop, she flew out. The ground blurred in front of her eyes, the dark, muddy browns mingling with the lighter shades of small stones, but she never landed. Waiting to hit the ground, she tensed for the impact. Anticipating intense pain.

Water logged fir limbs swept down, caught and cradled her, laying her on the soaked earth. Gasping, close to hysteria, Caitlyn raised her gaze to the fir tree. It had saved her.

"No, this didn't happen," she whispered. Hands trembling, she tried to stand. The muscles in her legs refused to stay strong enough to let her rise.

Marcy.

Adrenaline rushed through her veins. Weakened muscles gained instant power. She lunged toward the car.

Stopped on the side of the road, only a few feet separated it from a steep drop off the side of a ridge. When she reached Marcy's side, her friend sat frozen behind the wheel.

Jerking the door handle, Caitlyn tried to force it open. It wouldn't budge. Fear gave her strength. She braced a foot on the side of the vehicle and pulled. The door came free with a metallic screech.

"Marcy. Are you okay?" She leaned in and gazed at her friend's white face. Tear tracks covered the blonde's pale features. Fear and shock radiated from her. "Oh, Marcy, it's all right. We're safe."

"C-c-catey," Marcy whispered. "Catey, you're not..." Sobs erupted and her head lolled against the wheel.

Even as she wanted to comfort her, Caitlyn wanted to get them away. She glanced up the steep incline they were on. Just around the bend, the castle waited.

"Come on, Marcy. Let's get you out of here. Can you stand?" She wrapped an arm around her friend's shoulders and helped her struggle from the vehicle. Once Marcy was out, she checked her. Except for a few scratches from flying glass and bruises dotting her skin, her friend seemed okay.

"Do you think you can make it to the castle? If you can't, I'll go and bring help." Caitlyn brushed blond strands away from Marcy's face.

"No. Don't leave me." Her jaw jerked with the aftereffects of the accident. Was the other woman going into shock? Oh Lord, what if she had internal injuries?

"Let's go." She helped Marcy stand. Together, with her holding Marcy upright, they started up the road.

Each step grew more difficult. Caitlyn's muscles burned from the climb. Water drenched her sweater and plastered her hair to her skull. She shoved a lock of hair behind her ear. When she lowered her hand, crimson streaks marked her palm where she'd swiped at her forehead.

A tearful giggle escaped her. She was bleeding. Most likely, the blood had come from where the glass from the broken window had cut her. She hadn't even noticed.

Gasping for breath, she pulled and prodded Marcy to the entrance of Shay's home. The door swung open, and Fred greeted them. With one look, the older man stepped forward and picked up Marcy. He led the way, heading toward the nearest room.

"I'll be all right. Caitlyn, let me lie down in your room," Marcy pleaded.

Fred looked at Caitlyn, waiting for her answer. She nodded and followed behind him at a slower pace.

Despite being exhausted, she didn't stop in the sitting room but continued to the bathroom. She grabbed a couple of towels and returned to the small sofa where Fred had laid Marcy.

Glancing around, Caitlyn noticed Fred had disappeared. Great, now he'd tell the entire household. Of course, how did she expect to keep the wrecked car a secret? She helped Marcy stand, wrapped a towel around her head and led her to the bathroom.

Stripping the soaked clothes off Marcy was a nightmare, like undressing a mannequin.

Grazelda called her name and a wave of relief shot through her.

"We're in here. Can you help? Marcy's not doing too well."

Grazelda's worried gaze traveled over both of them. Caitlyn tried to smile, but when she glanced in the mirror, she realized no matter what she did or said, the old woman probably would not believe her. Blood ran in watered streaks down the side of her face. Without thinking, she dabbed at the cut. Already bruising, a knot the size of a half dollar rose just above her left eyebrow. Strange, she didn't remember striking her head.

"Oh, you sweet dearies," Grazelda murmured, clicking her tongue. "I'll tend to yer friend, love. You get yerself changed. Fred'll be bringing some hot tea up here in a bit. It'll help warm yer both while we wait for the doctor to arrive."

"That sounds wonderful, but I don't need a doctor. I'm fine. It's just a little scratch," Caitlyn said.

Frowning, Grazelda led Marcy out of the bathroom. Before she closed the door behind them, she looked over her shoulder and sent a small comforting smile to Caitlyn.

Peace came over Caitlyn and security surrounded her.

After a hot shower, she dried off and dressed in her nightgown and robe. Her muscles had stiffened and her body ached. By morning, she wouldn't be able to move.

By the time she'd finished dressing and returned to the sitting room, Dafydd had arrived. He held Marcy while she wept against his shoulder. Soft murmurs came from him. Caitlyn blinked to stop the sudden sting of tears.

Death had threatened a second time, since she'd arrived in Wales. She walked to the matching sofa across from the couple and sat down, tucking her feet under her. Wrapping the robe higher against her throat, she leaned forward and poured steaming tea into a china cup.

The hair on the back of her neck bristled. She glanced toward the doorway, and her breath caught in her chest. Shay stood bracketed in the door's frame, one hand braced on the wood.

She became lost in the deep purple eyes staring at her. He moved toward her, never releasing her from his concerned gaze. When he reached her, he sat on the table in front of her.

"You're hurt."

She tried to smile, fighting off the increasing need to cry. She swallowed, took a deep breath and said, "I'm fine."

Marcy stirred weakly before she sat up. A note of hysteria tinged her voice. "She could have died."

Shay stiffened. Caitlyn leaned forward and placed her hand on his knee. His head tilted, and he shot a glance at Dafydd. His words vibrated through her. "Perhaps, she should lie down until the doctor arrives."

Caitlyn met Dafydd's eyes. The music tech's throat worked, then he nodded. The way Shay suggested Marcy lie down left her feeling uncomfortable, but she was glad. Marcy's anxiety wore on her.

Without a word, Dafydd scooped up Marcy and walked out the door. A moment later, Rhys skidded to a stop at the opening. His features, lined with worry, were pale. "I just heard. Are you all right?"

Caitlyn took a breath and nodded, offering a weak smile to reassure both men. "I'm fine. I'm more worried about Marcy."

"You're injured." Rhys strode across the room and touched her forehead. He ignored her comment about Marcy, and Caitlyn wondered why. Of course, neither Shay nor Rhys knew Marcy very well.

Pulling away, Caitlyn shook her head. "It's just a scratch. I have no idea how I got the lump. It happened so fast. I suppose when I flew out the door--"

She clamped her hand over her mouth. The sudden widening of their eyes, and then the forward motion of their bodies told her she shouldn't have said anything.

Shay's whispered sentiments increased in volume with each word. "You were thrown from the vehicle? Caitlyn, your friend was right. You could have died."

"We both could have, but we didn't. I'm fine, and now that I think about it, I wanted to ask you something," she said, shifting toward him. Forgetting about his shoulder, she grasped his hand and pulled him to her. His deep groan caused her to release him. "Sorry."

She moved from the sofa to sit next to him on the table. Cupping her hand over his ear, she whispered, "Does Rhys know about what you told me the other day. You know, about being an e-l-f?"

He shifted to face her. Guilt filled her for not only scaring him with the accident, but because he still suffered severe pain from his own injury as a result of her last incident. "Yes."

That was it. No explanation, no excuses, just a plain *yes*. Great, now how to go about telling them about her suspicions without sounding like a lunatic? Unable to sit next to him any longer, she stood and paced for several moments. When she glanced at the two men, she caught them staring at each other. Shay raised a brow at Rhys and then faced her.

Sure she had both their attention, she said, "You know I don't believe what you told me the other day. Magic isn't real. Your performances are just acts. That's what I believed before I came here and I still do. But, let's just say, for the sake of argument, that what you told me was true."

She tried to keep her tone even when she continued. "If you are an--" She stumbled over the next word, forcing it out. "--elf, then what if your friends, fellow elves, didn't like me because I don't believe. Since you're one of them, do you think they would try to get rid of me?"

Shay stared at her. He cleared his throat, then said, "Uh, Rhys would be the best one to answer that question. After all, he taught me everything I know about--elves."

She turned to Rhys. The slender blond stood near Shay, and the heated look he gave the illusionist made Caitlyn think that maybe the gardener was not happy with Shay's comment. The older man met her gaze and opened his mouth twice before snapping it shut.

Shay stood and moved toward her. "Caitlyn, come sit down. You've had a terrifying afternoon. Maybe if you rest, then you'll be able to rationalize what happened."

Anger boiled within her, and she stepped away from him. "I'm thinking just fine, thank you. There have been two freakish accidents within the last two days. Both of them could have killed me. What makes it worse is that a damn fir tree saved my life today."

"You landed in a fir tree," Shay said, his body stiffening.

"Did I say that?" she snapped, crossing her arms over her chest. "The damn thing caught me. The limbs moved out and plucked me from the air and laid me on the ground. I did not land in the tree."

Rhys eased toward the door. "Perhaps, I should call my wife."

Caitlyn frowned at him. "What good will that do?"

Shay turned to him and grinned. "That's an excellent idea. His wife is an expert on the magic creatures in Wales. She'll be able to tell you if what you suspect about the other elves not liking you is true."

She rolled her eyes. Rhys leapt out the door and disappeared.

"Come, sit down and drink some tea," Shay said. He sat on the sofa and patted the seat. "Shouldn't take long. They don't live far from here. Who knows, she might even be on her way here now. They say she has the sight."

"The sight?" Her irritation came through with the question. What did they think of her? That she was crazy? All they've been talking was nonsense. "Don't patronize me. I'm not crazy. First the limb, and now a boulder. Both of them were coming straight at me."

One more pat, and she sighed. Shoulders slumping, she lowered her chin and went to him. Easing down next to him, she raised her gaze. Caught in the hypnotic pull of his amethyst eyes, she shifted nearer. He winced when he lifted his left arm over her shoulder and pulled her to him.

"I'm sorry. You're hurting, and I'm not helping matters with all this stupid talk," she murmured, resting her head on his shoulder. Her nose twitched at his musky scent. Shifting nearer, she buried it against his neck, tasted the saltiness of his flesh with her lips.

He whispered her name, and ducked his head. With his gaze centered on her mouth, he eased closer.

Rhys cleared his throat. Caitlyn jerked upright and glanced toward the door. Shay sighed.

"Myrielle will arrive shortly," Rhys told them. He stepped further into the room. "Would you care for fresh tea?"

Caitlyn released a shaky laugh. "Sure, why not?"

Chapter 26

Caitlyn let Rhys pour her a cup of tea. She started to lift the cup to her lips, but Shay, with a sweet grin, waved a hand over the brim. The aroma of cinnamon rose with the steam. She closed her eyes and breathed deep.

One sip, and she went to heaven. Rich flavor washed through her. She had come to love that spice. With a sideways glance at Shay, she asked, "Do you always carry cinnamon with you?"

He held up a small pouch and grinned wider. "I like it, and yes, I do."

She shook her head. This man was unique. She'd never met anyone like him before and she enjoyed his company. Too much. A nagging thought tried to push forward, but she was too tired to remember. Something familiar.

"If you don't mind, could you tell us about the accident? What exactly happened?" Rhys sat across from them, leaning forward in his seat. Arms braced on his knees, he clasped his hands together.

Caitlyn took a deep breath. "It's all still a blur. Marcy was driving, and I looked to the left. That's when I saw this boulder sliding down the mountain on that side. It was moving so fast. I remember thinking it was going to hit us, and then it did."

"Well, that explains one thing," Shay said.

She frowned at him.

"It's raining. Has been since last night. The rain caused the boulder to loosen and slip in the mud and water." He glanced from her to Rhys. "There's nothing sinister in that."

"Okay, but that doesn't explain about the tree." She took a sip, waiting for Shay to come up with an explanation for that.

He cocked a brow at her. "Sorry, that's beyond me."

She sank deeper into the sofa. Tightening the robe about her throat, she shook her head. "Me, too."

A soft rustling noise came to her. Her left ear twitched. Eyes wide, she swiveled toward the doorway. A woman stood framed in the opening. A coarse wool shawl covered her head and wrapped about her shoulders. She glided toward them. Caitlyn's mouth gaped. She had always thought Marcy was beautiful, but when compared to this woman, her best friend seemed plain. How did someone compare a diamond to a dirt clod?

Rhys stood and met the woman, took her arm and led her to Caitlyn. A gentle smile graced her bow-shaped lips. Tendrils of dark hair escaped from under the shawl. When she stopped a foot away, Caitlyn noticed the woman's hands trembled.

An introduction wasn't necessary. She knew the woman's identity--Rhys's beautiful wife. Caitlyn searched her memory for what Shay had told her about her name. Myrielle, a unique and lovely name for a beautiful woman. The memory of another woman flashed--a dark-haired lady riding on a unicorn. Shaking her head, Caitlyn didn't dwell on the memory when Rhys started speaking.

"My dear, this is my wife, Myrielle. Caitlyn is the reporter from Los Angeles I mentioned to you, Merry," he said as he stared at his wife.

Caitlyn tried to speak but her voice refused to work. When Myrielle touched her hand where it lay in her lap, and then wrapped her slender fingers around the back, Caitlyn jumped.

Shay stood. He took Myrielle's free hand and brought it to his lips. Holding her hand, he spoke in a low respectful tone. "Good to see you. We have something of a problem. Caitlyn believes elves are behind the accident. We thought you might be able to shine some light on the subject."

"Elves? Now, why would you think such a thing?" Myrielle's voice reminded Caitlyn of music boxes. Light and cheery, her voice helped Caitlyn relax.

"Because I told her I was an elf," Shay replied, matter-of-factly. "She doesn't know what to believe any more. She's confused."

"I am not." Caitlyn glared at him.

Myrielle laughed and Caitlyn smiled. Yes, she liked this woman. She liked her a lot.

Rhys's wife gave a gentle tug on her hand. "Come, Caitlyn. Let's get you settled. You should be in bed."

There wasn't any room for argument. A wave of exhaustion came over Caitlyn. She accepted Myrielle's assistance to stand and went with her into the bedroom.

* * * *

Shay narrowed his eyes, and listened to the soft comforting words Myrielle spoke to Caitlyn. He couldn't shake the impression he'd picked up ever since he'd met Caitlyn's friend. He might be jumping to the wrong conclusions, but anyone close to Caitlyn for most of her life would have at one time or another come into contact with Gwyneth. He didn't believe the witch would have simply allowed someone to become close to Caitlyn without having a measure of control.

When the door closed, shutting the two women off from them, he faced Rhys. "I want her friend out of the here before nightfall."

Rhys raised a brow. "Do you suspect her?"

"No one is beyond suspicion. Gwyneth is capable of manipulating humans. This woman might be a puppet for the witch. I don't want to take the chance, that if she stays, something else might happen to Caitlyn."

Rhys nodded, shut his eyes for a moment, then said. "Consider it done. Dafydd knows what you wish, and he will carry it out. The woman is more hysterical than injured. I sensed no real damage to her."

"Nor did I. This accident was meant to frighten us, not kill Caitlyn. I am certain of this. Gwyneth means to tease us, keep us off balance. You shouldn't have let Caitlyn leave this morning."

Shay moved toward the door. His entire body ached, but he refused to allow his physical limitations to defeat him. The last few days had placed a strain on him he was unaccustomed to after all those years imprisoned by Rhys's spell. The pain reminded him he was in his normal form and not solid wood. Better to hurt like this than live in the shape of a blackthorn.

Footsteps raced down the hall, and Shay looked up at Blake when he reached the doorway. He'd sent Fred to find the photographer as soon as he found out about Caitlyn. Too much time had passed since then and he was confident Fred had not been lax in his duty. The man had taken too long to find out about the accident. More worrisome, had he heard what Rhys and he had discussed?

Just another connection with Caitlyn that was open for Gwyneth to meddle with and he doubted she would have passed up the chance to do so.

The photographer nodded to him, opened his mouth to speak then snapped it shut. Relief surged through Shay when he sensed Blake's inner worry about his co-worker. "She's fine. She went to lie down. I'm sure she'll want to see you."

Blake nodded again, then stuck his hands in the back pockets of his blue jeans. "She tell you what happened?"

"An accident. A boulder slid down the ridge and smashed into the vehicle," Rhys answered.

Once more, the photographer nodded, then strode across the sitting room and tapped lightly on the bedroom door. At the soft response on the other side, he eased the door open and entered.

Shay cut his gaze to Rhys. "Him, too. Send your spies to keep a very close eye on him. He's all over the place, snapping his pictures. I don't like that."

Rhys studied him for several moments. "You are becoming possessive of her."

Pain sliced through Shay as he jerked his head toward his king. "What does that mean?"

"You are not her mate. Her protection belongs to me, not you. Bear that in mind, my muse."

Shay chuckled, moving toward the sofa. "I intend to go back to bed once Myrielle relieves her fears, sire. That is the only reason I have pointed out the areas for you to see too. Your daughter will be kept safe."

* * * *

Caitlyn smiled and gave Blake a little wave as he left. Poor man appeared shaken to his toes.

"He seems to be a nice person," Myrielle said. Her gentle gaze lingered on the closed door.

"Yeah, he's a great guy. Always trying to cheer me on. I think this scared him, though he'd never admit it to me."

Caitlyn leaned against the pillow propped against the headboard. She studied the woman sitting at the foot of her bed. Each time she looked at Myrielle, her beauty struck her all over again. The older woman turned toward her. Caitlyn smiled at her.

"You must be tired. Would you like to rest?"

She shook her head. "No, I'm not tired. I want to know if what I suspect is true. Shay said you were a sort of expert on magical creatures here."

Myrielle laughed. The sparkling sound flowed over Caitlyn. When Myrielle spoke, she leaned forward taking in every word, not wanting to miss a single syllable. "Elves do not usually try to kill disbelievers. No, I do not believe Shay's elf friends are trying to harm you. There are worse creatures in this world that are better suited for such vile deeds."

Caitlyn lifted a brow. Myrielle appeared to be a rational, calm person, yet the way she spoke about magical creatures made Caitlyn wonder. Just for the sake of argument, she prompted, "And they are?"

"Every once in a while, an elf is expelled from Sidhe because of their crimes there. In these beings there is the capability to create great havoc. Their spirits are tainted with madness, and they desire only to do wickedness. If you ask if one of those wished for your death, then I would fully agree that it is so. But you have never run across such a one, have you?" She raised an elegant brow, staring at her.

Caitlyn slowly shook her head. "No, not that I know of. The only e-l-f I've ever met is Shay. And I don't really believe that he's one."

"Perhaps. Shay has wondrous magic about him. He is a very talented e-l-f," Myrielle said, then laughed. "Enough of your worrying. The boulder hit your vehicle because of the rain. Nothing more. Now rest. You will be very sore in the morning."

Caitlyn nodded and eased under the covers. Her eyes drifted closed, and once more, the idea that Rhys's wife was as beautiful on the outside and as she was on the inside crossed her mind. And how much she resembled that woman on the unicorn of her dreams.

* * * *

Shay stood in the doorway and studied Myrielle as she watched her daughter sleep. His queen took a deep breath, then brushed strands of Caitlyn's hair over the pillow. The daughter was so like the mother. This close, he saw the strong resemblance.

Rhys passed him, placed a hand on Myrielle's shoulder and squeezed. "Come, my love. Let her rest."

Myrielle raised her hand and covered Rhys's. "You don't know how hard it was for me last night to see her, yet not grasp and hold her to me. Of all the things I have desired in my existence, not one, save your love, could match how I desire to have her home. Safe. Alive."

Shay heard the tears in her voice. He lowered his head as the ever-present guilt gripped him. Damn Gwyneth. He wanted the witch dead. If he didn't succeed, then in one more week, Caitlyn would die.

Determined to beat Gwyneth at her own game, Shay silently vowed to catch her. Without a word to the royal couple, he slipped from the room.

Chapter 27

The fourth morning after arriving in Wales dawned with golden splendor. In the blue sitting room, Caitlyn reclined in a chair turned to the window overlooking the gardens. She ran a brush through her hair, admiring the rainbow colors painting the early morning sky. Birds and insects sang to greet the new day.

Droopy-eyed, she smiled, pondering the peacefulness in Shay's home. For two days after the accident, she'd lazed around in her room. The time to rejoin the world outside had arrived. Today, she'd get dressed and go see Shay. She missed him.

It had been nice to have Grazelda and Myrielle to pamper her, but not anymore. She woke this morning feeling back to her old no-nonsense self.

She had a job to do. Resting didn't accomplish all she needed to do. She'd called Kramer the day after the accident and he assured her he understood. But how long would his patience hold out?

A knock on her sitting room door. She frowned, curious about who was coming to her room so early. Glancing at the clock on the far side of the room, she wondered who was there at six o'clock. Way too early for someone to visit.

She stood and walked to the door. The knob turned smoothly under her palm. Opening the wooden portal, she peeked out. A bright grin greeted her. Shocked to see Shay standing on the other side, she tugged the door wider.

"What are you doing out of bed? You know what the doctor said," she fussed, but Shay brushed past her. He stood in the center of the sitting room, gazing around.

"Shay?"

"Um?"

"What are you--"

"I'm better." He rotated his arm in a wide circle. "See. Just a little twinge every now and then. How are you doing? I couldn't stand it any longer. I had to check on you. Besides, I was wondering if we might start filming in the morning. We don't have much time left, and I want it done."

Caitlyn stiffened. Trying to appear nonchalant, she hugged her robe closer. A few steps, and she reclaimed her chair. "Are you that anxious to get rid of me?"

"What?"

"There isn't any reason for me to stay once the interview is over." She cut a glance at him. A frown creased his brow.

He tilted his head, and his amethyst gaze caught hers. "I don't want you gone. I was thinking more on the lines that if we finish with the filming, you could relax the last few days. I want to show you some of the local sights. That's all."

A warm glow lit within her heart. Her mouth twitched. "So you want to spend the last few days playing?"

"Can you think of anything better?"

She bit her bottom lip, trying to stop the smile from emerging. "No. But, I don't think my boss would like that. He sent me here to do a job."

"And you'll be doing it. Come on, you know you want to. Besides, it will add some flavor to your story." His tone cajoled a smile from her.

"I'm all for filming tomorrow. I have to think about what follows that," she conceded.

"Great. I have appointments set up for some people to come and fix you up. They're a lot better than the ones your station allotted to do the job." He strode to the window and sat on the sill. "They'll do something pretty with your hair and clothes."

Heat rose to her face and she snapped, "What do you mean by *fix me?*"

"I want to uncover your beauty." By his excited expression, he was serious.

Anger fueled by hurt forced her to speak. "So you don't think I'm beautiful the way I am."

He stared at her, studying her. "I think you're the most beautiful woman alive, but that's beside the point. You don't see yourself like I do. I want you to. And I want the whole world to see it too." His soft words soothed her.

"You sound like this is going to be a makeover. I'm not sure I want that. What's wrong with me the way I am?" Heat crawled up her neck as she demanded.

A lot of the people in her life had tried to do the same with her but she'd fought to keep her individuality. If Shay didn't like the way she looked then he could go to hell.

He stood, stretching out his hand to her. "Come here."

She eyed his hand for a second. With a huff, she placed hers in his and let him to lead her into the bedroom. He crossed the room to a stand-up mirror and pulled her in front of him.

He studied her in the looking glass. "Look, Caitlyn. Look close. Tell me what you see."

It seemed useless to try and dissuade him, so she stared at her reflection. As usual, nothing spectacular appeared. This wasn't the magic mirror he had hidden away in a storage barn, so she didn't expect major changes.

"I see me. Simple, plain, me."

"Open your eyes and look. You're not seeing with your heart." He squeezed her shoulders.

Her gaze met his before she focused on her reflection once more. A minute ticked away. She shook her head.

With a motion so fast she didn't have time to blink, he shot a hand up and slipped her glasses off her face. She gasped and jerked around, glaring at the blur he'd become.

"Give them back. I can't see without them."

"I don't think so." With a flick of his wrist, he tossed the glasses to his right. They flew through the air and landed on top of the armoire on the other side of the room.

The frames clanked against the wood and Caitlyn cried out, "What are you doing? They're the only pair I have. Don't you understand? I can't see without them. I need them back." Her voice rose with each word. Surprise and shock over his callous behavior coursed through her.

He touched her shoulders and leaned down to gaze into her face. His warm touch moved over her shoulders and neck until they cupped her face. Passing his thumbs over her eyelids, he closed them. She wanted to shove him away, but found her body frozen. A faint sound came to her, and she tried to comprehend the words but couldn't. All she heard was the breath leaving his body in almost silent words.

After several moments, he removed his hands and stepped back. She refused to open her eyes. Gently, he turned her around, and moved her forward one step.

His warm breath touched her skin as he murmured close to her ear, "Now look and tell me what you see."

Judith Leger

She opened her eyes. Blurry images swayed back and forth then joined. Her reflection came into focus. The blood in her veins vibrated. This was impossible. She could see without the aid of her glasses. As far back as her memory allowed, she had needed glasses.

"What did you do?" she whispered, disbelief emptying her mind of all other thoughts. Dampness coated her body. She felt lightheaded as darkness crept along the edges of her new-found sight.

Shay placed his chin on her shoulder, and caught her gaze with his. "I just believed in magic. Why can't you?"

"This isn't magic. I don't know what this is." She jerked away from him, fear biting at her. "This isn't possible."

Panic increased, until she heard his order.

"Caitlyn, be still."

She stopped instantly, her eyes drooping. Her chest heaved with slow breaths as her mind grew numb.

Caitlyn woke with the sun's rays caressing her skin. She smiled at the pleasurable heat. Sitting, she glanced at the digital clock on the bedside table. Ten o'clock. A chuckle escaped her. How wonderful had it been to sleep late. She glanced around the room. The many shades of blue seemed intense, brighter than she had ever seen. She reached for glasses where she'd placed them on the bedside table.

They weren't there. She scanned the room, searching, but didn't see them anywhere. Now where had she placed them? Shrugging, she stood and headed for the bathroom. She didn't need them.

Halfway there, she stopped and frowned. Something wasn't right. She eyed the full mirror in the corner of the bedroom. A fleeting memory passed through her mind. She stared at her reflection, her concern increasing. The tall shape of the armoire on the opposite side of the room caught her eye.

She turned and studied the upright chest. What was it about the piece of furniture? Her gaze traveled from the base to the arch at the top. With her intuition guiding her, she dragged a chair to the armoire. She stepped on the seat and reached on top of the chest. Her hand fumbled and then stilled. She pulled away, gripping her dark rimmed glasses in her palm.

She hadn't dreamed what had happened. Shay had come into her room. He had touched her eyes and now she could see. What had he told her? Seeing with Tylwyth Teg vision. With a shake of her head, she tried to deny his comment. She wasn't an elf.

Spinning around, she jumped down from the chair. He'd asked her once if her ears were pointed. She had told him no. Her ears had a nice shell shape to them. If she saw with elf sight, then she would see points on her ears.

Frightened, but determined, she marched to the looking glass and lifted her hair away from her ears. The curve of her ears angled up to a sharp tip. Her hands fell to her sides as her breath caught in her throat.

With her eyes squeezed shut, she jerked away. She needed answers, and she needed them now. She grabbed jeans and a pullover sweater. Tennis shoes on her feet, she ran from the room.

She had to find Shay. He would tell her the truth. He owed her that much.

Her search took her all over the castle. No one had seen the illusionist. He wasn't in his room. Jogging down the main hallway, she skidded to a stop in the sitting room at the back of the house. She would stay long enough to decide where to look next.

Anger simmered below the surface. Shay Evers had some explaining to do. Right now. Glancing around the room, she shot a look out the windows. There in the distance, his dark head showed above the line of shrubs. He walked along the path leading toward the lake.

She rushed to the French doors and threw them wide, leaving them open in her hurry. To hell with the mess. Shay Evers could stay up all night sweeping leaves for all she cared.

Running, she kept her eyes trained on the back of his head. When he reached the crossroad in the trail, he glanced over his shoulder, and then swung off toward the woods. She wondered why he was acting so strange. He must know that once she woke up she would search for him.

Caitlyn stopped to catch her breath. He was hiding something, and she intended to find out what. Not wanting him to see her, she trailed after him at a discrete distance. When he glanced once more toward the castle a moment before he disappeared into the dimness of the forest, she scrambled behind a bush. Once he turned away, she continued following him. He wouldn't get away from her. She'd discover what game he played.

She sprinted across the grass to where he'd entered the tree line. Noting how far ahead he was, she waited then continued shadowing him, keeping trees and undergrowth between them. After fifteen minutes, her newly rested muscles screamed for relief. The forest opened into a rolling meadow. Breathless, Caitlyn flattened her back against an oak tree. She peeked around the edge, searching for Shay.

He sat atop a boulder several feet from her. She frowned. What he was doing just sitting there, staring at the scenery? She scrutinized the sloping surface of the meadow. Bit by slow, blurred bit, the forms of young men and women appeared. A lilting song reached her.

Tightening her hands into fists to keep them from trembling, she watched as several youths danced while three played stringed instruments. They reminded her of the people she met in her dream. She shot a glance at Shay. No muscle moved, no sign revealed he witnessed the same scene.

He pulled his knees up and rested his cheek on them. The expression of sadness on his face tightened her chest above where her heart beat. It reminded her of schoolmates from her childhood who had always watched from the sidelines, but had never joined in. Like her, they never fit into the group, were never accepted.

She shook her head to rid herself of those ugly memories. Not wanting to believe what she saw was real, she decided to wait until he departed then corner him. He would tell her what was happening. She wouldn't allow him not to. He owed her big time for all the tricks and illusions he'd played on her.

Even though her eyesight was normal, she didn't believe he'd touched her eyes and healed them. Something strange was happening here, with her and him. She wasn't sure what, but this was real and though she dreaded admitting it, maybe, just maybe, magic was a little possible where he was concerned.

He'd led her down a twisting path, but no more. She was stronger than he ever imagined. She refused to let him continue to use her for his own means. The sun drifted toward the treetops on the opposite side of the meadow, and Caitlyn tensed. Shay stood on the boulder then leapt down, ducking his head away from the dancers.

She shifted to the other side of the tree and watched him enter the forest. Moving parallel with him, she stayed close enough to see him, but far enough away he wouldn't know she followed him.

He reached up and grabbed a low tree limb. He flipped over and landed in a squat on the branch. She gaped at the ease in which he'd accomplished the act. He didn't strain at all. He glanced about the area for a moment, then he stood and ran down the length of the branch, his balance perfect. When he reached the end, he jumped to a neighboring limb.

He moved too fast. She broke into a run, trying to keep up with him. With no time to check where he led her, she ducked branches and jumped over small bushes, keeping him within her sight. She glanced ahead and saw a huge gap in the trees. At least thirty feet separated the line of trees from where Shay headed. He'd never make that jump.

Fear filled her, shutting out the sound of her crashing through the brush. Exhaustion bore down on her. He reached the place and leapt. She cried out, falling to her hands and knees. She squeezed her eyes shut, unable to bear watching him fall to the ground. Magical being or not, he'd end up injured. Had been just three days ago.

She whispered his name.

Strong hands grasped her upper arms and lifted her off the ground. Fury blazed in his amethyst eyes. She curled her fingers into the front of his shirt.

"You were following me. Why?" he demanded, the muscle in his jaw flexing.

Taking a deep, shuddering breath, she glared back at him. "Don't ever scare me like that again. I didn't think you would make it."

"Why, Caitlyn?" He shook her a little.

"You lied to me. I remember, Shay. I remember this morning. You don't have any reason to be angry at me. I'm not the one who's been lying all this time," she cried, her anger refueled by her dwindling fear. "Tell me the truth. I want to know. You owe it to me."

He shifted nearer, his gaze locked with hers. "The *truth*? Are you sure you can handle the reality of it?"

"Yes."

"Then so be it." He gritted his teeth. Placing his palms on her jaw, he covered her eyes with his thumbs. No more than a second passed before he released her, turning her body away from him.

"You wish the truth. Open your eyes, and you will see it," he whispered. He rested his forehead against the base of her neck.

Without fear, without reservation, she snapped her eyes open and froze. The star-covered void spread out around them. Gasping, she tried to turn toward Shay, but he held her still.

"Look into the mirror, Caitlyn. What you see there will be the truth," he told her.

Before her, the same mirror from his performance in Los Angeles materialized. Once more, dressed in the radiant gown, she denied what she saw. To prove her point, she raised her hand and touched the glass. Ripples started where her fingertips brushed the surface, moved to the outer edges of the frame and disappeared.

Nothing changed.

"You are Princess Caitlyn of Tylwyth Teg. Stolen shortly after your birth, you have suffered a life without knowing your true identity." Shay slid his hands from her upper arms to her shoulders.

"You're lying. This isn't real. I don't believe it." She felt the warmth of his breath on the side of her neck.

He started to speak, but she jerked away. Keeping her gaze on the mirror, she watched him lift his head. The sight of his face built a scream in her mind. Cracked and peeling, the flesh appeared half skin, half wood. His hair streamed up and out about his shoulders and tangled with leaves and twigs. He lifted a hand to touch her, and his fingers were made of small branches.

Caitlyn pulled away, swinging about to face him. She stumbled when she saw what she'd witnessed in the mirror had not changed. She tripped as she backed up, unable to cushion the impact, she landed on her back with a jarring bounce to the rear of her head. Darkness surrounded her. Stars burst behind her eyelids.

Shay called her name. Moaning, she cracked open her eyes. Blue-gray sky and darkened treetops loomed over her. His concerned features came into view.

"Are you all right?" He brushed the hair from her brow. Tremors vibrated from his fingertips. He seemed frightened. She saw the fear in his worried gaze and felt it in his gentle touch.

The back of her head throbbed with sharp pains. Her memory returned, and she cried out. Scooting away from him, she scrambled with her hands and feet to escape. She didn't look back when he shouted for her to stop.

She had to escape from him. She needed to think, to figure out what was happening. Confused, hurt and frightened, she ran, swatting at the low branches until she broke free of the forest and felt the trimmed grass of the castle's lawn under her feet. She didn't stop running until she was locked behind her bedroom door.

Sinking to the floor, panting, she squeezed her eyes shut, wishing she could do the same with her memories. He'd said people saw their true form in the mirror. Well, she had just witnessed his.

He wasn't human. He wasn't, and even knowing it, she still loved him.

Chapter 28

Darkness covered the world outside her bedroom window. Caitlyn rolled her forehead against the glass. In the five hours since she'd run from Shay, she'd thought about nothing but what had happened in the forest. How could she have called him a liar? Yet, he had lied. All along, he had lied and used her. But why? What was his purpose? Did he even have one?

She stepped away from the window and wandered to the looking glass. The dark-haired woman gazing back at her was unfamiliar. The beauty of this woman amazed her. The Caitlyn Reiley she knew didn't possess such loveliness. This person was a stranger.

Her thoughts were muddled with how she felt for Shay. She still had trouble understanding the change in her vision. She shoved her hair over the tops of her pointed ears. She laughed. Yes, pointed tips.

Tears stung her eyes. No, she wouldn't cry. Tears never accomplished anything. She ought to know. They'd never helped when her parents beat her, left her alone days at a time and tried to feed her pills and alcohol. Tears hadn't helped her then, and they wouldn't do so now.

Maybe, she should go to Shay and talk to him. Just talk, calmly and intelligently. What could it hurt? She might end up telling him she loved him. What good would that do?

She shook her head. Would it matter? The way she felt wouldn't change just because he knew. It might complicate the situation, but it wouldn't change anything.

Taking a deep breath, she straightened her shoulders, and headed for the door. For some reason, a gentle premonition tugged at her. She headed for the library. Without knocking, she eased the door open and slipped in. Her assumption was right, he was there.

Thrown wide, the French doors behind the desk swayed back and forth under the force of the wind. The curtains rippled. Shay sat cross-legged in

Judith Leger

the center of the desk with his back to her. A bottle that looked as though someone flattened it while still forming it swung in his left hand. A tiny, thimble sized cup was pinched between his thumb and the index finger of the right.

"I didn't believe I would see you again." He grunted, raising the tiny cup and tossing a deep purple liquid into his open mouth. He never turned his head. How had he known she stood there?

Caitlyn walked toward the doors, keeping distance between them. She didn't want to get close. If she did, she would weaken. Become too wrapped up. She needed answers, not distractions.

She hugged her arms about her waist. "Probably won't believe me, but I couldn't stay away. You owe me an explanation."

"Um..." Dark hair threaded with silver-entwined braids shook. "I have no excuses for what I have done."

"Then explain it to me. Excuses won't change anything, but giving me answers might." She shifted and tilted her head, looking at him.

The bottle tipped, and he poured more of the purple liquid into the cup. His chest expanded after he emptied the thimble into his mouth.

"That's wine, isn't it? What kind?" She didn't really want to know, but he didn't seem inclined to answer her other questions.

The side of his mouth rose in a half smile. When he spoke, his Welsh accent changed to an Irish brogue. "Pixie wine from our cousins in Eire. Finest in the land. I've been saving it for a special occasion. What better time than the return of our clan's princess?"

For the first time since she'd entered the room, he lifted his gaze to her. He raised the cup. "Would you care for a bit? I should warn you, it's not as gentle as human drink. This will put stoutness in your heart."

"Shay..."

"No? All right, I don't mind drinking alone." With that, he downed another cup.

"Talk to me, Shay. Tell me what's going on. Please," she whispered, stepping closer.

"Don't--come any closer," he said, holding up the hand with the bottle.

She gave him a small smile. "And what will you do if I don't stop?"

"I'm the reason you were stolen. It was because of me. I enchanted your parents so that a witch could steal you," he muttered, glancing at the cup.

Her arms tightened about her waist, and she fisted her hands. She glanced about the room, blinking back the sudden sting of tears. "And you expect me to hate you because of what you did? How am I supposed to do that when I don't have anything to compare one world to the other? I can't miss something I don't remember. I worked hard to make a place for myself here, in this world. It might not count for much to most people, but it does to me."

When her courage increased, she looked at him. He watched her out of the corner of his eye. She took another step toward him. "Shay, I don't care where I come from. This is my world, my life, and you've turned it upside down. I don't know what to believe."

"Believe you will go home and live. Believe you will survive."

"I know I'll survive. Just tell me the truth." Battling to keep her frustration under control, she clenched her teeth. She wished he would open up and talk to her.

"The time is right. Tonight. I'll take you to the doorway, and you'll return home." He nodded. He spoke as though she no longer stood so close to him.

"And what will you do? You'll be with me, won't you?" She studied him. One more step.

He chuckled. The deep sound rumbled in his chest. He glanced at her, and then whispered. "No. I will stay here."

"Why?"

"Your father was very upset because of my part in your kidnapping. I will not return to resume my prison sentence. I've thought long and hard the last few days. It is best I stay here. Best that I fade away and am no more." He swallowed another cupful of the wine.

"What do you mean, 'fade away'? Shay, I don't know what scares me most. All the strange things happening or not having you with me-- helping me." She didn't understand. He sounded as if he would die.

"Help you?" He laughed then replied, exasperation in his words, "You don't need my type of help. I thought I was helping you twenty-four years ago. I was wrong."

His deep amethyst gaze rose and met hers. "From the first moment my eyes touched upon you, my heart left me and you held it in your tiny hand. Your aura extended so far, that when I stepped within its light, I felt as though my life became renewed. Helping you return home will give me a small measure of absolution. Just don't ask that I go with you. I cannot. I will not. Not even for you."

Caitlyn faced the open doors, biting her bottom lip. Didn't he realize how he hurt her? If he cared, he'd want to go with her.

He swore viciously. She jerked. The sound of him swinging his legs over the desk's edge and standing came to her. She shifted away, moving closer to the door.

The gentle touch of his hands on her shoulders sent shivers through her. He rested his cheek against her hair at the back of her head and whispered. "I've done it again. I'm sorry. I'm so sorry, Caitlyn."

"Don't be sorry. You don't have anything to be sorry for." She turned to face him.

The look of total defeat on his face stole her breath. A lump formed in the base of her throat. She raised her hands, cupping his cheeks. "Oh, Shay."

His strong arms enfolded her. She rested her head on his shoulder and nuzzled his neck. The warmth from his body seeped through their clothes to her flesh. When his arms tightened, she leaned her head back and stared into beautiful eyes that shone like twin bruises in his face. Full of hurt, full of grief.

"Shay." She reached up and pulled his mouth to her, rising to meet him half way. The wonderful flavor of cinnamon mixed with berries filled her senses as she dipped her tongue past his lips.

He moaned.

With a sweep of his tongue, he explored her mouth, and then applied suction. Caitlyn's knees gave out. Throbbing heat budded at the base of her belly. He held her close, kneeling on the carpeted floor. Spreading his legs, he caught her hips to him, holding her tight in the vee.

This was Shay, the real Shay, not a dream one. He kissed her, touched her. She wanted more.

Pulling away, they stared into each other's eyes. He raised a hand and motioned toward the open doors. They closed on their own, giving them some privacy from anyone looking in. She smiled. Arms crossed in front, she dragged the sweater over her head. Her hair swung free and settled over her shoulders, falling down her back. Silence reigned for several seconds. Her flesh heated.

Soft as a kitten's fur, he brushed his fingertips along the valley between her breasts where the lacy bra hooked. A swift movement, and the lingerie fell open. She shrugged her shoulders, sending the garment to the floor.

The slight widening of his eyes and flaring of his nostrils revealed he liked what he saw. His throat worked as he swallowed. Trembling, she waited, willing him to touch her.

He whispered her name. His lean fingers wandered over the curve of her breast and came to rest on the side, cupping their weight in the center of his hand. He dipped his head. She felt a puff of breath a moment before he captured her nipple between his lips. The muscles in her neck refused to respond, and her head lolled. Squeezing her eyes shut, she reveled in the sweet pull of his mouth.

His thick hair, threaded with braids, flowed through her fingers. She held him to her, never wanting him to leave. When he shifted, trailing soft kisses over her chest, she released a quiet cry.

Caught up in his touch, she barely registered when he drew her to the carpet. Laying her on her back, he leaned over her breasts, working his magic on her sensitive flesh.

Skin. She needed to touch. Explore his body. Wanted to feel the movement of his muscles and bones against hers. Wanted to simply feel. Breathing deeply, she ran her palms down his neck, glided over his shoulders and pulled his shirt down.

"Take it off. I want to see you, touch you," she murmured.

In that moment, she realized she'd never seen him bare-chested. Curious, she ran her palms over the sleekness of his back as he removed the shirt. Once the cloth barrier had disappeared, she slid her hands to the front.

Her breath caught in the back of her throat as she gazed upon the broad expanse of his chest. Beautiful, tanned muscles tightened under her inspection. Yearning flared in her core. Passion's sharp barbs pierced her belly to flow from her in a flood of longing.

Her fingers fumbled with the button and zipper that prevented her from viewing all of his body. Together, they stripped, clothes thrown, forgotten in their need.

Bare skin brushed against bare skin. Caitlyn gasped at the heated touch. She pulled him closer, needing to feel him over her, inside her. Panting, she whispered, "Now, love, I need you."

He nuzzled her neck, murmuring her name. He captured her lips as he rose above her, shifting between her legs. She lifted her hips, wanting him. Now. This instant. A gentle nudge and he slid, hard and deep, into her.

She cried out in joy. Pleasure rippled through every nerve ending, sending messages from the bottom of her soles to the top of her head. Unable to stop, she wrapped her legs around his, pulling him closer.

Slowly, he withdrew, only to enter her once more. Each movement propelled her nearer and nearer to the edge. Fighting to catch her breath, she rolled her head back and forth, holding his hands, moaning. His name echoed in her mind.

Her orgasm ripped through her, erupting her world with a flash of brilliant colors, draining her then refilling it. Her inner muscles clenched around him, pulling him tighter, further into her. Heated spasms raced through her legs and lower belly.

Groaning, gasping for breath, Shay braced his hands on the floor and straightened his arms, his back curled, his face pointed toward the ceiling. Deep inside her, he jerked once, then twice. Dazed, Caitlyn watched the look of satisfaction and pleasure cross his features as his completion pulsed within her.

Several moments passed, each frozen in the fierce reaction to the other. She lifted a hand and laid it flat over his heart. Sweat dampened her palm. He lowered his head and stared at the hand. She smiled. His muscles contracted under her touch.

When he met her gaze, he smiled and rolled to one side, keeping them joined. Exhausted and fulfilled, she closed her eyes as she settled her head on his shoulder. He held her tight against him. She smiled once more before sleep pulled her down into peaceful darkness.

Chapter 29

Shay's eyes snapped open. Lightning struck nearby. The crash and electrical sizzle echoed in the library, followed by a thunderous boom. He raised his head and stared out the open door. Clouds raced across the moonlit sky. Their shadows snaked over the garden like vile creatures intent on wickedness. Light flared through the clouds. Thunder cracked. A chill flittered up his spine.

He squeezed his eyes shut and concentrated. He didn't sense Rhys anywhere in the castle. The strength of the king's aura remained absent outside the house too. Where was he? He'd picked a fine time to disappear. Damn him.

All the guards Rhys left were in their proper positions, but Shay knew it wasn't enough. The power he discerned building outside surprised him. The witch approached. Her arrival was imminent.

He eased from Caitlyn's side, staring down into her peaceful features. There wasn't any time left. She'd never know how much she meant to him. Not now.

He jerked his jeans on. Two strides, and he swung open the double doors, scanning the gardens. A matter of time. It would be better to draw Gwyneth away. He glanced back at where Caitlyn slept, he had to stay with her.

Frustrated, he concentrated on music. As the beat built in his mind, he opened his mouth and the verses of an ancient battle song came out as an incantation. The winds whipped back around. Two bolts flashed diagonally on the horizon.

His hair floated about his head from the electricity in the air. He fisted his hands and continued to sing. The ground rumbled and boulders erupted from the dirt on the far side of the castle, splitting the earth of the lawns.

Behind him, the soft sound of Caitlyn whispering his name broke his focus. No. He couldn't stop now. The power he sensed rushed forward.

He opened his eyes and raised his hands, waiting until the witch revealed her location.

Vapors appeared in a line of shadows. Low laughter reached him. Underneath the sounds of nature and the arrival of the witch, the rustling of clothes came from behind him. In a flash of lightning, the vapor shot toward him. Not budging, he took the full force of the magical impact. Feet planted, he skidded back on the carpet.

"Shay, what's going on?"

He cut a glance to Caitlyn, where she stood next to the desk. Worry lined her face. With part of Gwyneth's spells removed, Caitlyn must have realized the magnitude of the danger drawing nearer. He wouldn't chance losing her. He'd never dreamed the witch's power had increased so much. A deadly miscalculation on his part. One he would never forgive if anything happened to Caitlyn.

"Come, we must leave now." He held out his hand.

She swallowed, and then ran to him, trust shining in her gaze. The feel of her fragile hand in his gave him little comfort. He caught her gaze and held it.

"At the next surge of power, we will run. Do not lag behind. Stay with me. If we get separated, go to the meadow. In the center is a faery circle. Step inside and say your name and Tylwyth Teg. The entrance will open. No matter what happens, do not stop. Your life depends on it."

He felt her fear beating in the rapid pulse in her wrist, but underneath, he sensed the rise of royal steel carried in her blood from her ancestors. She nodded and tightened her hold on his hand.

Laughter filtered through the doorway. A woman called his name. Gwyneth. He recognized the voice. "Come and play with me, Shay. Come. Bring the little princess with you. Think of the fun I will have as I watch the two of you die."

Caitlyn trembled. Waves of fear traveled up his arm from where she gripped his hand. In turn, anger rose inside him. So the witch wanted to play? Then, so be it.

The winds increased. He kept a watch over the shadows as his skin tingled with the magical charges floating in the air. He figured out the precise moment Gwyneth's power surged to release another volley of magic. Braced sideways, shoulder down, he took the brunt of the attack on his left. Twisting, he shoved the physical force away. Books and shelves shattered under the force.

Shay dove forward, through the door, Caitlyn following at his heels. He rushed toward vapors mixed with shadows, releasing a singular deafening note, sending a powerful thrust of magic to break through. The vapors dispersed in a blinding light.

A scream echoed in the darkness. He grinned. Good, he'd managed to strike her.

He plunged past the spot and continued speeding toward the woods. Uneasy at entering the trees with the scattering of underbrush, he refused to detour. Nature offered the witch many projectiles to stop them.

Leaping fallen trees, tearing through brambles, he ran, while doing what he could to protect Caitlyn from the worst of the abuse. They were half way to the meadow when he sensed Gwyneth bearing down on them. Growls and howls rippled through the forest. Dammit, the wolves were close. Trees moaned under the onslaught of the storm. A movement to his right brought his gaze around.

Several of Rhys's warriors raced a little behind them. Shay grinned. In turn, the lead warrior winked. Relieved he and Caitlyn would not fight alone, he increased his speed. Somehow, possibly because of the innate ability to run she'd inherited from her parents, she managed to keep up with him.

Lightning struck a tree to the left. Popping and sizzling, the burned splintered wood screamed in its dying throes as it tilted and started to fall. Almost upon the tree, he shouted to her, "Jump!"

Springing atop the tree before it impacted against the ground, they bounded off to the other side. Dark shadows leapt from the left, and the warriors intercepted them, enabling Shay to continue. The sounds of the Tylwyth Teg soldiers battling the wolves reached him above the noise of the storm.

A small measure of relief washed over him when he caught the sight of the meadow through the trees just ahead. Twenty paces and they would make it out of the darker forest and into the open. There, he could track the witch's location and deflect any attack aimed at them.

That's all he needed to do until Caitlyn returned to the Sidhe. He had confidence she'd figure out the riddle with Rhys and Myrielle's help. Once she entered, he'd kill the witch. She wouldn't escape him. Not this time. If he failed, Caitlyn would never be safe, even having solved the riddle.

Breaking past a narrow thicket, he heaved into the meadow. She stumbled and fell to one knee. He stopped, reached down and grabbed her under the arm. He pulled her to her feet. Seconds lost, never to be returned, he rushed toward the faery circle.

Something hit the ground behind them. He glanced over his shoulder. Magical power bounced in rays of greenish beams toward them, ripping and tearing at the earth. He twisted to one side, tugging Caitlyn with him.

"There, do you see? Up ahead. Go!" he shouted to her as they neared the center of the meadow.

"No, I won't go without you. I won't!" she yelled over the growing winds and booming of thunder and magic.

"This isn't the time to argue. Go." One handed, he jerked her in front of him and shoved. As she passed him, she grabbed his wrist.

"No," she cried.

Seeing the stubborn glint in her eyes, he nodded once, intent on her escape. Leaping ahead, they sprinted the last few feet. He shot a look behind them and noticed the vapor bearing down on them.

Flowers, their stems buffeted by the storm, formed a perfect ring. Shay stepped into the center, pulling Caitlyn close, and murmured the words needed to enter the Sidhe. Rays of light rose from the ground beneath their feet. The moment they were encased in the light, the vapor reached and joined them in the circle.

For several seconds, they were coated with searing blackness, and then the world of the Sidhe materialized. The royal gardens spread before them. Caitlyn's legs gave out, and she sank to the ground, her gaze wandering over the new environment.

Shay sent out mental probes to check if any of the mist had managed to succeed in following them. Nothing. Panting, out of breath, he looked down at Caitlyn.

She must have felt his gaze on her because she raised her eyes and stared at him.

"What the hell was that?" she muttered, her voice vibrating from the exertion of escaping, and perhaps, a tinge of fear.

"I can't stay." He needed to return to the human world. Gwyneth was there, and he intended to kill her. Now that Caitlyn was safe, he would leave.

Before he opened his mouth to answer or even move, his feet slid across the stone path. Realizing the spell controlling his imprisonment was renewed upon his arrival in the Sidhe, he concentrated on breaking free. The harder he fought, the faster he was propelled, until his feet were pulled into the spot he had been rooted in almost twenty-five years ago. Frustration, anger, and then defeat filled him.

He refused to cry out for mercy. He did not expect any. His bones shifted, his skin split and cracked, peeling back to reveal the hardened wood beneath. The look of utter horror on Caitlyn's face would haunt him forever. His last thought before pain took over was how cruel Rhys was to allow his daughter to witness this.

Caitlyn sat, frozen on the ground where they'd come into this different world. What had Shay called it? The Sidhe. She tried to convince herself that her imagination ran away with her. On shaky legs, she managed to gain her feet and stumble to where Shay had transformed. She couldn't deny what she saw. Traces of blood mingled in the twisted bark. Strands of dark hair fluttered in the gentle breeze.

A half laugh, half sob escaped her and bounced off the garden wall. "I'm mad. That, or I'm having a horrible nightmare. Please, tell me you're not Shay. Please." She raised a hand and touched the trunk of the tree. Sharp thorns pierced her fingertips.

She stared at the drops of blood coming from the puncture wounds and giggled. "I'm dreaming. That's it. I'm--"

Rhys called her name. She twisted and faced him. The gardener's long-legged stride ate up the distance from the arched doorway of the building to her left. He wrapped his arms about her shoulders and pulled her close to his chest.

"Shay turned into a tree," she murmured. Instead of finding relief in the security of Rhys's arms, she pulled away and turned back to the tree. "He really turned into a tree."

"It is his punishment." Rhys squeezed her shoulders.

Anger sparked a burning fire in her. She jerked her gaze to the tall blond. "Punishment? He brought me back, why should he be punished?"

"I cannot reverse my judgment. He knew this when he returned you. His sentence would resume."

"Resume? Change him back now. Do you hear me? I want Shay back, the way he was." She eased away from Rhys, taking several steps to the right.

"I can't do that."

"You don't want to," Caitlyn accused, wrapping her arms about her waist.

His back stiffened, and he scowled at her. "No, I don't."

"You know, I don't like you right now. Not at all."

Before she continued, a movement behind him caught her attention. Myrielle glided toward them. Memories flared to life. "You're the queen? I remember now, you're the one I saw in my dream. I knew I saw you somewhere before I met you."

"Come, Caitlyn. Come, dearest. You will rest for a spell then when you arise, I am sure you will feel much better." The woman in the flowing dress held out her hand to Caitlyn. This was Rhys's wife. The same woman who had sat beside her three nights ago, calming her fears after the accident. Now this woman wanted her to leave Shay.

No way was she going to follow them like a lamb to the slaughter.

"I don't think so. Who are you to me?" She waited and watched as the couple cut a glance at each other. "Well?"

His blue eyes reflected his worry and concern for her. "We are your parents."

Unable to feel any more shock, she stopped breathing for a minute. Finally, feeling secure her voice wouldn't break, she drew in a deep breath then asked, "You expect me to believe that?"

Myrielle raised a hand, reaching for her. Caitlyn backed up another step and said, "My parents are dead. They were useless losers. No matter how much I wished for our lives to change, it never did. Now, you think you can waltz in here and believe I'll fall all over you because you say you're my parents?"

She glared at him. With one jerk of her head toward the tree, she continued, "You want me to believe in magic so bad, change him back. Now."

Rhys's jaw tightened. "No."

She tilted her chin up. "Then leave me alone. I need to think, sort through all of this. If I am your daughter, and I possess magical abilities, then I'll figure out a way to free him myself."

"Caitlyn, my love," Myrielle started, but Caitlyn cut her off by turning her face from the queen.

"Don't beg," Caitlyn said. A low laugh escaped her. She was insane. "It's not becoming of you."

Silence reigned in the garden for several moments. The scent of wild flowers and green grass filled her senses. A feeling of belonging washed over her. Battling with her inner heart, she refused to budge on what she had told them. He released a sigh. Yes, she'd won.

His words verified it. "Come, Merry. Let us give her a bit of time. Not much, though, Caitlyn. Your life depends on you finding the answer to a riddle."

"Yeah," she muttered, refusing to soften in her actions and words. How dare they expect her to believe them? All of what had happened seemed like a dream. Was this real? The dreams with Shay always felt real, yet they were only dreams.

Without another word, Rhys took Myrielle by the arm and led her away.

Caitlyn's shoulders slumped. What now? Despite what she told them, how could she believe this was a dream when she still wore the same clothes she had in the real world? How could she feel so normal and this place have so much substance?

Deep in her heart, she believed what she experienced was real. That didn't change the fact she had no idea what she should do next.

She glanced at the tree. Black bark. White flowers. Was this the tree Shay told her about in Los Angeles? Positive it was, she walked over to a stone bench situated at the base of the trunk and sat. No wonder he spoke about the tree with such anger and hatred. This had been his prison for all her life.

"Oh, Shay, why didn't you talk to me before now? Why didn't you tell me?" she whispered, then laughed, shooting a look at the tree. "I know. I wouldn't have believed you."

A soothing breeze washed over her face. The cool air helped calm her. Once she settled, she heard a murmur and stiffened. Tilting her head, she frowned and studied the tree. There. Again the sound, barely above a whisper, came to her. Like tender fingers brushing through her hair, the wind lifted the strands, blowing them about her face. Above her, the branches of the tree swayed.

Her heart leaped in her chest. Was that her name she heard in the gusts? She stood and looked around. No one was with her. Turning, she faced the tree. "Shay?" she whispered. She lifted a hand to touch the bark.

An almost indiscernible reply came to her. "No. Do not. 'Twill only inflict more hurt on you. Stay away."

For a brief second, joy filled her heart. He was alive. In the form of a tree, but at least he still lived.

"I'm going to get you out of there. I promise. Just be patient." Her words sounded hollow to her ears. Ignoring his warning, she placed her palm on the trunk, careful not to press too hard. "Do you know how to stop whatever Rhys did to you? It's a spell, isn't it? Can we break it?"

Once more the wind brought his soft voice. The limbs rattled, giving emphasis to his words. "Go away. Think only of the riddle. Save yourself."

"How do you expect me to do that if I don't have you to help me?" she cried. Frustration grew. His insistence that she leave him alone battled with her need to help him.

The wind touched her heated cheeks, soothing her. His next words caused her to pause. "Please, Caitlyn. Live. For me."

She didn't have a choice at the moment so she slowly nodded. "All right. I'll figure out the riddle no matter how difficult it is. Then, I intend to free you, Shay Evers. Believe in me and don't give up hope."

With those words, she sighed and glanced at the building Rhys and Myrielle had entered. She might as well go see them. Maybe they knew something to help her come to terms with what had happened. She squared her shoulders and marched to the doorway, determined to find the answers she needed. Answers that would not only free her, but also release Shay.

Chapter 30

The archway leading into the building was supported by the same columns she'd noticed in her dream, a twisted sapling design carved into solid stone. Instead of feeling amazement over the intricate craftsmanship, she understood now why these same motifs echoed throughout the castle.

Dread pounded through her with each step. Her known world had shattered into a billion pieces, and she didn't know how to fix it.

When she entered the room, Myrielle faced her. Sitting in an armchair near an empty fireplace, the other woman tried to smile. The smile did nothing to hide the grief reflected in the queen's emerald eyes.

A surge of guilt came over Caitlyn. She tensed, her body taut. No, this would not affect her. Steeling her nerves, she approached them.

Rhys stood behind his wife, his hands resting on her shoulders. The tender moment touched Caitlyn's heart. When he noticed her, he straightened and asked, "How are you?"

She gusted out a low laugh. "How do you think I am? I've been living between the real world and this one for almost a week. Reality is shot out the window."

"Here, sit down. All will be explained." He gestured to the chair next to Myrielle.

The seat was covered in brocade, and Caitlyn studied the Celtic design as she sorted through what she wanted to say. She lifted her gaze to Myrielle. "It's not that I don't want you as my mother. I just don't know. All of this is confusing." She released a sigh and sank onto the seat.

For several moments, no one spoke. Happy that the older couple didn't pester her with questions or undying declarations of parental love, she leaned her head against the back of the chair. When a measure of peace returned, she looked at him. "Tell me. Everything. Who's the woman and why does she want me dead?"

He shut his eyes and lowered his head. Caitlyn watched him swallow. He raised his gaze and nodded. For the next several minutes, he spoke of the night she was kidnapped, explaining what had occurred.

"You never suspected either of them?" She needed to find out more than just the details.

"Perhaps Gwyneth, but never Shay." He turned his back to her. "I loved him like a brother. He was closest to me. I trusted him, and he betrayed me."

Her attention perked as she heard the emotion thickening Rhys's voice. He told the truth. She felt it. "Okay, you didn't suspect something was going to happen. Did Gwyneth have a motive for doing this? Shay told me he thought he was helping you, but instead he ended up helping to kidnap me."

Myrielle shook her head and answered. "We have searched for a reason, but we've never found any clue as to why she would commit such a hideous crime against us. She was always quiet, lurking about, watching. I didn't care to have her here, but she was one of the true bloods from our home planet."

"What do mean? True bloods?" Caitlyn straightened in her seat.

"She came here on the colonizing ship," Myrielle said. "There are still many who live that traveled to Earth on the ship. Your father and Shay are of undiluted blood lines."

"I see. No human blood was mixed with theirs. Okay, I know I probably shouldn't ask this, but I can't help it." Caitlyn rubbed her forehead, trying to ease the sudden tension building there. "How long ago was that?"

Myrielle frowned and glanced at Rhys. "How long? Three or four, would you say?"

"Almost four," he grunted.

"Four what?" She looked from Rhys to Myrielle.

His face remained expressionless as he answered. "Four thousand years ago."

Caitlyn felt a surge of bile in her throat. "That's not possible. You only look a few years older than me."

Pride rang out in his voice when he pinned her with his gaze. "Possible? We are the Tylwyth Teg. Space voyagers from the planet Vanir. All things are possible for us. Magic is a way of life, and only through the threat of arms and enchantments are we destroyed."

Realization dawned. "What about fading away?"

A flicker of pain deepened the creases in his face. Myrielle lowered her gaze to the clenched hands in her lap.

He continued with low tone. "And-- We can fade away. That is a last resort. Many become disenchanted with living, so they allow themselves to disappear."

"Physically disappear?"

"Yes."

"Great." Caitlyn had trouble catching her breath. So that was what Shay meant when he'd spoken to her in the library. He was willing to vanish rather than return to his prison. Guilt ate at her. She was the reason he'd entered this place. She winced as she recalled how she'd begged him not to leave her.

No longer able to sit, she came to her feet and paced, trying to relieve some of her tension. "Okay. Gwyneth traveled with you and Shay from your home planet. She had to have known how close you and Shay were. That's the only reason she needed his help. Right?"

Rhys frowned. Myrielle raised her brows and glanced at her husband. Taking their silence as agreement, Caitlyn continued, "She knew if she failed to steal me, then she would still hurt you through Shay. In a way, she was giving a double whammy with one blow. Right?"

His head tilted. "You're assuming her actions were aimed at me. I've thought of that, but I still don't understand why she would want to hurt me."

"Maybe you did or didn't do something that ticked her off a couple of thousand years ago and she took offense," Caitlyn rattled off, pacing. She stopped and gazed at Rhys, the information she'd gathered snapped into place. "What if it wasn't you that she wanted to get even with? What if it was Shay?"

She studied her parents' reactions to her words. Rhys opened his mouth to speak, but he stopped. Myrielle sat forward in the chair, staring up at her husband.

"I don't know," he said, slowly shaking his head. He cast a glance at Caitlyn. "Would you care to see what happened that night?"

"What? Did you video tape it?" She asked. That was not something she'd been prepared to hear.

A low chuckle came from Rhys. The tension seemed to ease. "No. There is a mystic fountain in the garden. You may witness what occurred on that night. Perhaps, you will notice something we failed to see."

"What are you waiting for? Show me. After that I want to hear this riddle," Caitlyn said, grabbing his wrist and tugging him out the door.

Once on the stone path, she allowed him to lead. They passed near the blackthorn tree in the center. She was drawn to the twisted form. The muscles in her chest squeezed around her heart. A fallen bloom lay along the path and she bent, picking it up. Following him, she brought the white flower to her lips.

Her father continued to the opposite side of the garden. Strange how easy that title came to her. He didn't look old enough to be her father. Shay certainly didn't look like he was almost four thousand years old. All this new information played with her mind. The whole situation was beyond her comprehension.

As they approached a small fountain, a chill crawled up her spine. She stopped and glanced around her. Nothing caught her attention, yet unease built within her.

"What's wrong?" Rhys twisted about, his eyes narrowed.

She shook her head. "Nothing. Imagination, I guess. For some reason, it's like my senses are more acute."

He smiled at her. "As they should be. Shay believed the curse Gwyneth placed on you wasn't as strong as we assumed. If you are experiencing extra sensations, perhaps your Tylwyth Teg blood is fighting to come alive. That's good."

"I suppose," Caitlyn murmured, still uneasy. The very air felt wrong. Like an unseen menace watched her. "Where is Gwyneth?"

"Somewhere in the human world. Why?"

"She attacked us tonight. Could she have returned here?" Caitlyn wanted to make sure the presence she sensed wasn't the woman who had threatened her.

"I doubt it. She knows what would happen if she did. My punishment to Shay is mild compared to what I would do to her," Rhys responded without hesitation.

He sounded so confident. Was he that in control of this world? Obviously not, since Gwyneth had managed to kidnap her all those years ago. One lesson Caitlyn had learned growing up, never underestimate someone with a burning desire to achieve a goal. Right now, Gwyneth's goal centered on taking her away from Shay.

Rhys stopped at the fountain and waved a hand over the top of it. "Come, peer into the water. You will see whatever you ask."

Shiny black, the fountain appeared more of a birdbath than a water spouting mechanism. No more than two feet in diameter and about three feet high, the rim consisted of carved orbs. The gaps formed where the spheres connected to the basin overflowed with water and cascaded over the sides into a stone trench encircling the slender pedestal.

"What kind of stone is it carved out of?"

"Onyx. 'Tis fashioned from the best magical quality. Come, look into the basin." He motioned for her to come nearer.

Squeezing the blackthorn bloom in her fist, she questioned if she really wanted to do this. Her dream experiences with Shay came to mind. They weren't so bad.

She leaned over and glanced into the dark water. "Is this like watching television?"

"In a manner."

"Well, that relieves me. In what manner isn't it like TV?" she muttered. Cutting her eyes to her father, she saw him smile.

"It's more personal."

"Oh. That way, huh?"

He nodded.

She took a deep breath and said, "Show me what happened the night I was stolen."

Seconds ticked by, and she concentrated on the mirrored surface of the water. The flower's waxy petals turned to gooey liquid in her palm. Fitful light moved across the water. All sound faded. Caitlyn felt sucked into the light.

Images formed, revealing the glittering clothes of her clan. From the corner of her vision she saw her hand resting on the smooth carved surface of a pillar. No, not her hand. Long and lean, the fingers appeared to belong to her, yet that was impossible.

Her head swerved to the left, and she watched a man approach. He spoke a name and realization shot through her. This wasn't her body. At that moment, she became aware of another's thoughts.

Shay.

This hand, body, they belonged to Shay. She watched through his eyes.

Refusing to allow fear to control her, she focused her attention on him. Then, like a door opening, his thoughts rushed through her mind. Boredom. Intense dissatisfaction spiraled in his head. The joy of living no longer existed in him.

Steeling her emotions, she mentally eased back to experience the night with him.

Chapter 31

Shay tilted his head and glanced past the queen to the petite infant in the bassinet. He marveled at how so much magic existed in such a small body. Radiant light enveloped the babe to a degree that her aura extended several feet.

Beautiful as a pure spring morning, her deep green gaze touched his and held. In that instance, the supreme boredom in his life lifted like a veil, revealing a new and wondrous path for him to follow. Never had he experienced such a surge of excitement as when he stared into the babe's eyes. She smiled at him. His heartbeat halted, and then pounded.

He did not stop to consider the onslaught of new emotions flooding his senses. A need to touch this child one time came to him and he stepped forward, not caring about and without fear of the growing frown on her father's face.

The queen, a gentle smile gracing her beautiful face, eased to one side and allowed Shay to draw near. The newborn princess gurgled in glee and bounced her dainty arms and legs. Going down on one knee, and unable to stop, he reached out. In the bare second it took for her to grasp his finger in her tight clasp, his heart was lost forever.

"I swear 'til my dying hour, I will protect you from all harm," he whispered. The baby's face puckered at the serious tone for only a moment, then she smiled again, causing the aura to increase.

Basking in the power evident in the babe, Shay stayed longer than was usually permitted. The princess was new and many had yet to pay homage to her.

"We have named her Caitlyn, my muse. What think you of it? Is this name fitting for our most precious daughter?" The queen touched the crown of his head, bringing his attention from the babe.

"Aye, it is more than fitting. Pure beauty is truly befitting for her name."

With a deep courtly bow, he stepped off the platform where the bassinet stood. He moved to the shadows surrounding the terrace. Thoughts of Gwyneth and her plans to play a practical joke on the royal couple flooded his mind. Perhaps he should warn the king, yet as he watched, he noted something Gwyneth spoke of. There was a laxness in the king's attitude toward the princess's security.

Anyone with vile intentions could harm the babe if they so chose. Yet, because of the peace within the Tylwyth Teg realm, why should the king worry? Several hundred years had passed since the last war. Their enemies in this dimension and in the human world were no longer a true threat.

"Are you prepared?"

The alluring voice carried a hard note. Shifting to one side, Shay gazed at the self-acclaimed beauty of the Tylwyth Teg court. Gwyneth's cold and calculating eyes studied the princess. Foreboding crept through him.

"Why do I feel you are plotting more than you claim?" He leaned closer, anger rising in him.

The scent of sweet lilacs coated the female elf, but another scent lurked underneath. Slight, but still there, she carried the smell of fresh blood on her. Shay remembered the smell. Its prevalence thousands of years ago when their people fought against the humans was as clear to him now as it was then.

"Nonsense. Do you believe me so stupid as to dare to cross our king? Rhys would have our heads if the babe came to harm," she whispered as she darted a look from side to side.

"I smell blood on you. What have you done? What spells do you plan that I do not know of? Speak now, or I will bind you with my magic and give you over to Rhys." Shay hated liars, and he feared Gwyneth lied to him.

"I cut my finger earlier. Nothing serious."

He frowned. Her explanation was simple and easy to prove, yet his inner senses warned him to beware.

She leaned closer, brushing against his arm. Her scent sickened him. He swallowed against the surge of bile.

"Come now, muse. I have no ill feelings for our liege and his queen, and I have no reason to have any for our new princess. I am beginning to wonder if you are acting the coward, seeking ways to break our contract. Do you wish me to release you?"

Shay stiffened and clasped her wrist. He squeezed, and she released a pain-filled breath. Her eyes widened as he spoke. "I will fulfill my word to you, but I swear, if you harm the babe in any way, I will be the one who removes your beautiful head from your body. So fear not our king, Gwyneth, because I will seek you out and take the life from your body. Heed my words, for I do not foreswear in vain."

"Fool, do you take me for one also?" She slid her gaze toward the queen, before raising her other hand and caressing his cheek. "Be still, they will notice us and grow suspicious. The queen is staring."

Gwyneth stretched up and kissed him on the mouth. He shut his eyes, but kept his lips sealed.

When she drew back, he noticed a callous glint in her eyes. Her words verified her anger. "Why do you draw away from me?"

"We are not lovers, nor shall we ever be. Now leave me. When all are gone from here, we will carry through with your little prank. Just remember, I will be watching." He stepped back into the shadows.

Though he cared little for the witch, proving to Rhys he should take better care of his loved ones served to justify agreeing to this jest. At least, that is what he continued to tell himself. He'd tried several times to approach Rhys but his king had laughed off his concerns as if they were nothing.

The night aged, and many visitors wandered away to seek their own homes and beds. Soon, only the royal family sat on the terrace enjoying the peaceful evening. Shay strode forward and bowed before them.

"With your permission, sire, might I sing a lullaby for the princess?" he spoke evenly, glad that his voice did not crack under the strain of deception. This lie weighed on his soul.

"Oh yes, my muse, sing for us." Myrielle beamed at him, the light in her eyes shining on him.

He bowed once more, then lifted the small harp he held and began to strum a soft melody. The lyrics of the ancient song rolled from his tongue as his magic twined with them. He sent waves of his spell toward the royal couple.

Holl amrantau'r sr ddywedant
Ar hyd y nos.
Golau arall yw tywyllwch
I arddangos gwir bryferthwch
teulu'r nefoedd mew tawelwch
Ar hyd y nos.

The words filtered through his mind. *Sleep, my child, and peace attend thee, all through the night, soft the drowsy hours are creeping, hill and dale in slumber steeping, I, my loving vigil keeping, all through the night.*

Within moments, Myrielle drifted to sleep. Rhys, the stronger of the two, listened to several more lines before his eyelids closed and his head drooped.

The second both slept, Shay, heart pounding, scanned the garden as he continued to strum the harp. Gwyneth stepped from the shadows near the scrying fountain. A satisfied smirk of pleasure covered her features. She crossed the garden, brushing past him on her way to the bassinet.

Shay heard a soft cooing before she bent and lifted the babe. Wicked, scalding laughter erupted from her, and she began to speak.

"This babe will suffer the torments of the human world until her twenty-fifth birthday when the curse is fulfilled and she dies. At that time, my vengeance will know satisfaction. For until she returns to her people, the Tylwyth Teg, and solves the riddle binding the curse, she will have no hope."

The words sent ice rushing through his veins. He shook his head. No, he must stop her. He raised one foot to move forward, but halted when the woman, clutching the babe, disappeared into a thick black mist. A sulfuric stench filled the air, burning his eyes and nose.

A shout from Rhys, King of the Tylwyth Teg, echoed through the walled garden.

The harp Shay strummed moments earlier fell from his fingers to shatter on the stone. He opened then closed his mouth. Coherent words refused to form.

Gwyneth had lied to him.

Used him, and now, deserted him.

He shifted his gaze toward Rhys, standing on the terrace. An ice blue stare, shimmering with frozen fires locked with his. The king's face appeared waxy, but then flared with heat.

"Traitor. You aided her." He moved toward him, past the bassinet, to the terrace's edge.

Sorrow traced the queen's cry when she reached the bassinet and lifted a bundle. "She has left a babe. A dead human baby--a changeling."

Myrielle looked toward Shay. Tears filled her emerald green eyes to fall. Her misery, so great over her loss, was palpable. He opened his mouth once more to deny Rhys's accusation, but the words refused to pass his lips. He was at fault. There was no one else to blame for this. His heart ached for the wrong he'd done to the very ones he adored above all others.

Movement from the outer edges of the walled garden forced his gaze away. The royal guard stepped nearer, their weapons ready to prevent his escape. Fools. Dry, gasping laughter erupted from his mouth. Pride prevented him from fleeing his rightful punishment.

Stupid youths. Did they not know who they dealt with? A true Tylwyth Teg who remained from the ones arriving in ships of clouds on this world over five thousand years ago, his power could match that of his king if he desired it. But he did not. At this, he chose not to prove his abilities to the young warriors.

Thunder bellowed. Lightning flashed in a brilliant flare. Shay shuddered and looked back at Rhys. The king, muttering ancient words, rose and levitated several feet above the ground. His golden hair drifted and swirled around his head and body. The strands joined with the next bolt until Shay could not separate them.

The stone beneath his feet cracked and split. He dropped six inches into a rip, and his feet ached from the slight fall. He glanced down. Long coiled roots tore through his boots.

"No." He jerked his head up, his gaze riveted on his king's features. "I did not know what she would do. I beg mercy. Let me find her."

Thunder roared. Rhys pointed at him. "Liar. For some time, I have felt a wicked restlessness in your spirit. I hoped it would pass, but no, you desired to see what bedevilment you could stir. Your punishment will last for eternity, even until the stars fade. This is my wish for you, betrayer." He raised both hands, palms out, and spoke three last words.

Shay tried to shake his head, but his spine solidified, the bones fusing. He lifted a hand in supplication to his king. Flesh cracked and peeled before turning black. Thorns erupted from his tightened skin. He opened his mouth and felt his face fracture under the dry, hardening effect of Rhys's spell.

"Live your life in this hell, for into a blackthorn you will go, never to be released, unless I decree it. Here you will stay to remind me of my error in keeping faith with one such as you."

Shay shouted but the sound fell silent, a last gust of breath as muscles and bones knotted and his hair rose outward. His body hardened, narrowed with twigs and leaves sprouting from his skin until he was a mass of solidified wood. Blinded by pain, struggling for breath, he tried to fight the spell engulfing him.

When the transformation finished, he was aware of Rhys standing in front of him. He saw all around him at once, yet could not move. The pores and cells of his new form gulped much-needed air. He would live.

The queen approached, her eyes filled with sorrow. For him? No, only for her lost child. He did not expect pity or understanding from the royal couple.

"She left this on the babe," the queen spoke, handing a parchment scrap to Rhys.

Shay listened to the words of the riddle as the king read them aloud.

"A key you need to unlock the heart, look ye close to the peeling bark. For beneath the roots lies the key to unlock the heart for eternity. Two powers unite and be as one. True and strong, it will be done, if you trod the right road to pay the price for which you owe."

When he finished, his ice blue gaze shifted to Shay.

"Do not fear, *my friend*. We will find my beloved daughter. She and I will tend you with the utmost care so your years will be long. I would not want you to wither."

Rhys had never spoken to him in such a cruel manner in all their years together. Now, he verified how deeply the pain went with the sarcastic words. The queen sobbed, and her husband wrapped his arms around her. He lifted her and turned away.

A windy gust swirled through the branches on the tree, tearing several leaves free. Spiraling to the stone ground, they scattered across the garden, slowly withering, death bearing down on them. Shay envied them.

* * * *

Strong hands gripped Caitlyn's upper arms, pulling her from the fountain. Her mind tore from Shay's like Velcro coming apart. She wanted to scream, shout and rail at Rhys.

The pain Shay suffered shredded her heart. She experienced every fraction of the ripping wounds on his body. Because of what he'd no control over, he bore the wrath of her father. He'd realized too late the choice he'd made was wrong. Now, he was doing what was right and still Rhys refused to forgive him.

Chapter 32

"What did you see?" Rhys said, holding her by the arms.

Steely fingers pried Caitlyn's from the surface of the spheres surrounding the fountain's rim. She tried to draw in air but found it almost impossible. Shay's agony remained in her mind. His dissatisfaction threaded through the pain, followed by the rise of emotion when he'd reacted to the baby exploded through it all to bring swift enlightenment to her.

She was the one he'd given his heart to all those years before.

The muscles in her body refused to work. Numbness filled the tendons and cords, making it difficult to speak. A sob left her in a gush of air.

She opened her eyes and sought Rhys's. "He loved you. Wanted to keep you and your family safe. Oh, there was so much going on inside him. There were so many doubts about what Gwyneth planned but he wanted you to see there was true danger lurking around. He only wanted to help you."

Her hoarse voice echoed with misery and sorrow as she struggled to speak. "How could you do this to him? He suffers right now because of the wounds and guilt he experiences. It's nonstop for him while he's in that form. How can you live with yourself?"

Rhys didn't answer right away. With his arms about her shoulders, he guided her to the bench near the blackthorn. Caitlyn stared at the tree. Tears threatened.

Shay.

Rhys knelt in front of her, bringing her attention to him. A glimmer of sorrow reflected in his blue gaze. "I cannot rescind my judgment. Chaos would follow. Remember, my daughter, I am king to the Tylwyth Teg. My duty to the protection and well-being of my clan must come first. If one attacks the clan, I must, and will, retaliate in a manner befitting the action. What Shay did violated not only the clan and our system of life, but it was aimed personally at me. I cannot relent on this matter."

"He wanted to you to strengthen your guard. He was trying to help you but you wouldn't listen." No matter how hard Caitlyn tried, she doubted she'd convince Rhys. Stubborn man. "This is exactly what Shay went through all those years ago."

"Because one wants to help does not mean that their help is right. Shay knew the chance he took. He knew. Because of this, he did not fight his sentence. Even now, he could have chosen not to return. He did so with the full knowledge that his sentence would resume."

Rhys reached up as he finished speaking and gently tucked a strand of her hair over her ear. Not only did grief radiate from his gaze, but something more. Caitlyn sensed that he wanted to release Shay.

"He brought me back. Isn't that grounds for a possible pardon? He is changed. He won't do something like this ever again. I know he won't," she cried, then stopped. "Great, now I'm begging. I don't beg. Not to anyone."

Spine stiff, she scooted sideways on the bench. The stone edge beneath her rear pressed into her skin, waking up numbed nerve endings throughout her body. A cool touch on the nape of her neck caused her to jerk around.

Myrielle leaned over her. "Come, Caitlyn. Rest for the night. When morning comes, you will be refreshed so you might solve the riddle quicker. Come, daughter."

Numbness returned, only this time instead of her thoughts remaining clear and focused, a strong desire to sleep washed over her. More magic. Her eyelids drooped. She hated magic.

Strong arms encircled her shoulders and slid under her knees, lifting her up. Eyes heavy, she rolled her head against solid muscle covered by fine velvet. Rhys's blue gaze caught hers and he smiled.

"Sleep, Caitlyn."

With the soft spoken command, she closed her eyes and drifted off.

* * * *

Birds trilled and Caitlyn stirred within the warm cocoon of blankets. Sluggish, she cracked open her eyes. Sunlight streamed through the open windows and doorway across from her. The arched entrance revealed trees swaying in the gentle breeze.

She smiled and stretched. A sharp stab of awareness shot through her. Someone was with her. She sensed their life force. Frowning, she remained still, listening. Several moments passed with the buzzing of the insects and the chirping of the birds the only sounds around her, then a faint noise reached her. Wood shifting.

An accented voice came to her. "I know ye be awake, princess. Are ye planning to stay abed for the rest of the morn, or do ye wish to rise up and help yerself and yer Shay?"

Grazelda. There was no mistaking the woman's voice.

She sat up and searched the room. Drawing her knees to her chest, she saw Grazelda. There before the empty hearth, Shay's housekeeper sat in a straight-backed chair. After a deep breath, Caitlyn questioned her, "You're one of them, too?"

The elderly woman cackled. "One of them? We, all of us that were closest to Shay, are ones. As ye are, sweetling. Now, up with ye."

Resting her cheek on her bent knees, Caitlyn sighed. "Get up for what? As soon as I find out some new information that upsets me, Rhys and Myrielle will put me to sleep. I wish they wouldn't do that."

"Then tell 'em not to. They may not like it, but they will abide by yer wishes."

Caitlyn shifted so her chin dug into her kneecap. She studied the old woman. "Tell me about Shay and Gwyneth."

"Tell ye what?"

She waved a hand around. "What were they like? What made them do what they did? Do you believe Shay is innocent?"

Grazelda glanced at her. An audible gush of air escaped her as she rose from the chair. "Shay is a loving, sweet-natured youth."

Caitlyn lifted a brow at the old woman's last choice of word as she described Shay. At almost four thousand years old, he was not a youth. Deciding not to argue the point, she prompted Grazelda. "And Gwyneth?"

A look of disgust washed over the old woman's features.

Grazelda ambled to the bed and stood gazing at Caitlyn. When she spoke, she left no doubt of her feelings for Gwyneth. "She thought too much of herself. Always with airs about her. She considered most of the clan inferior. She, after all, is the youngest sister to the ruler of our home planet. Overlord Tyr taught Gwyneth all she knew about status and order. She never understood, that when we arrived here, what always served on Vanir did not apply to this new and wondrous planet."

"So, she was more or less an outsider with the clan. Didn't fit in?"

"Aye, never tried."

For a moment, Caitlyn considered this. "Do you think she wanted to? That, maybe, she thought this would be a way of getting someone to notice her?"

"If so, 'twas strange indeed. She liked the dark arts, always brewing potions and whatnot. Rhys reprimanded her many times for dabbling into what she ought not to. I always thought this was her revenge on him for doing so." Grazelda held a length of material. "Here, get dressed, dearie. The king has decided to allow you to speak with every clan member."

"How kind of him," she muttered.

The deep emerald green cloth turned out to be a dress. Fitted across the top of her body like a second skin, it flared in flowing skeins to her feet.

Grazelda brought a gold ringed belt and encircled the top of Caitlyn's hips with it. Bands of beaten gold were added to her arms above the elbow. The final touch came in the form of a thin gold band placed across her brow. With her hair down, she almost didn't recognize herself in the standing mirror. The shade of the dress echoed her eyes, intensifying the color.

She glanced at the vines cascading down the walls behind the mirror, tensing as she waited for one to aim at her hair. Nothing happened. Breathing a sigh of relief, she faced Grazelda.

"I'm dressed. Now what?

The old woman cocked her head. Her movements were spryer here than they had been in the human world.

"I don't mean to be nosy, but how old are you?" Caitlyn studied the woman's features.

Yes, she was right. The deep age lines were not as distinct here. Also, her accent seemed more pronounced. Was this a carryover from her home world, or had the elderly woman preferred the old way of speaking to the modern world's?

Grazelda cackled. "I be much older than any in this place. I came here as nanny to the fledglings on board. I was already close to ten thousand Earth years at that time. Now, you must understand. The passage of years here and on our birth planet is different from each other. What would be a thousand years on this Earth is roughly five years on Vanir. So by human standards, we, the Tylwyth Teg, are considered immortals. By human standards, I am almost fifteen thousand years old."

Caitlyn swallowed. "Has anyone ever returned to your home planet?"

"Ah, nay, sweetling. 'Twould serve no purpose. Shortly after we arrived here, we felt a great unsettling in the life force of the universe. Our home is no more. The surge of grief and pain coming from Vanir has led us to believe the ones left behind were destroyed." The old woman grasped Caitlyn's arm and steered her toward the arched doorway. "Come along. Ye must see the riddle and begin to search for the answer."

Her heart remained torn between disbelieving all that had occurred and wanting to figure out not only the riddle but how to free Shay. Confused, she allowed Grazelda to lead her from the room. The gardens spread before them in a glorious array of colors.

Unable to stop herself, she looked at the blackthorn tree. The breeze swayed the top branches. There weren't any leaves on the limbs, just the white blooms. So odd. What had Shay said about the tree? *It blooms in spring before the leaves come out.*

Men and women roamed the stone paths winding through the gardens. None went near the tree. Did they fear Rhys would do to them what he had to Shay if they approached the tree? Or did they despise Shay for his part in her kidnapping? Of course, they probably were used to seeing him in the tree form. After all, twenty-five years had passed since she'd been taken.

"Where are my parents?" She searched the people, but didn't see Rhys or Myrielle.

Grazelda waved an arm toward a building further down the covered terrace, to the left of her room. "They wait in the hall. First, though, ye must read the riddle. 'Tis there. Rhys had it carved onto a stone and placed at the foot of the tree as a reminder to him and all the clan of Shay's crime."

Caitlyn pulled her arm free and hurried to the blackthorn. The darkness last night prevented her from seeing the plaque. There, in granite next to the bench, was the riddle. She focused on the strange letters covering the angled surface. They blurred, then came into focus.

At first, she didn't understand the meaning of the foreign words. Then, as if a light switched on, they appeared in English. A chill raced up her back. She didn't know if she would ever get use to this bizarre place.

She read out loud, the words slipping from her tongue. "A key you need to unlock the heart, look ye close to the peeling bark. For beneath the roots lies the key to unlock the heart for eternity. Two powers unite and be as one. True and strong, it will be done, if you trod the right road to pay the price for which you owe."

Great. The meaning stumped her. How could she figure this out before her birthday? Only a few days remained until she turned twenty-five. Every line reminded her of what Shay had said in the small office in Los Angeles. Poetic phrases. This topped everything that had happened to her.

"What tree has a peeling bark?" She shot a glance at Grazelda.

"Might not be a tree, dearie. That's one thing about riddles, sometimes the simplest ones are the hardest to unravel," the old woman commented. She winked at the tree and continued. "Good morn to ye, young Shay. How are ye today?"

The breeze rattled the branches and his voice, low and weak, washed over Caitlyn. "Been better. How are you, Caitlyn? Rested some, since last evening?"

She swallowed around the sudden lump in her throat. It took her several seconds before she was able to fight back the sting of tears in her eyes. "Yes, I did. I'm ready to start unraveling this puzzle. Do you have any ideas what the answer might be?"

No sound came to her on the breeze. Realization hit her. "You can't tell me, can you? I have to figure it out by myself."

She took a deep breath and faced the garden, turning her back to the tree. "Okay, where do we start? I need paper, pens--my computer would be great. Can you get those for me, Grazelda?"

"Don't need yer computer. We have no way of making it work here," Grazelda commented as she moved to the building where Caitlyn's parents were.

"Wonderful." One less helpful tool. She trailed behind the woman.

Chapter 33

Caitlyn entered the stone archway leading to a huge room. At the far end stood two regal high-backed chairs. Inlaid with gold, the chairs radiated a brilliant glow. Rhys and Myrielle rose from the seats and approached her.

They each greeted her with a kiss on her cheek. Myrielle clasped her hand and led her to a round table on the far side of the hall. Three chairs awaited them. Rhys pulled one out for Caitlyn, then another for Myrielle.

For a few seconds, she studied the couple. They claimed they were her parents. Would she ever see them that way? Shaking her head, she stopped that train of thought and spoke. "I've read the riddle, now what do I do? I'm lost here, so a little help is appreciated."

"What do you want to know?" he asked, his eyes bluer than normal. A light shone from them. It suddenly occurred to her, it must be a reflection of his joy at having her here with them. They loved her. The proof lay in their gazes.

"How do I start? What is the key she's talking about? Where's the tree that is peeling? What are the two powers to unite, and how do I know that I'm on the right road?"

He glanced at Myrielle before he answered. "The peeling bark, we assume, is a sycamore tree. We've searched all in the Sidhe and found nothing. The key could be anything, as could the two powers. We are as lost as you. The only way to solve it is to work together."

"Well, that cheers me up." Caitlyn didn't try to keep the sarcasm from her voice. Frustrated, she continued, "What about the clan? Do you think any of them might help solve this puzzle?"

"They are all willing to help you. There is not one of them who wish you harm," he said, standing. "I will ask the first to come in to speak to you."

"Not one? You're wrong. There was one and there could be others. I want to talk to them alone. I have a feeling they'll open up more if you and Myrielle aren't there," Caitlyn said. She glared up at the tall blond for several seconds, waiting for him to respond.

The muscle in his jaw twitched. He bowed his head and said, "It will be as you wish. But there will be guards close by. I will not risk the witch having a spy among us."

He turned to Myrielle and held out his hand. She rose and glided to him, placing her fingers on his palm. "I will send the first one in to you."

"Thanks." Caitlyn didn't allow them to see how torn she was by all this.

She certainly didn't want to argue about the guards, when he'd conceded to her about interviewing the others alone. Clasping her trembling fingers together, she waited for the first person to arrive.

Paper and pen arrived with a handsome man. He looked like a normal teenager. Long dark hair fell about his shoulders, the right side braided in a five strand plait. His sweet, innocent smile reminded her of Shay. A pang of grief flashed in her chest. "How old are you?"

His blue eyes sparkled and a wide grin split his face. "I'm a hundred and fifty, your highness."

She winced. "Don't call me that. My name is Caitlyn."

He only grinned wider before striding toward the door.

For the rest of the morning, she questioned each of the clan members. A tray of food appeared with a bevy of women. They laid the plates of raw vegetables, fruits, cheeses and bread on the table within reach. Goblets and a pitcher stood in the middle of the round surface.

Glad for the break, she ate. One woman filled the goblet, and Caitlyn realized with the first sip, it was water. Clear and clean, the liquid was ice cold. She frowned. More magic.

The afternoon passed in much the same way as the morning. With the light fading, she glanced out a window and watched the sun sink over the horizon. The day had gone by too fast.

Gathering the papers and pen, she returned to her room. Working by candlelight, she went over all the notes she'd taken during the day. Nothing struck her as important in all the things the clan told her. Of course, she still had quite a few to speak to before she was finished, but she'd hoped to have something to work with by tonight.

Exhausted, she stood and stretched. She moved toward the door. Without thinking, she walked into the garden. Several minutes later, she stood next to the blackthorn.

She sat on the bench and stared at the tree.

"Hello," she whispered.

The breeze washed her over. "You look tired."

She drew her knees to her chest and wrapped her arms about them. "I am. I'm not any closer to the answer than I was this morning."

A low chuckle reached her.

She glared at the tree. "There's nothing funny about this situation, Shay Evers."

"I wanted the fires to blaze in you. Like now. You need to feel, not just exist."

Had that been how she lived her life? Existing and not living? Yes, she supposed so. "Why can't you help me with the riddle?"

"I don't want to cloud your mind. You must discover it on your own."

"Without your help?" She tilted her head back. Stars filled the clear sky. She laid her cheek on her knees and whispered, "I miss you."

Silence answered her.

Knowing he wouldn't comment, she changed the subject. "Are you in pain?"

"No more than usual. Go to bed, Caitlyn. Rest for the night. You need all your senses fresh, and to be at ease so you can live."

Refusing to respond right away, she sat in silence. Several minutes later, she fought the sudden urge to fall asleep. She jerked upright and accused, "Stop trying to make me sleep."

"Go."

"All right. I wish everyone would stop trying to make me go to sleep. Especially when I don't want to," she muttered. Shoving away from the bench, she stood. With her back to the tree, she whispered, "Good night and sweet dreams."

Silence reigned in the garden as she strolled to her room, accompanied only by the fragrance of the flowers blooming. Once she entered the door, she glanced at the papers strewn over the top of the table on the far side of the room. She considered working more on unraveling the riddle.

So far, she hadn't received any new information. She'd do as Shay wanted, and hopefully, tomorrow something new would come to her. Stretching, she undressed and climbed under the silken spread and fell asleep.

She woke the next day, groggy and disoriented. Her sleep had been filled with strange dreams and images. A faceless woman had pursued her through a maze of hallways. When she finally reached the middle, she saw a blackthorn tree in bloom. Joy had filled her at the sight, but before she could reach the tree, it exploded in a burst of flames and cinders.

Sorrow had gripped her. At that moment, the woman had found her and blackness filled her.

Was this dream a premonition, or with all the strange occurrences, was she losing her sanity? Exhausted, she rose and discovered a different dress placed over the back of the chair in front of the hearth. The burgundy velvet bordered with gold and silver inlay draped her body much as the dress from yesterday. Bell sleeves reminded her of drawings of medieval attire from her art history class. The golden band had disappeared and in its place, one of filigreed gold and silver waited for her on the dressing chest next to the mirror.

Shrugging, she placed the band on her brow. She gathered her materials and headed for the hall.

* * * *

Six days later, and no nearer to an answer, Caitlyn sat at the table. Frustration stayed with her and made the tension in her increase every day. She waited as an old man approach. Silver hair hung down his back to his knees. A thick, five-strand braid held his hair away from his face. His clothes glimmered with greens and reds as he walked toward her.

He bowed low and when he straightened, he cocked his head. Keen gray eyes seemed to bore into hers. "So, ye've not discovered the answer, have ye?"

Caitlyn winced. She felt hopeless enough without having someone voicing it out loud. "No. I haven't. Do you know something that might help me?"

"Perhaps. I am Saurian, uncle to Shay. 'Tis a fine predicament you're in, my lovely." He pulled a chair out and sat across from her.

Surprised, she stared at Shay's uncle. She didn't know if she liked him or not. His eyes seemed to laugh at her. "And you find that funny?"

"Aye, indeed. Ye're spending all this time and effort in asking about Shay, Gwyneth and what everyone else thinks the answer to the riddle is, but ye've never looked to your heart to solve it."

His words froze Caitlyn. She studied him. Though his skin was smooth and his eyes bright, an aged wisdom radiated from him. He was probably older than Grazelda. She shook her head. "So, how do you suggest I do that?'

"Think of what you desire the most. Can you name it?" He leaned forward, spreading his hands on the table's surface.

He allowed her only a few seconds to think about his question then he snapped, "Answer me, princess. Of all things you could desire, what is the most important? What have you wanted most in all your life?"

Judith Leger

She locked gazes with him. Images of Shay filtered through her. No, that wasn't realistic. They were daydreams, not real.

"I don't know." She took a deep breath. What did she want? "I guess a normal life. It'd be nice to have friends and family and..."

"And Shay? Do you want him, or do you wish only to free him?"

"I want to free him."

"Do you? And for what purpose? Do you want him? What would you do if you had him? Think about these questions, my dear. Think long and hard, for you have only 'til midnight to solve the riddle. If you don't, then you will lose all you hold dear, including your life." With those words, Saurian rose and strode from the hall.

Caitlyn watched him leave, contemplating his questions. What did she want? To free Shay, of course. But what happened after that? She frowned and worried her bottom lip with her teeth. She didn't know. How could she? All her goals and dreams of becoming a top reporter had ceased being important. Without that, what did she want?

She motioned for the next person to come forward. After several minutes of the same repetition of information she'd heard over the last few days, Caitlyn ended the interview. She told the youth to send the remaining clan members away. Compiling all the sheets of paper, she cleared off the table and wandered to her room. Saurian's questions whirled through her thoughts. What did she want?

Shay.

Did she really want him? Did he want her? In the dreams she'd experienced, he'd shown he cared for her, but did he feel the same way out of the dream?

Should she take the chance and tell him how she felt? She rubbed her throbbing temple. She loved him, but what if he didn't feel the same way? How could she open her heart to him and take the chance he might reject her? She stopped walking. The papers and pens she gripped dropped to the stone path.

Open her heart.

Blood pounded through her veins.

Open her heart.

She shot a glance toward the blackthorn. If she didn't tell Shay how she felt, her heart would remain locked. Excitement and fear whipped through her. Was this the answer for the riddle? But what did this have to do with a peeling tree and roots? What were the two powers? Magical powers? Hers and Shay's uniting? The pieces of the puzzle fell and locked into place. Only two were missing, and she hoped as she rushed toward the tree that they, too, would come to her.

Dark clouds formed in the sky. She frowned, throwing a glare over her shoulder. The weather had been perfect the entire time she was in the Sidhe. Now, today, her last if she didn't solve the riddle, it looked as if the perfect weather was at an end. Thunder rumbled and a fork of light speared from the black clouds. The wind carried the scent of moisture to her. Rain would soon come.

Worried the weather would catch her, she sprinted the distance separating her from the tree.

"Shay?"

"You're early today."

"It's my last day."

"I know."

Tears threatened to stop her. She swallowed, fighting the sentimental weakness. "I have to ask you a question. I need to know the truth."

Silence came to her.

"Shay, please."

Low laughter echoed across the garden. Caitlyn stiffened. The sound came from near the fountain. She shifted her gaze and searched for whoever was there. Thunder boomed, and she jumped. A malicious force radiated from the darkened area around the fountain. Lightning flashed and she saw the outline of a woman.

Caitlyn stepped back. She glanced over her shoulder toward the hall and the living quarters. Nothing stirred. Where was everyone? The guards? Rhys? Myrielle?

"Tell me, Caitlyn, what question do you wish to ask of Shay?"

The sweet lyrical words soothed her frazzled nerve endings. The voice sounded familiar, but she couldn't recall where she'd heard it. Fear built in her.

"Who are you?" she whispered, facing the fountain once more.

"You know who I am," the woman said. Shadows dispelled and she glided into the light.

Black spots appeared before Caitlyn's eyes. Her heart raced, and she had trouble catching her breath. Never in all her imagination would she have believed the true identity of her enemy. Now the woman stood before her and there wasn't any doubt.

When she spoke, the name came out sounding more like a croak. "Marcy?"

Ringing laughter prickled the hair on the back of her neck.

In low tones, Shay commanded her to flee. But fear rooted her feet to the ground, as secure as the blackthorn to the soil.

"And who else did you expect?" Marcy's golden hair billowed about her head and shoulders. She wore faded jeans and an old t-shirt. Caitlyn blinked, struggling to catch her breath. Marcy's favorite perfume reached her on the wind. Nausea roiled her stomach.

Her friend's figure shimmered and reformed. Blake's ruffled dark hair fell across his forehead. A deep-throated chuckle escaped him.

Caitlyn, surprised and frightened, shook her head. "How?"

He smirked. "I have a touch of faery blood in me. Very simple, really. Why do you think your precious Shay and your most haughty king couldn't sense me?"

"Where are they? What have you done with them?" Caitlyn demanded. Fear for her own safety was forgotten, replaced with concern for her friends.

The photographer's body rippled and another figure came into focus. More beautiful than Marcy, hair longer, the woman wore a long scarlet gown. The front dipped, revealing a great amount of skin and the top curve of her breasts. When she glided nearer, Caitlyn noticed the skirt was split on each side to reveal the slender length of her legs. Gwyneth had revealed her true form.

"Oblivious to what is happening around them. Marcy's lying in that traitor Dafydd's arms, and Blake is sitting in front of the movie screen in the castle's viewing room. It's a replica spell. They are unaware I took their places when needed. And with enough thought replacement, they'd never know what happened to them. Don't worry Caitlyn, they served their purpose and are now free from my spells. But please, don't let me stop you. What did you wish to ask Shay?" Gwyneth smirked, a cold glint shining in her eyes.

"Why? How could you use my friends? I thought-- You were-- Why?" Caitlyn shook her head. This couldn't be happening.

"You thought what? That I was your friend? I was. Wasn't I there for you every time you needed someone? Didn't I tell you how much help you needed to improve your looks? What about all the time I told you how hard it would be for you to ever find a man? But for you not to worry, because I was there for you?"

Gwyneth finished speaking and laughed. An insane note rang out with the laughter, and Caitlyn shivered. "I thought for sure when you were thrown from the car the other day you would die and this would all be over, but you didn't."

"Was that why you were so rattled after the accident? You were upset because I lived?" Anger lit in Caitlyn. The flame flickered then burst to a burning torch. "What did I ever do to you? Why are you doing this to me?"

"Not to you, Catey, dear," Gwyneth said, cutting her gaze to the blackthorn. "This was never aimed solely at you. You are simply a stupid, innocent pawn."

Chapter 34

"You're trying to hurt Shay? Through me?" Caitlyn stared in horror at the blonde. "I guess you're going to tell me that you love him and if you can't have him, no one can?"

"Isn't that the way of things? I've always wanted him, but he never desired me. I hoped every day he would have a change of heart. I even consulted the fountain. Normally, it will not show the future, but I have knowledge of how to make it reveal its secrets. I saw in the scrying fountain weeks before the night you stole his heart. I knew then I would never have him. So if he doesn't want me, then why should he have you?"

Incredulous, Caitlyn shouted above the next rumble of thunder. "You're nuts. What made you think that I would fall in love with him? I was only a baby."

"Ah, but Shay has a wonderful way about him, doesn't he? I knew it was just a matter of time, and you would be grown and he would court you. Now, what do I do with you? Have you figured out the riddle?" Gwyneth stopped a few feet from her. She tilted her head, studying Caitlyn.

"As a matter of fact, I have. Once I say the answer you won't be able to hurt us anymore. Rhys will come any minute, and he'll punish you for what you've done."

Caitlyn stiffened her spine and raised her chin, gazing down the line of her nose at the woman before her. This person wasn't her friend. The woman had used, lied and betrayed her. She didn't care what Rhys did to the crazy woman.

Gwyneth laughed. "Your father is behind the shield I placed around the garden. He cannot enter and you cannot leave. Interesting, wouldn't you say? I hold the power over you now, Caitlyn. Poor dear, all your hope is gone."

She edged to the side, keeping an eye on Gwyneth but still able to see Shay. As she moved, she noticed movement from the tree. Unable to stop herself, she glanced in the direction and saw a thin layer of the bark peel from the top branch to the bottom of the trunk. The layer dissolved into sparkling dust. Her mouth fell open. "What happened? Shay, what was that?"

Shay had remained silent during her confrontation with Marcy, but now she heard his voice in the wind. "'Tis my skin. It sheds every so often. Quickly, Caitlyn, solve the riddle. Save yourself. Now, do not wait."

Shocked by what she'd just seen, she took a deep breath and started to speak, but a flame burst at the foot of the tree. She gasped, fear escalating. Gwyneth cackled behind her.

"No," Caitlyn cried.

She grabbed handfuls of soil and threw them on the fire. The flames licked higher up the sides of the trunk. Desperate, she tried covering the fire with the bottom of her skirt, hoping to smother it, but the blazing tongues only increased. The odor of singed velvet permeated the air.

Panic rose in billowing waves inside Caitlyn. From behind her, Shay spoke. His beloved voice rang out reciting a chant. The lyrical words rose on the wind. Rain began to pour from the black clouds.

"Oh, very good, Shay. I wondered if Rhys had completely shut off your powers. I suppose not. They won't help you, though." Gwyneth sneered and raised a hand. She brought it down toward Shay. Lightning struck midway on the left side of the trunk. The wood splintered. He screamed.

Caitlyn, thrown by the force of the strike, landed on her rear several feet away. She shouted his name as the tree tilted. Rain, mixed with her tears, streamed down her face.

Fury filled her. With a cry, she struggled to her feet. "Leave him alone."

"And what will you do? Use your magic on me?" Tilting her head back, Gwyneth cackled. "Oh, I am so frightened."

Without thinking, Caitlyn leapt toward her. Raising a fist, she swung with all her rage behind it. Gwyneth, not expecting a physical attack, went down under the hit. Breathing hard, Caitlyn loomed over her, waiting for Gwyneth to make another move.

Instead of cringing in fear, the fallen woman chuckled and swiped the back of her hand across her mouth. Blood smeared over her lips and cheek. In a fluid movement, she kicked out at Caitlyn's right thigh. Numbness filled her muscle, and she went down to her knee.

Gwyneth rolled to her feet and stood several feet away from her. "Big mistake, Catey, dear. I'd hoped to finish this without too much blood and grief, but you have sealed your fate."

Her eyes widened and she raised both hands. Caitlyn struggled to rise. When she gained her feet, she hopped and limped to stand in front of the tree. The air crackled and surged with an overabundance of power.

"No, you won't harm him. I won't let you." She spread her arms out to the side. Her blood pounded, and she closed her eyes in concentration. She let go of her worldly viewpoints and attitudes, calling forth the abilities etched on her soul, whispering, "For Shay."

A bolt came down from the left and Caitlyn, sensing it, opened her mouth. The words flowed out of her to redirect the current. She cracked open her eyes, and watched it sizzle across the garden before landing against a stone column. Dust and stones flew from the granite.

The witch howled and sent more lightning toward them, but as she shouted, she kept her focus on Gwyneth. Three jagged lances of electricity flashed toward Shay. Determined, Caitlyn didn't stop. The lightning curved and struck Gwyneth with an explosion. A high pitched cry ended in a choking gurgle.

The ground shifted beneath Caitlyn's feet, and she fell to the side. Gasping in the smoke-filled air, she stared at the burned body of the woman who had been determined to destroy her. She took a shallow breath, hoping to calm down, and turned toward the blackthorn. Tilting more to one side after the blast, the tree had come loose from the soaked ground.

The tree was falling. She bounded to her feet. She had to stop the tree. Shay. Ignoring the thorns digging into her skin, she wrapped her arms around the slender trunk and held on, but the weight jerked her to the ground.

Sobs tore through her.

"No," she cried. "I haven't told you yet. Don't die on me, Shay Evers."

Blinded by tears, she tried to cover the roots with dirt. She grasped the trunk closer to the branches and worked to upright the tree. Her hands and arms bled from a thousand tiny cuts where the thorns pierced her skin.

Exhausted, she fell to her knees. Sobbing, hysterical, she smeared the mud over the roots, mixing her blood and tears.

Finally, giving up, she placed her cheek against the black wood and whispered, "I never told you how much I love you."

A gentle hand touched her shoulder. She refused to look. Rhys spoke, ordering Gwyneth's remains taken from the garden. Caitlyn didn't care. Shay was gone, lost to her.

Rhys grasped her upper arms. She whimpered. "Caitlyn, come, love."

She pulled away with a growl. "Leave me alone. Haven't we suffered enough? Let me stay with him for a while."

As she spoke, a low humming vibration came from the trunk. She frowned and stared. Lights flickered all around the tree.

Rhys gripped her under her arms and hauled her several feet away. She glanced up at him. Surprise lined his face. He met her gaze. "Watch, Caitlyn."

The vibrations increased, as did the humming. The sound and movement raced across the ground and rushed over her body. A force tugged her toward the tree. Her father let go of her and she was pulled back to the tree. With barely two feet separating her from the wood, the blackthorn rose upright. Rays of light burst from the twisted bark. She gasped.

Heat gathered in her fingers. She glanced down to see the rays coming from her. The light intensified until it blinded her. Her chest grew tight around her heart as if the organ would explode. A second later it did. White hot beams blasted from between her breasts.

Knowledge filled her. She sensed every molecule of matter, to the tiniest atom. She was physically blinded by the light as her eyes opened wider. She saw with an inner sight.

Past images appeared of the Tylwyth Teg arriving on this planet. A younger, innocent Shay walked the pristine meadows and forests, striding beside a golden-haired youth. Her father, Rhys, sharing his hopes and dreams for the future.

In a flash of brilliance, the future appeared. A small boy raced ahead of her toward a meadow. The green grass and bright yellow flowers fluttered with a gentle breeze. When he turned and grinned, her heart stilled for a moment. He possessed Shay's features, but looked at her with eyes of deep emerald green.

A sob escaped her. Intense joy swept over her, and the force of the light slowly dwindled. Standing before her, bruised and bloodied, and no longer in the form of a blackthorn, Shay lifted a finger and followed the line of her nose. She gasped, taking a step closer.

He lived.

"Hello," he murmured, tracing her eyebrows, and then her lips with a lean finger.

She smiled through her tears, unable to pull her gaze away from his bright amethyst eyes.

"So, you love me, do you?" he asked, a shy little boy smile gracing his lips.

"More than life," she whispered, then laughed through her tears. "So, do you love me?"

He nodded slowly. "Without you, there is no magic in my life. Stay with me, here in this place. Give me a reason to go on and not to fade away."

"Oh, don't worry about that. If you even consider doing that, I'll turn you back into a plant. Only I won't make you a good plant. Maybe, a mold or fungus." She lifted a brow, trying not to grin at him. "You'd better be on your best behavior with me."

His eyes widened. "A mold?" He cupped her face in his palms. "I won't mind as long as I can grow on you."

She leaned closer, her eyes drifting shut as he covered her lips with his. Cinnamon exploded though her senses with the first stroke of her tongue against his. Oh, she loved the taste of him. Savoring him, she deepened the kiss.

He groaned and pulled away. A flash of pain flickered in his eyes. Caitlyn moaned, becoming aware of his injuries. She wrapped his arm about her shoulders and took hold of him around the waist. When she glanced down at his body, bloody cuts and bruises slashed across his chest and arms. She sucked in a sharp breath when she noticed the damage to his leg.

A jagged rip in the side of his thigh ran across the front to the stop at his knee. Blood oozed from the tear in deep purple-red drops. A sweet odor rose, mingling with the rancid aroma of singed hair and the burned cotton material in his jeans.

"Come on, you need a doctor." She glanced at Rhys. "Well, what are you waiting for? Help me."

Her father grinned, gave orders to prepare a bed for Shay, then grabbed Shay's other arm. Together, they managed to make it to the living quarters. Caitlyn refused to allow Rhys to take Shay to a different room. He belonged with her--for eternity.

Once she and Shay were settled, Myrielle tended to the damage inflicted by Gwyneth to both of them. When she finished, she turned and smiled at Caitlyn. "He will heal nicely. There will be a scar on his leg, but I'm sure you won't mind, will you, my daughter?"

Tears in her eyes, she smiled and shook her head. She wrapped her arms around her mother and hugged her. With her newfound abilities, she remembered her time with her true parents. For the first time since she'd arrived in Sidhe, she knew the truth. When she drew away, Myrielle, a sheen of tears in her gaze, nodded, then pulled Rhys from the room.

Drowsy from the potions Myrielle had insisted he drink, Shay lay on a stack of pillows propped against the headboard of her bed. The silken bedspread covered only his lower body, leaving his chest and arms bare. Caitlyn tilted her head and studied the slowly fading bruises and cuts.

"Come here," he said softly, holding a hand out to her.

She smiled and carefully sat at his side on the edge of the mattress. She brushed a lock of hair off his brow, and then whispered, "I love you."

"Here, lie beside me. I want to feel you next to me," he murmured.

She slid down on the bed and rested her head on his shoulder. "Why wouldn't you answer me when I questioned you about the riddle? Did you know the answer?"

"I suspected it, but I couldn't say, in case I was wrong. If what I suspected was incorrect and I told you, then you would have spent time traveling down the wrong path. I didn't want that to happen." He brushed a kiss on her brow. "I love you. So much. I just couldn't see past today."

"You've loved me for a long time," she said, smiling against his shoulder. "I saw that night through your eyes. I wondered why it was your eyes, though. Why didn't I see it through my sight, when I was a baby?"

"You picked up the flower. When you looked into the fountain, you had a piece of me with you."

She laid her palm on his belly, enjoying the feel of his skin beneath her hand. "Rest, and when you're better, I want you to take me to the stars again. I don't think I'll ever tire of feeling you in me, loving me."

"I hope not," he said, then grinned lazily. "So, do you believe in magic now, Caitlyn Reiley?"

She laughed. Rising up on her elbow, she kissed him. "I suppose so. Of course, you'll have to keep reminding me. Did I understand we have an eternity to live? If so, then you have a long time to convince me over and over again."

"It will be my greatest pleasure," he murmured.

Judith Leger

Born and raised in the South, I make southwest Louisiana my home. My writing is a doorway to my imagination that I love to share with the world. Reading--living in other worlds--has always been a part of my life, and I decided to let others visit the places in my imagination. My muse set free, I write mostly paranormal fantasy and futuristic stories, but I also dabble in contemporary fiction.

I am happily married to a full-blooded Cajun. We have three sons, a horse and a very, very spoiled dachshund. When I'm not busy writing, I work in higher education and enjoy reading fantasy, romance and playing video games with my sons. Favorite Saturday evening consists of bowls of buttered popcorn and watching tons of anime with my boys and Gracie (the dachshund).

Judith's Website:
www.JudithLeger.weebly.com
Reader email:
www.judithleger@hotmail.com